# Heir to the Underworld

# The New Gods of Olympus

# Book One

JB Dennis

# Heir to the Underworld

# The New Gods of Olympus

# Book One

JB Dennis

**Heir to the Underworld**

Copyright © 2019 Jaxom Price

**Content Editor:** Mallory Miller
**Copy Editor:** Callie Waterson
**Cover Design:** Krystina Grey
**Editor-in-Chief:** Kristi King-Morgan
**Formatting:** Kristi King-Morgan

All rights reserved. This book or any portion thereof may not be reproduced or used in any manner whatsoever without the express written permission of the publisher except for the use of brief quotations in a book review.

ISBN: 978-1-947381-20-9

Dreaming Big Publications

www.dreamingbigpublications.com

To those who helped me along the way I say, "Thank you."

# Prologue

Zeus, King of the gods, lord of Olympus, and god of the skies, sat upon his heavenly throne and brooded over all of creation. For countless millennia he had ruled over the heavens above and the mortal world below. But now times have changed, and the god of thunder and lightning has grown bored of his reign. The time of the gods had passed, but, bound by duty, Zeus, once the greatest of kings and lord of the heavens, was now reduced to nothing more than a glorified weatherman.

Bolts of lightning flashed through the night sky as Zeus glared down at the world below him. Rising from his throne, Zeus paced about, the clouds around him darkening as his temper grew. Thoughts of massive storms and disastrous tornadoes raced through his mind. Visions of deadly blizzards and catastrophic hurricanes danced before his eyes. But he knew that it was all for not. Gone were the days when he could visit divine retribution upon those who displeased him. Gone were the days when his name commanded fear and awe. Gone were the days when he was the most powerful being in all of creation. Now he was but a legend: a myth to be told about in storybooks.

More bolts of lightning flashed through the sky. A strong wind whirled about him, carrying with it the roaring sound of rolling thunder. With a howl of rage, he unleashed a storm upon the mortal world below. He watched as his tempest grew, covering the landscape in a blanket of torrential rain. Bolts of lightning screamed through the air, splitting trees with reckless abandon. A massive cyclone of turbulent air laid waste to what was once a tranquil field, ripping up plants and mounds of earth as it tore through the countryside.

And yet, as Zeus watched his savage squall unfolding before his eyes, he felt nothing. No great swell of pride at his work. No sense of vengeance against those who had wronged him. No feeling of righteousness as he expressed his will upon the world of man. It was all hollow and empty. That's all his actions were. Hollow and empty. There was no recognition to be had for his work. Sure, some would say it was God's work, but he wasn't the god they were referring to. Zeus let out another howl of fury.

"You seemed troubled, my lord," said a soft, quiet voice. A figure, dressed all in white, appeared next to Zeus' throne, their face covered by a hood.

"I am not troubled," replied Zeus in a voice like rolling thunder. "I am frustrated! What is the point of being the King of the gods if there is no one to worship me? The mortals have forgotten us. They pray to false saviors and naked idols while we endure eternity, keeping their precious world from crumbling. WE ARE GODS! We could wipe them from the Earth if we so chose. And yet we serve them. They should be the ones serving us! After all, it was by our grace that they were created in the first place!"

"Is that all being a god is to you, my lord, the adoration of mortals?"

"What other reason is there for their existence? It is why they were given life in the first place: to worship at our feet while we rule on high. And now, it is they who rule while we bend to their whims."

"But, my lord, it is still you who controls the winds and the rains and the storms. It is still you who ordains the will of the gods. It is still you who rules over all of creation. How can you say that mortals rule when it is you with all the power?"

"What is the point of power if no one knows you have it? I may rule over the storms and the gods, but what does that matter? I'm but a myth to these mortals, a legend from a bygone era of no more significance than a drop of water in a vast ocean. To dictate what is true and what is false, that is real power. As long as the mortals see me as not but a figment of their imaginations, I am their servant."

"Perhaps it is time for a change, my lord. If you are unhappy with the current situation, perhaps you should do something about it."

"Had I the option to wipe man from existence I would have done so ages ago. But I am duty-bound to protect the people of this world. Had I not sworn a divine oath all would be different now, but, alas, I gave my word. If they destroy themselves, all the better, but I cannot be the one to end them. My storms may take a life, here and there, perhaps, but I cannot cause their complete extinction."

"Have you considered a different approach than death and destruction, my lord?"

"What other approach is there when dealing with man?"

"I would not presume to suggest anything to you, my lord. You are the great ruler of the gods, and I am just your lowly and humble servant. But if there is a way for you to resolve this matter to your satisfaction, I have every confidence that you, mighty Zeus, will be able to come up with it."

Silence fell as Zeus looked down upon the world below him. After a time, Zeus spoke again.

"What a blessing it must be to be an ignorant mortal," he mused. "Look at them. They live their lives unconcernedly, with no care toward any matters of importance. What care they of the great powers that govern the world, so long as the sun comes up in the morning? What care they of the toil involved in managing the seasons, so long as they have pretty flowers to look at and vegetables enough to eat? I almost envy the freedom their stupidity allows them."

"My lord, are you saying you wish to join the mortals? To live among them?"

Zeus snorted with laughter. "No. I have no interest in living with mortals. They are petulant creatures, lacking in dignity and understanding, full of woe and misery. And yet, their lack of responsibilities, real responsibilities, is a pleasant prospect to consider. They know nothing of true duty. When all is said and done what are jobs and mortgages when compared to the burdens of commanding the forces of the universe? They are not but the foolish concerns of close-minded children."

"Could you not give up your responsibilities, my lord? You are the King of the gods; anything should be within your power."

"You are just as stupid as the mortals. You contradict yourself without even knowing it. As you just said, I am the King. How would I go about giving up my power? What mechanism is there for me to do so? None. There exists no precedent for a King of the gods to give up his authority. Were I a mortal king perhaps I would have the option to abdicate, but no. I am the King of the gods, and I will be as such for all of eternity."

"But why can you not abdicate, my lord? Why can you not find someone else to take on your divinity and give you the freedom you so crave?"

"As I already said, no King of the gods has ever abdicated his throne before."

"Begging your pardon, my lord, but no King of the gods has ever had the option to do so. First, your grandfather

## Heir to the Underworld

Ouranos was cast down by your father Cronus, and then you yourself cast down Cronus. Of all the Kings of the gods that have ever existed, you have not faced any attempted insurrections."

"And what am I to do if I give up my godhood? Languish in Tartarus with my tyrannical father? Become a hermit and wander the world?"

"I believe that the point is that you could do anything you wished, my lord. You would have true freedom. Freedom to live any life *you* choose. Freedom to be anyone *you* wanted. Freedom to go anywhere *you* desired. Freedom to do anything *you* pleased."

"And the other gods would simply sit by and let this happen? They would just allow me to give up my powers to another. Can you imagine the power struggle that would ensue from such a decision? Each and every god would be vying to be my replacement. It would start another divine war."

"You are the King of the gods, my lord, the greatest and most powerful being in existence. Your word is law. Were you to decree that any such individual was to be your successor, I'm sure your fellow gods would not dare to countermand you."

"There is truth in that," said Zeus with a self-satisfied smile.

"Besides, my lord, from what I understand you are not the only one who is feeling underappreciated."

"What do you mean?"

"Merely that some of your fellow Olympians have expressed disappointment with the current state of affairs, my lord."

"Which ones?"

"The Ladies Hera, Demeter, and Athena, and the Lords Poseidon, Apollo, and Ares, my lord."

"Over half of the Olympians wish for a change," Zeus muttered to himself as he paced about in contemplation. "Perhaps there is something to this abdication idea of mine. After all, if mere mortals can do it, why not I?"

Zeus strode back to his throne and sat down upon it; his mind abuzz with possibilities. The sky around him went from dark to light to dark again and still, Zeus sat in deep contemplation. Finally, as light began to shine through the clouds once more, Zeus spoke.

"Call for Hermes. I have a message for him to deliver to my fellow gods. We have much to discuss."

# Chapter One

The original campus was constructed in 1985 using only local artisans and materials. Since that time, M.O.U has steadily grown in reputation. By 1995, it was the most prestigious institution of higher learning here in Greece, and by 2010, it was considered to be on a par with the likes of Oxford, Cambridge, and the Ivy Leagues. Some would say that M.O.U even surpasses them."

"Now the building we are currently in is the Pasithea Student Center, the main student recreational center for the entire campus. On the ground level, you have the campus café, a few franchised restaurants, several common areas, a computer lounge, and galleries for various art pieces. On the upper floor, you'll find a gym, as well as several meeting rooms and movie theaters."

It was the same spiel that had been given to countless freshmen their first day at Mt. Olympus University, a premier international university that catered to students from around the world. Every year a new class of freshmen was subjected to the same speech, word for word, as they were given a tour of the university, and every year the freshmen ignored it. This year was no exception. The students traipsed along listlessly behind their equally unenthusiastic tour guide as he pointed out various aspects of the campus.

"This room is dedicated to the fourteen major gods of Greek mythology. Though we are accepting of all faiths here at M.O.U., the Greek pantheon has influenced much of the school's architecture and curriculum. For example, the communications department is located in the Hermes building. For those who are unaware, Hermes was considered to be the god of communication, as well as the messenger of the gods. Likewise, this building is named after the Greek goddess of relaxation. Now, if you would like to, you may take a moment to appreciate the majesty of these legendary figures. They are the inspiration for everything we do here at M.O.U."

Most of the freshmen milled about the room aimlessly, staring at the marble statues around them, texting on their mobile devices, or simply just chatting with each other. One especially studious girl was examining the statues intently, taking notes on their artistry and composition.

"He could inspire me anytime," said a beautiful boy with blond hair and brilliant blue eyes. He was staring at the statue of a particularly handsome god, his eyes roving over the statue's fine contours.

"What about you, cutie, you get any inspiration off this hottie?" He turned to look at a smaller boy who was standing only a few feet away from him and who had been giving him surreptitious glances throughout entire the tour.

"I-I-I," stammered the smaller boy. He was incredibly thin, with sandy brown hair and green eyes behind square-framed glasses.

"Or maybe you'd rather have me for a muse," teased the blond boy, his eyes twinkling. The smaller boy blushed furiously.

"Leave him alone," snapped a girl who was standing near them. Even compared to the bespectacled boy she was tiny. Standing no taller than five feet, she was a petite, wild beauty with dark brown hair, deep brown eyes, and light olive skin.

"I'm just having a little fun with him," said the blond boy with a charming smile. "No harm meant."

"Well he's obviously uncomfortable," said the petite girl. Her voice had the twang of a southern from the United States. "So, back off."

The blond boy held up his hands in acquiescence. "Very well. I'll leave the poor boy alone."

"Thank you."

"If you don't mind my asking, what is your name, my dear? Or would you prefer to be called defender of the meek?"

"I'm Sophia," said the girl coolly.

"Well, Sophia, if I've offended you in some way, I apologize most profusely."

"I'm not the one you should be apologizing to," snapped Sophia.

"You make a fair point." The blond boy turned to face the smaller boy again, whose face turned red immediately. "If I've made you uncomfortable, I am sorry… what's your name?"

"G-Ga-Gavin."

"Well Gavin, I'm truly sorry for any discomfort or awkwardness I may have caused you. I'll leave you to get on with whatever you were doing before I so rudely interjected myself into your life." As the blond boy turned to leave Gavin managed to pluck up enough courage to ask him a question.

"What's your name?" The words tumbled out of Gavin's mouth faster than he had intended, which made Gavin's face burn redder than before.

Fortunately, the blond boy had understood him. He turned to face Gavin again.

"Matthew. Matthew Golden."

He gave a theatrical bow. Sophia's eyebrows rose.

"Wait, aren't you—"

"Yes, I'm the son of Charles Golden and Elizabeth MacKenzie. And if you want an autograph from either of them, I'll be happy to get you one."

"I'll keep that in mind," said Sophia. "At least I know where you get your flair for the dramatic."

"Nothing wrong with being a little dramatic from time to time, my dear."

"Just from time to time?" asked Sophia with a raised eyebrow.

Matthew chuckled lightly. "Well, perhaps I am a touch overdramatic. I blame genetics, and I've never been accused of being a little anything." Matthew gave Gavin a wink as Sophia rolled her eyes.

"Come now, there's no need to be so stiff. It's all in goo—" Matthew broke off mid-sentence as his eyes scanned the room.

"What?" asked Sophia.

"Correct me if I'm wrong, but didn't there use to be more people in this room?"

He was right of course. There had been at least thirty people on the tour, but now, besides Gavin, Sophia, and himself, Matthew could only spot ten other people in the room.

"Where the hell did everyone go?" asked Sophia loudly. At her words, the others in the room noticed that they had been left behind as well.

"It seems we've been abandoned," said Matthew. "I can't say I'm disappointed. That tour guide was about as engaging as a brick wall."

"It's very unprofessional of him to leave us behind," commented the girl who'd been taking notes. She spoke with a Hispanic accent. Her skin was a warm coppery brown, her hair was long, black, and disheveled, and she wore large glasses that obscured most of her face.

"It's not like we can't just catch up to them," said one of the remaining boys.

He was handsome, tall, and physically fit, with dark brown hair and sharp, green eyes. He walked over to one of the doors leading out of the room and pushed against it. The door remained closed. He tried pulling at it, but the door refused to budge.

"Or maybe we can't," he said in confusion as he pushed against the door with more force.

"Here, let a real man try," said another boy.

While not as tall as the first boy, he was considerably more muscular. He had close-cropped black hair, hard brown eyes, and several tattoos along both arms. The larger boy walked over to the door and gave it a hearty shove. The door remained immovable. With a grunt of frustration, the boy slammed his shoulder into the door. Still, it stayed firmly closed.

"Maybe you should try ramming it with your head next," called out a boy who'd laid himself out upon one of the stone benches, a flask in his hand. "Doesn't look like there's much there to damage in the first place."

The larger boy gestured rudely at him before pulling at the door to no avail.

"Like what you see?" asked the boy on the bench as he caught Matthew giving him an appraising look.

He was indeed attractive, with wicked blue eyes and hair dyed a quartet of different colors. He'd intentionally left the top three buttons of his shirt open so as to expose his chest.

"Well, you're no Greek god," said Matthew as he walked over and sat down next to the boy, "but I'll take what I can get. I'm Matthew."

"Vincent," said the other boy with a mischievous smile.

"I have a feeling you're going to be trouble."

"Oh, you have no idea."

"As much as I like to see ro-mance for-ming, I zink we 'ave a pwoblem."

A truly gorgeous girl with clear blue eyes, a willowy figure, and long blond hair that fell past her knees had glided over to Matthew and Vincent. She spoke with a thick French accent.

The problem she was referring to was that both sets of doors out of the room refused to open. Two more boys had joined in the attempt to force open the doors. One was a muscular black boy, with short curly hair and gentle black eyes. The other was tall and slender, with wavy dirty blond and deep blue eyes. Together the four boys were currently pushing against the same door, which stubbornly continued to resist their efforts to open it.

"That is a problem," said Matthew, before adding in French, "*mais au moins on obtenir un spectacle.*"

"*Oh, vous parlez Français?*" asked the girl, brightening up at once.

"*Oui. Matthew, au fait. Et vous?*"

"*Je m'appelle Reneé. C'est un plaisir de vous rencontrer.*"

There was a loud yelp. The bulkiest of the boys had charged at one of the doors, slamming painfully into it with his shoulder.

"One of them is gonna get hurt."

A group of three girls had wandered over to where Matthew, Vincent, and Reneé were sitting. The speaker was a girl with flaming red hair, mint green eyes, and an Australian accent. Her two companions, a bleached blond with unnaturally blue eyes and a mousy brunette with warm brown eyes, could not have been more different from each other. The blond was artfully made-up and dressed in fashionable and expensive clothes, while the brunette looked as though she'd fished her clothes out of a thrift store clearance bin.

"Hey," yelled the blond girl. "The doors obviously aren't going to open. So, stop trying to prove how macho you are. We can just call the maintenance crew, and they can figure out what the hell is wrong with the doors. Unless you want to dislocate a shoulder."

"You got their number?" asked the boy with brown hair and green eyes.

"No," said the blond girl as she pulled out her cell phone. "But the school does have a website, and the number is

# Heir to the Underworld

probably listed." As the blond girl tapped away on her phone, the others in the room gathered around her.

"Okay, here we go," said the girl after a few seconds, "got the number. Now everyone be quiet while I call them. With thirteen of us in this room, it shouldn't take long for them to respond."

"Fourteen," said a quiet voice.

Everyone jumped and whipped their heads around. Lurking next to one of the statues was a tall, darkly handsome boy. With his black clothes, hair, and eyes, he'd completely blended into the statue's shadow.

"How long have you been standing there lurking?" asked the blond girl coldly.

"I've been here the whole time," said the boy in black. "People tend not to notice me."

"I wonder why?" asked the blond girl sarcastically as she called the maintenance number and put her phone to her ear. "Just keep quiet. Not that you need help with that."

There was silence for a few seconds and then she lowered her phone. "Call can't be completed my ass. This phone is supposed to be the best available. Someone else try. Here's the number."

The assembled students all pulled out their cell phones, each trying to get a hold of the maintenance crew, only to find that none of their phones could get through.

"I can access the internet, but I can't make a call," complained the blond girl. "How does that make any sense? Hey, you, little guy, you look like you would know. What the hell's up with our phones?"

"He has a name," snapped Sophia in annoyance. "It's Gavin. Use it."

"Well good for him," replied the blond girl, equally annoyed. "I also have a name. It's Ashley Queen. Does that change anything? No. So, do you know what's going on with our cell phones or not?"

"Sorry, no," said Gavin. "I've tried everything I can think of on my phone to see what's wrong, but it's just not working."

"Well, you're useless then," said Ashley.

"I don't see you coming up with any ideas," chided the girl with the Spanish accent.

"Come on everyone, just chill out," said the tall boy with dirty blond hair. "There's no need to fight with each other. Obviously, we are gonna be here awhile so let's try and get along and get to know each other. I'm Samuel Poole, but everyone calls me Sammy."

An awkward silence fell as Sammy waited expectantly for someone else to introduce themselves. Finally, the Spanish girl spoke.

"Fine, I guess I'll start. I'm Ana Maria."

"Cool," said Sammy. "Nice to meet you, Ana Maria." Sammy turned expectant eyes on the rest of the group.

"I'm Andrew St. Cloud," said the green-eyed boy.

"Lance," said the black boy with a friendly wave of the hand. His voice had just a hint of an accent, though no one was quite sure where it was from.

"Johnny," said the muscular boy shortly.

"I'm Sara," said the Australian girl. She nudged the girl next to her who was trying to remain unnoticed. The girl sighed.

"My name is Irene Holmes," she said in an English accent.

"I've already introduced myself once," said Ashley haughtily. "Don't expect me to do it again."

"Got it," said Sammy nonchalantly. "And we already know Gavin. How about the rest of you?"

"Reneé."

"Matthew Golden and yes, I'm that Matthew Golden."

"Vincent."

"Sophia Hunt. It's a pleasure to make y'all's acquaintance."

"Great. Now we all know each other's names."

"Not everyone's," corrected Matthew. He pointed over at the boy in black.

"Oh crap, I'm so sorry dude," said Sammy.

"It's fine," said the boy. "I'm used to it. Name's Benjamin, by the way."

"Well, glad to meet ya, Benny," said Sammy with a smile.

"Please don't call me that," said Benjamin.

"How about Benji?"

"God no."

"Benito?"

"No."

"Benster?"

"How about just Ben?"

"I guess that works too. Well, now we officially know everyone, unless there's another person hiding under a bench or something."

"Whoopie," said Ashley as she twirled her finger through the air. "We know each other's names. Good for us. Doesn't change the fact that we are still stuck here."

"Yes, but it makes the atmosphere a little better," said Sammy with a smile.

Ashley rolled her eyes and walked purposefully away from Sammy.

"*Savez-vous ce qui rend l'atmosphère meilleure pour moi?*" said Reneé, leaning over to talk to Matthew.

"*Qu'est-ce que c'est?*"

"*Tout le monde est magnifique à regarder.*"

"*Ah oui, très vrai. Surtout les garçons.*" They both began to giggle.

As Matthew and Reneé continued to chatter on about cute boys in French, the others in the group broke off from the huddle to find ways to pass the time. Most talked, learning more about their fellow captives and making new friends. Some inspected the doors or fidgeted with their cell phones, trying to find a solution to their problem.

Finally, after several minutes had passed, Ashley, in a loud carrying voice, complained, "Oh for heaven's sake, how long are we going to be trapped in here? What kind of school is this where fourteen people can get locked in a room in the middle of the day and no one notices? Not to mention the fact that they obviously have malfunctioning doors. This is absolutely ridiculous. I have a mind to call my attorney about this. If I miss lunch, I'll make this school pay, believe you me. I'll—"

A new voice interrupted Ashley's tirade.

"Enough already, we get it, you're pissed."

# Chapter Two

"Who said that?" asked Ashley her eyes flitting angrily from one face to another.

"That would be me," said the new voice.

"Is someone on an intercom or something?" asked Ashley, her eyes now scanning the room.

"Look up," said the voice.

The trapped students raised their eyes upwards.

"No, over here. To the right. The other right. There ya go."

Floating several feet above their heads was a small ball of bronze light.

"Hi there," said the ball of light as it bobbed up and down.

"Is everyone seeing this, or am I going insane?" asked Johnny.

"If you're insane then so am I, bro," said Sammy.

"What? You've never conversed with a ball of light before? How boring your lives must be."

"Can someone explain what the hell is going on?" demanded Ashley, a hint of panic in her voice.

"Oh, pipe down," said the ball as it soared around the group of confused students. "I'll explain everything."

The ball flew towards the center of the room and then exploded into a swirl of sparks. There were several loud gasps from assembled students. A second later the sparks vanished to reveal a man hovering several feet in the air. He was lean, fit, and clad in a bronze chiton. Attached to each of his sandals were pairs of small, white wings. On top of his sandy brown hair was a bronze winged helmet and his hazel eyes twinkled mischievously out of his roguishly handsome face.

"Allow me to introduce myself. I'm Hermes, messenger of the gods and god of trade, communication, and travel. Now, do we have everyone here? I'm sure I managed to arrange it so that only the fourteen we wanted would be here, but it never hurts to double-check. And yup, looks like that's everyone. And uh, Ben, could ya stop lurking about? You look like a serial killer."

Hermes paused as he caught the looks of shock and confusion growing on everyone's faces.

"Is there a problem?" he asked, a small smile playing across his face. Only silence met his words.

"Hello? Earth to mortals. You still with me?"

"*Pardonnez moi, monsieur,*" said Reneé hesitantly, "but, did you just call yourself a god?"

"Yup," said Hermes cheerfully. "I know it's a bit hard to accept but —"

"There's no fucking way you're a *god*," interrupted Johnny. "You look about as intimidating as a twig."

Hermes turned to look down at Johnny, the mischievous twinkle in his eyes more obvious than ever, and snapped his fingers. Johnny opened his mouth to speak again, but no words came out. Instead, he let out a donkey-like bray. His eyes widened in shock. He tried to speak again but all that he was able to manage was more braying. Johnny closed his mouth in frustration and glared at Hermes.

"Well I hope that puts to rest any other doubts you may have," said Hermes in satisfaction as he snapped his fingers again. "Your voice has been restored. I would suggest that if you insist on speaking, do so with a little more respect, lest you find yourself turned into an actual jackass. Now if there are no further interrupts, I need to get things ready for the congregation. They'll all be here soon enough."

"Congregation?" asked Ana Maria. "Who else is coming?"

"Just the other fourteen major Greek deities, you know: Zeus, Hera, Hades, Poseidon, Athena, Ares, Apollo, Artemis, Demeter, Dionysus, Hephaestus, Aphrodite, Hestia – oh, no wait, not Hestia – she never leaves Olympus."

"This is not possible," said Andrew. "There's no way that the Greek gods exist."

"And yet," said Hermes, his arms spread wide, "here I am for all to see."

"What about the Bible?"

"Bestselling work of fiction ever written."

"What about the Quran?" asked Ana Maria. "Or the Torah? Are they fiction too? What about Hinduism and Buddhism? Is it only the Greek gods that exist, or are the Norse and Egyptian pantheons also real? What about that the Asian and Aztec deities? And the—"

"Whoa, whoa, whoa, slow down," said Hermes. "Look, I'd love to answer your questions, but I can't. Trust me, as a god of communication I love to talk but I've been told not to give out too many details until after everyone arrives. Zeus wants everything to be a big surprise. That being said, I understand that you need some answers. Since your questions seem relatively safe, so I'll give you a quick rundown. The Quran and the Torah are both fictional too; Hinduism was created by the Muses; Buddhism by the Charities; the Norse gods were a bunch of demi-gods who wanted to be worshipped in their own right; the Egyptian pantheon was the result of we Olympian deities drinking far too much of Dionysus' ten-thousand-year-old spiked nectar; the Asian deities were the work of Selene; and the Aztec deities were the work of Helios."

"What—" began Ana Maria but Hermes cut her off.

"No, no more, please. I don't want to risk accidentally saying too much."

"But—"

"Ana Maria, please, work with me here. There will be time for questions later but not now."

"How do you know her name?" asked Matthew.

"See, now that is a question I can't answer," said Hermes. "So please, no more questions. I beg of you."

"This is unreal," said Sammy.

"Real or not, the other gods will be here soon, and I've got to get things ready for them. They can be so picky. Eh, what are you doing over there, little girl?"

Everyone turned to see Ashley frantically pressing buttons on her phone.

"I'm trying to call the police, but this stupid phone isn't working. I told my mother we needed to get an upgraded plan."

"Um, you do know that I'm the god of communication, right?" asked Hermes. "Your phone isn't working because I don't want it to work."

"You... how... what?" sputtered Ashley angrily.

"I can see that you are all freaking out a little, but I don't have time to hold your hands through this. The Greek gods exist. Accept it and move on. Now, if you will excuse me, I have work to do."

Floating down to the ground, Hermes raised his right hand above his head. A wing-topped, bronze staff with two snakes entwined around it appeared in his hand. Bringing his hand down he struck the floor with the butt of his staff. The wings on the head of the staff flapped, and the snakes began to writhe about, hissing softly.

There was a series of loud rumbling sounds as the fourteen statues of the Greek gods began to move on their own. Slowly the statues marched around the room until they formed a large circle around Hermes. Once the circle was complete, the statues began to change, slowly morphing into large marble thrones, each decorated with different objects, sigils, weapons, and ornamentations.

"Holy shit," said Sammy as he stared around at the thrones. "That was awesome."

"I do good work," responded Hermes, as he flew around admiring his handy work. "Not as good as Hephaestus, but considering he's the god of craftsmen I think my ego can take the hit."

"What are the chances that we are all having a mental break down at the same time?" asked Lance.

"Nonexistent," said Ana Maria.

"Great."

"So, are we actually going to meet the *real* Greek gods and goddesses?" asked Ashley.

"Technically you've already met one. Just because I'm the messenger doesn't mean I'm not a real Greek god. But yes, you'll be meeting the others. In fact, here's one right now."

At his words, there was a flash of gray light and a woman appeared in the middle of the room. There were several yelps of surprise, which were accompanied by a loud exclamation of, "What the fuck?" by Johnny; an awe-inspired "Holy hell," from Sara; a shocked "Jesus!" by Andrew; and a whispered "*Ay dios mio*," from Ana Maria.

The woman was at least three times the size of an average human. She wore a bronze breastplate over a gray peplos. In her left hand, she held a massive bronze shield, upon which the monstrous face of a hideous, snake-haired woman was embossed. In her right hand, she held a beautiful spear of dark, glossy wood, topped with a spearhead of gray crystal. A helmet rested on top of her raven black hair like a crown. Her beautiful face wore an austere expression as she gazed around the room with calm gray eyes.

"Presenting Athena, the goddess of wisdom, intelligence, and strategic warfare."

Athena strode over to one of the marble thrones, around which was littered scrolls, books, charts, and various weapons. An owl was perched upon the back of the throne. As Athena sat down, the owl sprang to life. It swiveled its head about, observing the gathered students and hooting softly.

"Hey lady," called out Johnny, taking the opportunity to interrogate someone who had yet to threaten him, "can we get some answers here? We've been stuck in this room with the flying guy for a while now and we've gotten nothing. You wanna tell us what the hell is going on?"

Athena turned to look down at him, her gray eyes cold and her expression, if possible, even sterner than before. Johnny gulped.

"Patience is oft extolled as a virtue, albeit one of the many you evidently lack. In any event, the reason for your assemblage here will be explained to you by Zeus himself. No other god, myself included, shall do so. As such, if I were you, I would consider it wise to keep silent until such time as I am directed to speak, lest I be confirmed for a fool."

There was a ripple of laughter from the other students as Johnny blushed furiously.

A soft breeze whipped around the room, bringing with it the earthy smell of a forest. The space in the center of the room seemed to glitter with silver stars. A moment later a woman materialized into existence. Though smaller than Athena, she nonetheless towered over the gathered students. She was young and pretty, with eyes like shining droplets of silver and brown hair that seemed to dance in a nonexistent breeze. She was dressed in a silver chiton, and she wore a crown of antlers and thorns upon her head. A bow of beautifully carved wood was slung across her back.

"Presenting Artemis, goddess of the hunt, the moon, and the wilds."

Artemis loped on unshod feet to a throne surrounded by deer, rabbits, squirrels, and birds. As Artemis took her seat, the animals came to life, gamboling about her ecstatically.

# Heir to the Underworld

The sounds of music filled the air as a sparkling golden light fill the center of the room. When the light and music faded, an astonishingly handsome man was left in their wake. Though he greatly resembled Artemis in face and size, they differed in attire and presentation. Where she was subtly dressed in pale silver, he was bedecked in radiant, shimmering gold. His skin, his eyes, his hair, and his chiton all shone like miniature suns. He even sported a luminesce, golden halo.

"Presenting Apollo, god of light, music, and healing."

"Sister!" cried Apollo dramatically as he floated over towards Artemis, leaving a glittering trail as he went. "So nice to see you."

"Must you always turn everything into a production?" asked Artemis coolly as she surveyed Apollo with disdain.

"But of course," replied Apollo with a broad smile. He turned his glowing eyes upon the assembled students, all of whom were shielding their eyes from his blinding brilliance.

"So, this is our little band of mortals," said Apollo as he floated over towards the students. "Well, I must say, they are an attractive bunch. We picked well, didn't we."

"Apollo," chided Athena warningly.

"Don't worry, sister mine," said Apollo with an airy wave of the hand. "I won't spill the proverbial beans."

"Hey, can you turn off your brights?" demanded Johnny. "We are going blind over here." Apollo looked down at Johnny in amusement.

"More brawn than brains and the manners of a donkey to boot. No need to wonder whose you are. I suppose there's no accounting for taste."

"What are you talking about?" asked Johnny, but Apollo merely raised a finger to his lips.

"It's a secret little one," he said with a wicked smile. "So, don't ask."

Apollo turned and floated over to his throne, dimming the intensity of his magnificence as he went. His throne was decorated with many musical instruments. As he sat down upon it, the throne turned gold and translucent. It looked as though it were made of solid light rather than marble. The instruments around him sprang to life at once, filling the air with their soft melodies. Between the hooting of Athena's owl, the music of Apollo's instruments, and the various noises of Artemis' horde of animals, the room was becoming very noisy.

"Excuse me, but are you really telling us not to ask you any questions?" demanded Ana Maria.

"Yes," said Apollo.

"How can you expect us not to be curious?" snapped Ana Maria. "Your very existence changes everything we all thought we knew about the world."

"I didn't say you couldn't be curious," said Apollo. "I just said you couldn't ask questions."

"How is that fair?" demanded Sara.

"No one ever said life is fair," replied Apollo. "You should know that better than most." Sara's eyes widened in surprise.

"What do you—" she began, but Apollo raised a delicate finger.

"No more questions."

"Apollo, stop tormenting the mortals," chided Athena.

"It's beneath you," added Artemis.

"Everything is beneath me," said Apollo loftily. Artemis rolled her eyes.

"Guess I know which god's statue I was looking at earlier," muttered Matthew to Reneé. "Pity he's a bit of a prick." Reneé chuckled and nodded in agreement.

"How are you two taking this so well," demanded Andrew.

"Well, it is happening right in front of our eyes," said Matthew, gesturing towards the gods. "How else are we supposed to take it?"

"We could always hide like Gavin," suggested Vincent, nodding towards Gavin, who was cowering behind the others.

There was a sudden flash of red light and man appeared, standing in the middle of the room like all the others had. He was handsome, in a brutal way, with fierce black eyes and extremely short-cropped black hair. Like Athena, he wore bronze armor over his red chiton. A war-helm of Grecian design, topped with a long, red, horse-tail crest, rested under his arm.

"Presenting Ares, god of war, violence, and bloodshed."

There was a trace of distaste in Hermes's voice as he announced Ares' presence. Ares seemed not to notice or care. He simply moved forward to take his seat upon his throne, around which was littered numerous battle-worn weapons.

"I do hope everyone else gets here soon," said Ares, as he lounged upon his throne. "There's a battle happening in Syria in two hours that I want to watch."

"Heavens forbid our divine business get in the way of your sport," mocked Apollo disdainfully.

"You will not have long to wait," said Athena, cutting across Ares before he could respond to Apollo's barbed comment. "In fact, Aphrodite comes now."

As if on cue a plume of thick, glittering, pink vapor rose up out of the ground, swirling sensually upwards. For a moment the vapor hung, twinkling, in the air before fading away to reveal the most beautiful woman any of them had ever seen.

"Presenting Aphrodite, goddess of love, beauty, and passion."

No words existed that could accurately describe the beauty that was Aphrodite. It was as if she was under her own personal spotlight. She seemed to draw the attention of everyone in the room toward her. In her presence, all else looked common and vulgar. She radiated desire and allure. Her movements were so poised, so graceful, that she seemed not to walk but to glide. Her pink, semi-transparent peplos hugged every curve perfectly and left very little to the imagination, and her glittering, jeweled crown framed her face perfectly.

She sat down upon her throne, which was surrounded by bouquets of flowers and twittering doves, and looked over at the assembled students, all of whom gazed upon her in complete rapture. Matthew was the first to awaken from her entrancing presence. He blinked several times before glaring down past his navel.

"Traitor," he muttered.

Slowly the rest of the students regained their sense of self. Several tried to avoid looking at Aphrodite for fear that they would again fall under her spell. Others found that they couldn't resist taking a peek every few seconds. Their attention was finally pulled away from Aphrodite when a pillar of fire erupted in the middle of the room, from which a man stepped forth.

"Presenting Hephaestus, god of the forge, fire, and craftsmanship."

Up to this point, all the Greek gods had been extraordinarily attractive. Hephaestus, however, was somewhat of a different story. He was very ordinary in his appearance which, when compared to the other gods, made him look ugly, especially when he was compared to the ravishing beauty that was Aphrodite. He had a large, tangled black beard and long, tangled black hair. His eyes looked like burning coals, and his chiton was orange and covered in soot. A simple circlet of iron rested upon his brow. In his right hand, he held a massive smith's hammer, which he used as a cane as he limped towards his throne, which was ornamented with several smiths' tools. As he sat down, Aphrodite, who was seated to his right, reached over and began brushing off the soot stains on his chiton.

"Leave it woman," snapped Hephaestus, pushing her hand away. He spoke with a deep Scottish brogue.

"You're a mess," said Aphrodite, her musical voice as seductive as her appearance.

"I don't bloody care," said Hephaestus. "Ya should be happy I came at all. Now leave me be."

Aphrodite clicked her tongue in annoyance but stopped fussing with Hephaestus.

"Why does he sound like a leprechaun?" asked Johnny in a whisper.

"I may be the lame god but that does not mean I'm deaf," roared Hephaestus, his eyes blazing with fire. "And I do not sound like a leprechaun, ya brainless twit. This is a Scottish brogue. Leprechauns are of Irish legend. If ya're goin' to open yar mouth, perhaps it would be better if ya knew what the blazes ya were talkin' about. Or, better yet, just shut up and don't speak, ya witless moron."

"Scottish or Irish, whatever," said Johnny, his tolerance for being insulted finally reaching its limits. "Aren't you Greek gods?"

"Who the bloody hell are *you* to tell a god how to speak?" bellowed Hephaestus as he rose up from his chair. "I think that, as a god, I have the right to talk in any way I choose."

"It just doesn't make sense."

"MAKE SENSE! Did yar mother drop ya on yar head when you were a child? We are gods. Just because we were most active in Greece does not mean we didn't travel around. Gods existed long before there even was a Greece. I've been part of every civilization since the dawn of bleedin' time. We can look and speak any way we bloody well please, and I'll not have some upstart mortal with half a gnat's brain tellin' me how I should talk."

"You know, I'm getting sick of you people calling me an idiot," snapped Johnny.

"Well maybe if ya thought about what ya were gonna say before ya opened yar bleeding mouth, we wouldn't call ya a blitherin' idiot."

"Perhaps it would be best to end this before it gets out of hand?" suggested Athena.

"Nothing wrong with a little lively discussion," said Ares.

"This isn't a lively discussion, Ares," commented Artemis coldly. "This is a fight."

"Even better. I do love a good fight."

"This fight is liable to end with the mortal getting burnt to a crisp," muttered Hermes.

"I don't care what you all think of me!" shouted Johnny. "Call me an idiot all you want, but this guy doesn't sound like any Greek god."

Hephaestus let out a deep, thunderous roar. His jaw elongated into a reptilian maw, his hands grew into long, sharp claws, and his skin began to sprout scales. A pair of large, leathery wings exploded out from his back as a long, scaly tail thrashed about behind him. In a matter of seconds, Hephaestus had transformed into a colossal dragon. He turned to gaze at Johnny with burning eyes and opened his mouth wide. The other students all bolted as a torrent of fire roared out of Hephaestus and enveloped Johnny in searing flames.

"Well, that complicates matters," said Ares. "Guess we have to scrap the lot of them?" As Ares rose up from his throne, his hand reaching down to grab a battle-worn sword, an unseen voice rang out.

"Not so fast, Ares."

There was a soft pop as a hazy, glittering mist cascaded down out of thin air in the center of the room before taking the form of another god.

"Presenting Dionysus, god of wine, celebration, and ecstasy."

Dionysus, like all the other gods except for Hephaestus, was very attractive. Though perhaps not as fit as Hermes, Apollo, or Ares, he was still somewhat slight, with a charming smile and glittering green eyes. He wore a crown of grape leaves upon his head of sandy blond hair, and the chiton he wore was amber in color.

"Hef, stop breathing on the poor mortal, I think he gets the point."

Hephaestus closed his mouth, cutting off the stream of fire, and reverted back to his original form. The flames subside to reveal Johnny, perfectly safe inside a bubble of amber energy. Dionysus snapped his fingers. The bubble popped, releasing Johnny from its protection. Though he hadn't been incinerated by the flames, it was clear that he had felt at least some of the heat. His skin was red, his lips were chapped, and sweat was pouring down his body.

"Now, will you behave and stop acting like a petulant child?" asked Dionysus. "Or do we have to feed you to Hephaestus?"

Johnny, knees trembling, nodded. Slowly, the others started to move back towards Johnny, all of them shooting furtive glances at the gods, Hephaestus in particular.

"Good," said Dionysus as he walked over towards his throne. The floor around it was littered with bottles of wine. As he sat upon his throne, he reached down, picked up one of the bottles, and took a long draft from it.

"Excuse me," said Ashley, stepping forward, "but are we all supposed to just ignore the fact that the Scottish god just tried to barbeque one of us?"

Expression of fear flitted across several of the faces of the assembled students but others, spurred on my Ashley's indignation, joined her in chastising the gods.

"I thought you were here to talk to us, not attack us," said Andrew.

"Yeah, that's not cool," chimed in Sara.

"Totally," agreed Sammy.

"You can't just go around trying to set people on fire," snapped Ana Maria.

"Well, well, well," chortled Dionysus, "isn't this a fiery lot."

"They've got nerve," agreed Ares.

"*They've* also got names," chided Ashley coldly. "And *they* would prefer it if you didn't speak as if *they* aren't in the room."

Ares leaned over from his throne so that his large face was within a few inches of Ashley. His furious black eyes found her defiant blue ones.

"You'd best watch your tongue girl. You are speaking to gods."

"I don't care," retorted Ashley. "If you are going to act like a bunch of jackasses then you can rest assured that I'm going to call you out on it."

A tense silence filled the air as everyone gazed at Ares in trepidation, unsure of how the war god would react. After what seemed like an eternity of silence, Ares began to laugh.

"I like you girly," said Ares, straightening back up. "You've got a fighting spirit within you. Please, accept my apology for my brother's actions. He can be a touch hot-headed."

"No," said Ashley. "He's the one who has to apologize, not you."

Everyone, gods and mortals alike, turned to face Hephaestus.

"Oh, fur the love of . . . fine. I'm sorry I lost my temper. Ya happy now?"

"Yes," said Ashley haughtily.

Several of the gods chuckled. Hephaestus, growling and grumbling to himself, sank despondently down his throne.

"Presenting Demeter, goddess of nature, Lady of the seasons, and Queen of the harvest," said Hermes, drawing the student's attention back to the center of the room before Demeter had even appeared.

Unlike the other gods, Demeter had a rather sedate entrance. She simply grew up from the ground like a stalk of corn. She was taller than the other gods, with a lovely, healthy look about her. Her hair was a deep shade of auburn and her bright green eyes matched her green peplos. Upon her head, she wore a crown of leaves. As Demeter walked towards her throne, which had various plants clustered around it, her eyes caught sight of the scorch marks around Johnny. She cocked an eyebrow at the sight of them.

"Hephaestus you must work to control your temper," said Demeter as she sat down upon her throne, filling the room with the scent of nature as the plants around her seat came to life. "They are only foolish mortals, no need to try to burn them alive."

"Don't start," chided Athena as Hephaestus opened his mouth. "We don't need anyone getting into a furor over this."

"At least things are picking up," said Ares, straightening in his seat. "The big guns are finally arriving."

"How nice to be included as a *big gun*," said Demeter primly. "Even if it is by you, Ares."

"Has the bickering started already?" asked a disembodied voice.

A hole opened up in the middle of the room, and a man erupted out of it. He was taller still than Demeter, with hair as black as midnight and eyes so dark you couldn't see his pupils. He wore a black chiton, trimmed with gold, and a crown of black stone upon his head.

"Presenting Hades, god of the riches of the earth, Lord of the dead, and King of the Underworld."

Hades' dark eyes roved the room and caught sight of the scorch marks around Johnny.

"Ah, that explains it. It seems that I've missed the excitement."

"Only a minor disagreement," said Ares. "Nothing to be concerned about."

"I would hardly call anything that involves the use of fire minor, Ares," said Hades testily. "And I definitely wouldn't call it a disagreement."

"It's been handled," said Dionysus. "No need to drag it back up again."

"Very well, I'll leave it be," said Hades as he took his seat. "I wouldn't want to add to the infighting." His throne was the plainest of all. It had no ornamentation upon it or paraphernalia around it. In fact, the only thing that happened when he sat down upon it was that it turned black as pitch.

As Hades took his seat, several torrents of water swirled through the air to join together in the center of the room to create a miniature waterspout, which collapsed to reveal yet another god. He was just as tall as Hades, though much more muscular. His hair and beard were both brown, and his eyes were the same greenish-blue as the ocean. His chiton was a mellow blue and the crown upon his head seemed to be made of coral. In his right hand, he held a golden trident.

"Presenting Poseidon, god of earthquakes, Lord of horses, and King of the Seas."

When Poseidon took his seat, his throne filled the room with the sounds and smells of the sea.

"What happened there?" asked Poseidon, nodding toward the scorch marks.

"Oh, here we go again," muttered Artemis.

"Apparently it's a matter that we should drop," said Demeter, "lest we cause conflict."

"Which would be totally out of character for us," said Hades with a smirk.

"Okay now I really have to know what's going on," said Poseidon eagerly.

"I tried to roast the little arse over there because he was bein' an impertinent shit," explained Hephaestus moodily. "I let my temper get the better of me. There I said it. Ya happy now?

"I just wanted to know what was going on," said Poseidon, raising his hands defensively as Hades and

Demeter tried to hide their amusement. "No need to bite my head off."

"Why is it that every time we all assemble for a meeting everyone ends up fighting?"

There was a flash of purple light as a woman appeared in the center of the room.

"Presenting Hera, goddess of marriage, Lady of Olympus, and Queen of the gods."

She was as tall as Hades and Poseidon, with sharp purple eyes and glossy brown hair tied up in a tight bun. Her peplos was purple, trimmed with gold, and far more elegant than anyone else. She wore a crown of woven gold and silver, set with shimmering diamonds.

"I see nothing wrong with some friendly banter," said Ares.

"*Friendly?*" commented Hera as she sat down upon a particularly regal throne. "If this is what you call *friendly*, Ares, I would hate to see what you call antagonistic. And would someone please remove those unsightly scorch marks from the floor. If Zeus sees them then this *friendly banter* will most definitely become a full out argument. I'd rather not have to deal with him hurling bolts of lightning left, right, and center."

Hephaestus let out a sigh and gave a quick wave of his hand. The scorch marks vanished, returning the marble floor to its previously pristine condition.

"Excellent timing," said Hera. "Here he comes now."

A bolt of lightning struck the center of the room, leaving a man standing in its wake. Zeus, dressed in a cyan chiton, was taller than any of the other gods. He was more muscular than Hades but not as muscular as Poseidon. His eyes were a vivid shade of electric blue, and his hair was gray, though he looked no older than any other deities in the room. He sported an impressive beard that looked more like a large bank of clouds than anything else and the crown upon his head was made to resemble the jagged shape of a lightning bolt.

"And finally, I present, Zeus, god of the skies, Lord of Olympus, and King of the gods."

Having now finished his duties as herald, Hermes flew over to his own throne, growing in size as he went. By the time he reached his throne, which was surrounded by scrolls, he matched the other gods around him in size.

Zeus had yet to take his seat. Instead, he was looking down at the mortals below him with something akin to contempt in his eyes.

"You are in the presence of the king of gods," he said, his thundering voice shaking the walls and ceiling. "At least show some respect." The other gods rolled their eyes as the assembled group of mortals looked to each other to figure out what to do. Finally, they all inclined their heads in a bow. Zeus let out an exasperated sigh that was reminiscent of a windstorm.

"I suppose that's better than nothing," he grumbled as he took his seat upon a throne composed entirely of storm clouds. "Well let's get this over with. We, the gods of Olympus, have decided that you fourteen mortals are to take over our divine duties as the new gods of Olympus. Do you accept?"

# Chapter Three

"You want us to be what now?" asked Andrew incredulously.

"We want you to be the new gods of Olympus," said Hermes. "You know, take on the powers and responsibilities we each hold. You will be the new gods for a new generation."

"And what if we refuse?" asked Ana Maria. "What if we don't want to be gods?"

"Refuse?" bellowed Zeus, his thunderous voice increasing in volume. "We are giving you the opportunity to be the most powerful beings in the universe! Why would you ever refuse such an offer?" Zeus stopped yelling and turned to look at Hera, who had reached over to place a hand on his arm.

"Perhaps it would be better to allow another to explain the situation to them. We cannot force them to take on this responsibility, and your *passion* could prove to be more of a hindrance than a help."

"Very well," said Zeus as he sank back into the throne grudgingly. "Athena, you do it." Athena nodded, rose from her throne, and turned to face the confused students.

"This is a legitimate offer. I feel I should clarify that. This is not some crude divine comedy. If you agree to replace us as gods, you will be granted powers beyond your wildest imaginings. With the exception of a few minor details, all things will be within your collective powers. In short, together you will hold the universe in the palm of your hands. But this decision must be yours, made of your own free will. And it must be unanimous. All fourteen of you must agree."

Athena gazed down at the fourteen mortals below her, eyes scanning their faces intently.

"I can see some of you have already made up your minds to accept our offer. As such, I beg your indulgence as I endeavor to convince your comrades to accept our proposal. I know that some of you are hesitant to acquiesce for several reasons including, but not limited to, the deferment of your lifelong goals, lack of self-confidence in your ability to take on this monumental task, or a general disinterest in becoming a divine being. While these are all perfectly understandable reservations to have, I would, if allowed, like an opportunity to rebut them."

"In regard to the deferment, or alteration, of your life goals I would like to point out that, as a god, it will be within your ability to do whatever you desire including any career, profession, or endeavor you see fit to undertake. What's more, you will not be constrained by limitations such as old age, injury, monetary restrictions, or fatigue. As a god you will be immortal and nigh-invulnerable, meaning that you need not concern yourself with such trivial matters like death, disease, physical complicates, or even exhaustion. Furthermore, as a god, you will have access to a considerably vast amount of capital, which makes financial complications a non-issue."

"For those of you who believe yourself unqualified or inadequate for the task of being a god, I hope that you will take our confidence in your abilities as a sign that you are, in fact, fully capable of taking on the mantle of godhood. We did not make our choices lightly. This plan for our retirement has been a hundred years in the making. We have observed you, your parents, your grandparents, and your great-grandparents. We believe you all have within you the strength and capacity to not only undertake this prodigious responsibility but also excel at it in ways that we could never dream of."

"You've been watching us?" questioned Ashley.

"We are gods," said Zeus bluntly. "We reign upon high and look down upon the mortal world below. We watch everyone and everything."

"Hope you enjoyed the show," said Vincent with a smirk.

"I can understand you feeling somewhat violated," said Athena, shooting a look of exasperation at Zeus, "but we had to make sure that you truly were worthy of this prestigious appointment. We could not just hand over what would effectively be the keys to the universe to any odd person off the street. So we waited and selected fourteen individuals who we felt could not only fill our proverbial shoes but also reinvent them for a new generation."

"Can we ask you a few questions?" inquired Ana Maria.

"Of course. Feel free to pose any query that you may have."

"Ok," began Ana Maria, "so you've intimated that we will have the power to do as we please. From this, we can assume that you already have the ability to do as you please. As such, I must ponder the question as to why there is still suffering and hardship in the world. As gods, why have you allowed such things to continue?"

Several of the gods shifted uncomfortably in their seats.

"I wonder who you've been chosen to replace," said Apollo with a knowing smile. Athena glared at him reproachfully.

"As gods," explained Athena, "we do not believe it is our place to intervene in the everyday lives of mortals.

Hardships and adversities have their place, as do pleasure and accomplishments."

"But—" began Ana Maria but Apollo cut her off.

"This is the cost of free will. Yes, we gods could hover around you and keep you all safe and secure but then you would be little better than puppets on strings. The misery and pain in the world is not caused by we Olympian deities, it is caused by you mortals. You make the decisions, not us."

"But you influence it," challenged Sara. "You allow it to happen."

"We do our duty," countered Artemis.

"Don't you care about people at all?" asked Sophia.

"Do you care about the ants you trod underfoot?" countered Ares. "Or the flies you swat from the sky?"

"Are you comparing humans to insects?" asked Sophie in indignation.

"Of course, I am. To us, mortals are nothing but slightly more intelligent specks of dust under our feet. Your lives, your existences are but a fleeting, insignificant moments in the fullness of time, hardly worth notice or consideration."

"You can't just—" began Sara but Zeus interrupted her.

"Who are you to tell us what we can and cannot do!" he roared, rising up from his throne to tower menacingly over the mortals below him. Storm clouds began to form above him, blanketing the ceiling with dense, dark vapor that was crawling with crackling lightning.

"We are gods! We created mortals! We brought you into existence, gave you life, gave you purpose. And yet, how were we repaid for our generosity? We were forgotten, cast aside as myths and legends. We, who were you creators, are now figments of your imagination. And now, you dare to dictate what we may do or say. Your arrogance knows no bounds. If you ever dare to chastise us again, I will put an immediate end to your short existence." Zeus glared menacingly down at the cowering students before resuming his seat.

"Ya have ta understand," said Hephaestus, "we are gods. We were born of power. As a result, we are vain and vengeful. We care little for anything but ourselves. It's our natures."

"But don't let this influence your decision," chimed in Hermes. "If you accept, you'll be the ones in control. You can make the decisions on how the world works. You can be as involved as you want. You could end all disease, stop all hunger. You could even make it rain real cats and dogs, though I would suggest against that because it could get a little messy."

"Enough of this prattle," snapped Zeus. "Make your decisions. We have much to attend to."

"We have some time still," countered Athena. "If they have more questions, they should be permitted to ask them.

"What about our families?" asked Andrew.

"What about them?" asked Ares dismissively.

"Will we still be able to see them?"

"Of course," said Hermes. "You can see them whenever you want. There's no rule against gods fraternizing with mortals."

"Although, if there were, it might certainly have helped things," muttered Hera.

"What will happen to all of you?" asked Ana Maria. "Will you all just fade away?"

"We are granting you our divine authorities, not our lives," said Athena. "We were born with power long before we acquired our respective domains. Once those domains have been transferred to you, we will simply be as we were before, immortal beings of divine energy.

"Also, something you should note, we will be passing along only a portion of our powers to you. This is for your protection. If we were to endow you with our full, and considerable, divinity you would be incinerated by its sheer unadulterated might. This spark of power will continue to grow inside you, slowly increasing in strength until you have completely acclimated to our powers and become a god. This may take some time. The exact amount of time is unknown to us as this has never been attempted before. During this period of adjustment, we will remain in our positions of authority. As you become more and more accustomed to your powers, we will educate you about the various duties that you will be required to perform. Hopefully, by the time our powers have completely transferred to you, you'll be ready to reign as the new gods of Olympus."

"Can we move this along?" demanded Zeus. "We gods do have somewhat busy schedules. We've spent too much time on these pointless questions as it is. This should be a simple decision; do you want power or not?"

"Well I'm in," said Johnny immediately.

"*Quelle surprise*," muttered Matthew so that only Renée could hear him. She chuckled lightly.

"I'm game too," said Vincent raising his flask in assent. "Sounds like fun."

"It's a no-brainer for me," said Ashley haughtily. "After all, I always knew I was destined for great things."

Sophie, Ana Maria, and Sara all rolled their eyes.

"So, I can still be a football player if I want to be?" asked Andrew.

"Of course," said Hermes. "I played a season or two myself, just for kicks."

"Alright cool. I'm in."

"And we really will be in charge?" asked Ana Maria. "Our decisions will be the final? No catches? No loopholes?

"Whatever decision you make, for good or ill, will be the word of law," said Athena. "But you will have to deal with any consequences that may arise from said decision."

Athena's steely gray eyes met Ana Maria's warm brown ones. For several seconds they stared intently into each other's eyes, engaging in a silent and intense conversation. Finally, Ana Maria spoke.

"Very well. For the good of humanity, I consent."

"If she's good, then I'm good too," said Sophia.

"And me," said Sara.

"*Je suppose que nous serions jeunes toujours*," said Matthew to Renée.

"*Suffisant pour moi*," replied Renée. "We are in."

"Guess I'll join the majority and say yes too," said Lance with a shrug.

"Sound like it could be cool," said Samuel. "Count me in."

Everyone turned to look at Irene and Gavin, who had yet to proclaim their intentions.

"I . . . I . . . I'm not sure," said Gavin hesitantly. "It's kinda a lot to take in."

"What's to be unsure about," snapped Ashley. "You get to be a god. I mean, I know someone like you might not understand how that may feel but—"

"Hey!" interrupted Sophia. "You don't know anything about him. So why don't you keep your opinions to yourself, bitch."

"Excuse me? Who the hell are you to talk to me like that?"

"I'm the girl who ain't afraid to kick your overly made-up ass all the way back to the States."

"Is that so you little c—"

"Enough!" bellowed Zeus, the clouds overhead thundering ominously.

"Killjoy," muttered Ares.

"Take your time," said Sara. "You heard what Athena said. This has to be your own decision. Don't let anyone influence ya."

"I guess," said Gavin after a minute's contemplation, "that it wouldn't be so bad."

"Great," said Ashley brusquely. She turned to Irene and demanded, "How about you?"

"I don't want to rock the boat, so I'll say yes if it's what you all want."

"It's not about what we want," said Lance. "You have to make this decision for yourself."

"Why is it always the riff-raff that makes things difficult," said Ashley in exasperation.

"Oh, shut up," snapped Sophie.

"Please, don't fight," said Irene quickly as Ashley opened her mouth to respond. "It's not just because everyone else wants to. I am interested. Really."

"You're sure?" asked Lance.

"Positive," said Irene with a smile.

"Well there you have it," said Ashley happily, "a full consensus. Now make us gods."

"Not quite," said Hades. "You are one short."

"What?" gasped Ashley. She turned to scan the group. "Who?"

"Me," said Benjamin raising his hand. He had been standing slightly apart from the group, completely unnoticed.

"Oh, well make up your mind."

"*Elle va être une poignée,*" muttered Matthew.

"*Convenu,*" replied Renée.

"*Les dieux nous aident tous,*" added Ana Maria.

"*Oh, vous parlez Français aussi?*" asked Renée happily. "*Vous devriez l'avoir dit.*"

"Would you three shut up?" demanded Ashley. "You answered already. You, mister doom and gloom, answer already."

"Who would I be replacing?" asked Benjamin, ignoring Ashley.

"Me," said Hades with a smile.

"So, I'd be in charge of dead people?"

"Correct. Your domain would be the Underworld."

"And if I just wanted to hide in the Underworld and not deal with anything else that would be fine?"

"Absolutely. It's what I've been doing for millennia."

"Alright. I'm in."

"Good," said Zeus, rising to his feet. The other gods followed suit. "Then let us get this over with. Hebe!"

A pair of pure white wings unfurled out of thin air, expanding out at least twenty feet before folding into a beauty, feathery dress, into which a young girl suddenly appeared. Though she too towered over the assembled group she was tiny compared to the other gods. No more than eight feet tall, she looked like a porcelain doll with her long, golden ringlets and mint-colored eyes.

"I am Hebe," she said in a sweet, innocent voice, "goddess of youth. I will serve as Lady Hestia's representative as she cannot be here herself."

"Why?" asked Ana Maria.

"Because she never leaves Olympus," replied Hermes. "I'm pretty sure I said that already. Now then, are you ready?"

"Yes," was the unanimous response.

"Then let us begin," said Zeus.

"Irene Adler, come forth."

Irene stepped forward to stand in front of Hebe, who held out her hand. A pure white flame erupted into existence in the palm of her hand. Irene looked at Hebe in confusion. The goddess of youth smiled comfortingly at her and nodded towards the flame. Slowly, Irene reached up with shaking hands and took the ball of white fire from Hebe. It hovered above her cup hands, its gentle warmth spreading through her and filling her with a great sense of comfort and safety.

"Vincent Hops, come forth."

Vincent sloped languidly forward and took the amber flame the Dionysus offered him. He immediately felt a giddy euphoria wash over him.

"Ooo, that feels good," said Vincent, shivering with enjoyment as his blood seemed to fizz about in his veins.

"Gavin Swift, come forth."

Gavin crept forward even more nervously than Irene, his hands trembling so much they were blurs. It took him several seconds before he could even look up at Hermes. It took him even longer to accept the bronze flame that was being offered to him. Once he'd taken the flame, however, a sense of excitement raced through him. His doubts and fears gave way to a fervent need for exploration.

"Hold up there, kiddo," said Hermes with a wicked smile as it looked like Gavin was about to make a break for the door. "We've got more to get through." Gavin, who was now shaking with excitement instead of nerves, gave Hermes a disappointed look but stayed put.

"Lance Smith, come forth."

As Lance took the orange flame from Hephaestus, an intense heat surged through him, bringing with it a burning determination to mold and shape the raw elements of the world into all manner of useful and innovative contraptions. Plans for new inventions quickly filled his head and he couldn't wait to get started on them.

"Reneé Hart, come forth."

Aphrodite's pink flame filled Reneé with an overwhelming sense of her own grandeur. She could feel all of existence gazing at her, yearning for her. She reveled in the exaltation of such universal adulation.

"Matthew Golden, come forth."

Matthew swept forward confidently and took the golden flame from Apollo, which sent a soothing heat danced through him like sunlight on a summer's day. He felt inspiration tugging at his heart and mind, urging him to compose astonishing pieces of music or create breathtaking works of art. All he needed to do to become the greatest artist that ever lived was follow the golden path that was shimmering in front of his eyes.

"Sophia Hunt, come forth."

The silver flame glittered mysteriously as Sophia stepped forward and took it from Artemis. A sense of wild abandon rushed through the tiny girl, filling her ears and nose with the sounds and smells of nature. At the same time, something strange stirred inside her. It was as if a great beast had awoken within Sophia and was now ready to claw its way to freedom.

"John Strong, come forth."

Barely able to contain his eagerness, Johnny arrogantly swaggered up to Ares to receive the red flame. The instant he took the fire, Johnny's world went red. A seething fury raged through his body, causing his blood to boil, his muscles to bulge, and his heart to hammer loudly in his ears. It was all he could do to keep himself from lashing out violently against those around him.

"Ana Maria Sabio, come forth."

Unlike the other, Ana Maria took the time to inspect the gray flame that Athena offered. After she'd examined the fire from all angles, she pulled out a pen and poked at it.

"What is this?" asked Ana Maria as she examined her pen, which seemed to be completely unaffected by the gray flames.

"It is the fire of the gods," answered Athena. "The source of our power."

"How does it—"

"Enough of your questions!" roared Zeus, his thundering voice bouncing deafeningly of the walls and ceiling. "Accept your flame so that we may continue!"

Ana Maria shot a disgusted look at Zeus before taking the fire from Athena. She let out a soft gasp as a massive amount of information immediately began to flow through her mind. Equations and theorems, facts and figures, the answers to every conceivable question, all began whirling about her consciousness. Ana Maria tried to snatch at a passing thought, only for ten more to take its place.

"Sara Gardener, come forth."

A sense of tranquility and comfort bloomed inside Sara as she took the green flame from Demeter. It was as though she'd been transported back on her family's farm in Australia. She could feel the hot noon sun beating down upon her, taste the warm summer's breeze on her tongue, hear the sounds of farm animals all around her, smell the scent of fertile earth under her feet, and see the fields of wheat stretching out in front of her as far as her eyes could see.

"Benjamin Darke, come forth."

Stepping out of the shadows of the remaining three mortals, Ben moved to stand in front of Hades. They locked eyes. To his surprise, Ben found comfort and strength in the dark eyes of the god of the dead. He reached out and took the black flame from Hades. A cold and silent darkness crept through Ben like a winter's night. And from that darkness, came a feeling he knew all too well, the feeling of isolation. And yet, this time, the sense of loneliness felt different to him somehow. He didn't hate it. He didn't recoil from it. In fact, he felt at peace. The hustle and bustle of the world had melted away, leaving Ben calm and contented in this solitary darkness.

"Samuel Poole, come forth."

Ambling happily forward, Sammy took Poseidon's blue fire. He felt the power of the blue flame flooding through him. He was no longer himself; he was the sea. His bones were coral, his muscles were kelp, and his beating heart was the breaking of the tide against the shore. All sense of who he was had been lost, washed away by the majesty of the sea.

"Ashley Queen, come forth."

With her back straight, her head held high, and a look of determination in her eyes, Ashley stroll forward and accept the purple flame from Hera. She was immediately overcome with a sense of regal dignity. She knew, in her heart of hearts, that she'd been born to rule. As she looked at the world around, it became clear to her that the world was in desperate need of her guiding hand. It wasn't just her birthright; it was her duty.

"Andrew St. Cloud, come forth."

Andrew stepped forward and took the crackling cyan flame from Zeus. Lightning roared through Andrew, charging every inch of his body with pure, raw power. He had never, in his life, felt more alive than he did at this moment. The world, the universe, all of existence was his, and his alone, to command.

"We," chorused the gods in unison as they raised their hand and eyes to the heavens, "the gods of Olympus, do bestow upon these mortals a portion of our power. May it take hold inside them and grow until they have gained true divinity."

The flames began to grow in size and intensity. Soon each of the young mortals was covered in their own fiery aura. As the flames intensified, so too did their effects. Soon all fourteen of the young mortals were double over, gasping in pain as the divine power of the flames coursed through their veins.

"We declare you the new gods of Olympus!"

The gods clapped their hands together as one. The fourteen fiery auras all flared at once. There was a blind flash of light and the flames vanished completely. The sensation that had accompanied each flame vanished too, leaving the fourteen young mortals feeling the same as they had before they'd take them. Looking around the room, they found that all traces of the Greek gods' presence had vanished. The statues had returned to their original forms and locations, and the doors out of the room stood open. A new group of freshmen were already filling into the room as their tour guide explained the significance of the statues.

The new gods looked at one another, unsure how they should feel. For a moment, they all thought it might have just been a dream, but something inside them told them what had just happened was very real. Though they all looked the same as before, deep down they knew something had changed. And, though they didn't yet understand exactly what was different, they all knew that they would never be the same again.

# Chapter Four

Walking across the M.O.U. campus, Ben marveled at its architecture. Each building had its own particular style, though they were all built of polished marble and featured columns in some form or another. The geology building, for example, had been constructed to resemble a miniature mountain, its many entrances and windows disguised as cave openings or stony outcroppings. Meanwhile, the architecture department was housed in what could only be described as a five-story drafting compass.

Ben stopped, readjusted his grip on his armload of boxes, and continued on. He was moving from his dorm in the Zephyrus Hall to an apartment that the gods had created especially for him and the other thirteen new gods. The term, *new gods*, was still weird to him. In fact, the very idea that gods existed, in general, was difficult to wrap his head around, let alone that he would soon be one himself. Though they were of Jewish heritage, Ben's family was mostly atheistic. The few traditions they did practice were mostly cultural ones, like *Chanukah* and *Bar Mitzvahs*.

Spotting a nearby bench, Ben put down his boxes for a moment's rest. He'd been sent a letter that said that someone would come around 10 a.m. to help him move. That had been the first communication that he'd received from the gods since meeting them. What's more, 10 a.m. was four hours ago. After coming to the conclusion that he'd been forgotten again, he decided that, since his stuff was already packed up, he'd just move it all himself. After all, it was only one big box and four smaller ones. Unfortunately, the apartment was in Eurus Hall, which was on the other side of campus. Ben closed his eyes and took a deep breath.

"Problem?" Ben's eyes flew open and he turned to see Hermes sitting next to him. Instead of the ancient Grecian attire he'd worn when they had first met, he was instead dressed as a moving man.

"No one came to help me move," said Ben. "So I figured I'd do it myself."

"Sorry about that," said Hermes. "You just slipped my mind."

"I'm not surprised," said Ben. "It happens all the time. I'm used to it."

"That's not exactly heartening," said Hermes.

"I'm the invisible boy," said Ben. "At least, that was my nickname in high school."

"Well, I'll make a mental note to always remember you," said Hermes. "And when I make a mental note to do something, it sticks."

"Whatever you say," said Ben, though he didn't put much stock in Hermes words.

"So, how about we get you moved into the apartment?" suggested Hermes. "I'm afraid all the other rooms have already been selected so you're stuck with the one closest to the door."

"That's fine," said Ben. "I don't mind."

"How very obliging of you," said Hermes. Hermes snapped his fingers. The support of the bench immediately vanished, and Ben fell backward onto carpeting. His boxes dropped softly on the floor beside him.

"Ow."

"Sorry about that," said Hermes, who was sitting on air. "Should have warned you about that."

It only took Ben one look to see that Hermes was not sorry at all.

"Where are we?" asked Ben as he rose to his feet.

"This is your room," said Hermes. "We can deal with furniture and unpacking later. For now, a tour. That door is your closet, that door is your bathroom, and that knobby thing is your personal climate control unit. All the rooms have their own personalized heating and cooling. Also, there is a washer and dryer in your closet."

"How much more than Zephyrus is this going to cost?" asked Ben as he looked around at his empty, but spacious, room.

"Why does it matter?" asked Hermes. "You and the others are all here on scholarships."

"Yeah but mine was only for a specific amount," said Ben. "Any more than that and we had to pay out of pocket."

"You don't seem to grasp the point," said Hermes. "We, the gods, were the ones who arranged your scholarships. We've dealt with all the paperwork and even emailed your parents about your change of address. You don't have to worry about anything. Not even your grades. Oh wait, I'm not supposed to tell you that. Ignore what I just said. Do well in school."

Ben let out a snort of laughter. "Will do."

"Now, follow me."

Ben followed Hermes out of his bedroom. To his right was what he assumed was the front door. To his left was a small hallway. Based on the size of the room he'd just been in, he guessed that his was the only room that was actually in the hallway.

"Front door," said Hermes. "It faces west, in case such things matter to you. Oh, and here," Hermes hand him a key card. "This gets you in the building and then you have to swipe it on the elevator to get up here. Top floor."

"What about groceries?" asked Ben.

"The pantry, fridge, and freezer are all self-replenishing," said Hermes. "Come along."

Hermes led him down the hallway and into a wide, open living room. Two large sofas, one leather and one suede, and six armchairs in various fabrics were scattered around the room, all of them facing a fifty-inch HD television and accompanying entertainment center. There were thirteen doors set into the north, south, and west walls, while the east had a large archway that led into a dining room. There was also another door on the far side of the east wall, as well as three large shelves: one full of books, one full of DVDs, and one full of board games.

"Kitchen is through the dining room," said Hermes. "And of course, the other doors are your fellow new gods' rooms."

"There are fourteen doors," said Ben. "Who's the other room for?"

"Oh, that's a linen closet," said Hermes. "A very special linen closet."

"How can a linen closet be special?" asked Ben.

"You'll find out soon enough," said Hermes. "Let me see, the T.V. gets every channel, in every language, known to man. There is a rather extensive guide on that bookshelf over there. There is also one of every gaming console in the entertainment center and a selection of games for you all to choose from. You can already see the shelves with books, DVDs, and board games. The entire place has the best internet connection in the known universe, about one thousand and five hundred megabytes per second."

"That's . . . ridiculous."

"That's divinity," said Hermes. "I am the god of communication and speed after all."

One of the doors opened and Sara stuck her head out.

"I thought I heard a voice. Hello Hermes. Who are you talking to?"

Ben raised his hand and waved it about.

"Me."

"Sorry mate," said Sara, "didn't see ya there."

"Don't worry about it," said Ben. "I'm used to it."

"Get everyone else out here while I show Ben the kitchen," said Hermes.

"Why?" asked Sara.

"Because there is more for you all to know."

Hermes led Ben through the dining room, which had a circular dining table that looked big enough for all fourteen new gods to use, and into the kitchen. It was at least twice the size of Ben's bedroom. There were four separate stove tops, six ovens, three microwaves, two refrigerators (with freezers), and one freezer by itself. There was also a considerable collection of pots, pans, utensils, and other kitchen wares, many of which Ben had never seen before. There were also two doors, one slightly smaller than the other.

"That door," said Hermes, pointing at the smaller door, "is the pantry. The other door leads to Irene's room. Interestingly enough, she's the only one with two exits to her room. I suppose it makes sense that the future goddess of the home has easy access to the kitchen."

"Happy coincidence?" asked Ben suspiciously.

"Clever assumption," said Hermes with a smile. Having finished looking over the kitchen, Hermes and Ben returned to the living room, where the other thirteen occupants had been assembled.

"What is it?" demanded Ashley crossly. "I was unpacking. I have several designer outfits and I don't want them wrinkling."

"Calm yourself," warned Hermes, "or I'll turn you into a newt." Ashley glared at him.

"What is it you need Hermes?" asked Andrew politely.

"There are a few more things I need to tell you about the apartment and the rules. And I've been asked to make introductions as well. But that's for a bit later. Alright everyone, go stand in front of your doors please."

"Why?" demanded Ashley.

"So, Ben can see where everyone's room is."

"What, he didn't see us pick earlier?"

"He wasn't here when you all picked your rooms," snapped Hermes.

"Oh, well how long until he gets here?"

Hermes let out an exasperated sigh and gestured towards Ben, who was still standing right next to him. Ashley turned her unnaturally blue eyes upon him.

"You're late."

"Sorry," said Ben sarcastically.

"You should be," said Ashley with complete sincerity. Turning sharply on her high heels, she started back towards her room. The others followed immediately. Looking around the room, Ben saw that his closest neighbor was Johnny.

"Now then, everyone hold out a hand," said Hermes.

They all obeyed. Hermes snapped his fingers. Old-fashioned keys appeared in each of their hands. The bow on Ben's key was shaped like a skull and its two prongs resembled caricatured bones.

"These are your room keys," explained Hermes. "They have a couple of special properties. The first is that whenever you need them, they will always appear. So, don't worry if you lose it. The same goes with your key cards. But that's not the most important function of your keys."

Hermes moved to stand in front of the linen closet door. "If you would all gather around."

Once the new gods were assembled around him, Hermes opened the closet door, revealing piles of linens on every shelf.

"Under normal circumstances," said Hermes, "this functions as a normal linen closet. But if you insert your key into the lock, it becomes something much more. This closet is actually a portal. To activate it, you need only insert your key into the lock, think about where you want to go, turn the key, and open the door. You will then be connected to a door at or near where you wanted to go. And, to get back to the apartment, just insert your key into any key hold, turn it, open the door, and walk right back in."

"That's amazing," whispered Gavin softly.

"I know," said Hermes proudly. "I made it."

"What if we want to go somewhere we've never been before?" asked Ana Maria.

"As long as you have a general idea of where you want to go, you'll get there," said Hermes. "Now, there are two people I've been told to introduce you to. But, before we get to that, a few ground rules about the apartment and the whole future gods thing. First, this is your place. Do with it as you will. But remember, there are thirteen other people living here, so try and be respectful. Secondly, if you are ever in dire need, there is a stack of papers on the bookshelf. Simply write whatever your issue is and then set the paper on fire. That will alert us if it happens that we are too busy at the time to notice. Do try not to use them for everyday emergencies. You are going to be gods after all, you need to figure that kind of stuff out for yourself.

"Third, you must keep it a secret that the Greek gods exist, at least for now. What you choose to do once you are gods is up to you but as of right now, the rule is for secrecy. We defer to your judgment on what steps you would like to take to prevent the information from being leaked. As such, you can invite anyone you want to this place, so long as they don't find out about the gods. If complications should occur and the gods have to step in to fix it, we may revoke this privilege.

"And finally, you will be expected to participate in a daily, one-hour training session. I do not know what this will include or how it will be structured, but I do know that their purpose is to help you gain control of your new powers. Are there any questions?"

Reneé raised her hand.

"Yes?"

# Heir to the Underworld

"What are ze ruwez about dating, if zere are any?"

"That is entirely up to your own discretion," said Hermes. "So long as whatever paramour you are currently romancing doesn't find out about the gods, we couldn't care less. Anything else?"

"Yes," said Ana Maria. "All of our schedules are different so how are we going to all attend a training session? And, while you told us that the gods effectively made it so that we could attend this school, what are our academic requirements?"

"You are going to be a god," said Johnny. "Why do you still care about school?"

"Because she's an intelligent individual who understands that school is more than just about getting a degree," said Hermes. "It's about broadening your horizons and expanding your mind. Something you obviously need help with."

Johnny's face flushed.

"As for your questions, we have arranged it so that your classes will allow you a break period to attend training, without overwhelming you. And, we expect you to do well academically. There may be repercussions if you do not."

*Not a word.* Ben stiffened. Hermes' voice had just echoed through his mind even though Hermes' lips hadn't moved.

*How—*

*God of communication remember. No don't say a word, you'll spoil my fun.*

"Like what?" asked Johnny with a dismissive smile. "No spring break?"

"I was thinking something more along the lines of turning anyone who has below a two-point-five GPA into a turtle for the summer holidays," said Hermes coldly.

The smile slid off Johnny's face.

"Anything else?" asked Hermes.

No one raised their hands or said anything.

"Good, now to meet the two people who will be in charge of your training. I warn you now, you'll like one of them. The other one, not as much."

Hermes pointed at the door to the linen closet, which closed and then opened. To the amazement of the new gods they saw, not the shelves of linen as before, but the flat, grassy turf of a sports arena. Hermes stepped through the door and motioned the new gods to join him.

Following Hermes, the new goes found themselves standing in a massive, open-air arena that had to be at least ten times the size of the Coliseum. As far as they could see, the arena had everything. There was a basketball court, four tracks (each a different size), a football field, a soccer field, a baseball diamond, two Olympic sized swimming pools, a volleyball court, six different obstacle courses, a wrestling and fighting ring, a collection of gymnastic equipment, several targets for archery, a Zen garden, a tennis court, seven rock walls, a hockey rink, and several large open areas that could be used for any number of different activities.

"Whoa," was the collective response from the fourteen new gods.

"Welcome to Heracles' arena," said Hermes.

"Heracles?" asked Lance. "Don't you mean Hercules?"

"That was his Roman name," said Hermes. "His real name was Heracles. The media has been mucking that up for years. Seems they think Hercules is easier to say than Heracles."

"I can't exactly blame them. It can be a bit weird the first few times ya say it."

Two people, a man and a woman, had suddenly appeared before the new gods.

"Everyone, may I introduce Heracles, greatest of all heroes, and Hecate, goddess of magic."

If ever there was a man who deserved to be called a Greek god, it was Heracles. He was at least seven feet tall, with bulging muscles, wavy black hair, friendly brown eyes, a handsome face, and an olive complexion. He smiled at the group and raised a friendly hand in greeting.

"Nice to meet you all." He turned to look at his companion. Standing next to Heracles, Hecate could easily become lost in his shadow. She was incredibly thin, with skin as white as chalk, long hair the color of blood, and cold lime-green eyes. She wore a black dress so tight that it was almost possible to see her ribs.

"I will withhold my judgment until a later date," said Hecate haughtily.

"You'll have to excuse her," said Heracles. "This is the first time she's come up out of the Underworld in the past two thousand years. She's forgotten how to be nice."

"I do not need you to make excuses for me to a group of mortals," hissed Hecate coldly.

"These aren't just any mortals," said Heracles. "They are gods-to-be."

"I don't care what they *may* be in future. For now, they are mortals and, as a goddess, I need not explain myself to them."

"In case you didn't notice, they don't get along very well," muttered Hermes so that only the new gods could hear. Raising his voice, he said, "Shall I introduce the new gods of Olympus?"

"No," said Hecate. "I have no interest in becoming acquainted with mortals."

"You may not be interested but I am," said Heracles. "Go on Hermes."

"Gladly," said Hermes and he proceeded to introduce all fourteen new gods to Heracles, who shook each of their hands.

"Now that that's out of the way, why don't you explain to everyone what training will be like," suggested Hermes.

"Right," said Heracles. "When it comes to training, you'll have two options. You can either train in physical combat with me, or you can train you divine powers with

Hecate. The choice is up to you. And don't think you have to do the same one every day. You can switch around as you like."

"Do try not to disappoint," said Hecate, her lime-green eyes raking over the new gods in disdain.

"Now, I know there will be some questions about safety, since we will be using battle-ready weapons and your divine powers are still new to you but don't worry. Hecate will be able to heal you right up. Are there any questions?"

"When do we start training?" asked Andrew.

"We thought we'd give you the day to settle in," said Heracles, "so training starts tomorrow at three o'clock. Also, feel free to come and use the arena at your leisure. And if you ever want to talk, that little shed over there is my place. Come by anytime. Hopefully, I won't be otherwise engaged."

"I do not reside here," said Hecate, "and I will not be available outside of training. You would do well to remember this. If you lose a limb while I am not present, that will not be any of my concern."

"Thank you both for you time," said Hermes. "Back to the apartment. I still have to get Ben some furniture."

"See you all tomorrow," said Heracles, waving energetically as the new gods began to leave.

"Yes," said Hecate, "see you tomorrow when, I can only hope, you all prove yourselves capable to the task before you."

As the last of the new gods crossed the threshold back into the apartment, the linen closet door closed on the smiling Heracles and the scowling Hecate.

# Chapter Five

Gavin took a deep, steadying breath. Bending down into a runner's crouch, he looked down the track in front of him with unfocused eyes. He'd removed his glasses in case of an accident. The first time he had tried running the track he had ended up breaking his glasses, causing a shard of glass to become embedded in his eye. Though his eye had been healed, and his glasses repaired, he found it prudent to take them off so as not to repeat the same incident.

He tried not to think about that as he tensed his body, took another breath, and shot forward, moving faster than was humanly possible. In the blink of an eye, he had cleared a hundred yards. He tried to turn with the curvature of the track, but he was going too fast. Losing control, he tripped, flew several yards through the air, and then landed painfully on the long stretch of grass.

"Ow," moaned Gavin as he got shakily to his feet.

His clothes were stained with grass and his arms, face, and legs were covered in large scrapes. Sadly, out of all his attempts thus far today, this had been the most successful. At least he had been able to shift his weight a bit this time around. He hobbled back towards the starting line, his injuries and blurred vision hindering his progress. Finally reaching the starting line, he picked his glasses up off the small table next to the track and put them on. Immediately the arena came into sharp relief.

"Are you even trying?" Gavin looked around to find Hecate glaring at him.

"I am," said Gavin defiantly.

"You'll excuse me if I'm far from impressed."

Hermes had been right, no one liked Hecate. She was coldly judgmental and cruelly critical of everyone except Matthew, who she constantly praised.

"I'm new at this," said Gavin in an attempt to stick up for himself. "At least I'm moving fast. That's something right?"

"Power without control is not power at all," said Hecate. "Everyone else, except Benjamin, has at least some modicum of control over their powers by now. Honestly, why Hermes would pick someone like you to succeed him is beyond me."

"Oh come on, leave him alone." Matthew, who had been practicing creating light projections a few yards away, had wandered over with the intention of healing Gavin's injuries.

When they had first started training, Hecate had been the one to take responsibility for healing any injuries they may have received. Now Matthew, who was mastering his new abilities with astonishing speed, was the one who acted as the official healer for the group.

"You are too soft on people," snapped Hecate disapprovingly. "How do you expect people to grow if you are always coddling them?"

"I've made plenty of people *grow* when I coddle them. Or was that cuddle?" Matthew gave Gavin a sly wink.

Gavin could feel his cheeks turning red and determinedly looked the other way. Matthew reached out to touch the scrap on Gavin's face, his hand glowing with a soft golden light. The sting of Gavin's injuries began to fade away as Matthew gently moved his hand across each and every scrape, scratch, and cut. Goosebumps erupted all over

Gavin's body as he desperately tried to ignore the fact that his pants were getting uncomfortably tight.

"All done," said Matthew cheerfully.

"Thanks," said Gavin with an awkward smile as he tried to adjust himself surreptitiously.

"No problem cutie."

"Should I be jealous?" asked Vincent, who had been lounging on a nearby bench and drinking his way through a bottle of wine.

"I don't know," mused Matthew as he slid his arm around Gavin's waist. "I think that depends on Gavin."

Gavin's face felt like it was on fire. He quickly slipped out of Matthew's grasp and put several feet between them.

"Sorry," said Matthew apologetically. "Forgot you were shy."

"I'm not shy," said Gavin defiantly. "I just don't like being touched is all."

"If you are looking for someone to fondle, I'm available," said Vincent.

"And why would I be interested in a drunk like you?" asked Matthew teasingly as he walked over towards Vincent.

"Well, I am extremely sexy," was Vincent's brazen response. "As you well know."

"Can't disagree with you there," said Matthew with a smile. He leaned down and kissed Vincent.

Gavin watched their display of affection with a wistful expression in his eyes. Ever since the fourteen of them had moved into together, Matthew and Vincent had developed a very *close* relationship.

"Sexy or not, you are a lazy, drunken, miserable excuse for a god-to-be." Hecate was glaring at Vincent and Matthew, her hands on her hips and her lips pursed.

Vincent, unlocking his lips from Matthews, looked up at Hecate and asked, "Well then I'll make an excellent wine god, won't I?"

"You have done nothing for the past five days but sit and drink," snapped Hecate. "You have been granted a great power but, instead of learning how to control your new abilities, you spend your time drinking and flirting."

"That's not true," said Vincent in mock outrage. "I'll have you know that I've mastered a very critical aspect of my powers."

"And what might that be?"

"I can keep this bottle from running dry."

Matthew snorted with laughter as Hecate glared menacingly at Vincent.

"You are an insolent brat," said Hecate, her voice as cold as ice.

"And you're a frigid bitch who needs to get laid."

Hecate's eyes and nostrils widened in anger. Pale blue energy began to course around her clenched fisted and steam, literally, began to billow out from her ears.

"How dare you—" she began, but she was interrupted by the arrival of Heracles, Lance, Ana Maria, Johnny, and Sophia.

"Whoa there girl, calm down, no need to get so riled up," said Heracles.

"I am not a horse," hissed Hecate, turning to stare daggers at Heracles. "And this boy needs to learn respect."

"Somehow I don't think you casting a spell on him is gonna make him respect you any more than he already does. Besides, what do you think Dionysus is gonna do when he hears you cursed his protégée?"

"Were he here he would support my decision."

"Have you ever met Dionysus?" asked Heracles sarcastically. "If he were here, he'd join in with the insults."

"Be that as it may, these children need to learn that they have been given a great honor and they need to stop squandering their gifts on petty indulgences."

"I thought that's what gods do," said Vincent, "indulge in pettiness and superficial wants."

"Impudent mortal," screeched Hecate. "I should remove your tongue."

"Well he's not wrong," said Heracles. "I mean look at my dad. He's not exactly the poster boy for restraint."

"Have you any respect for the gods?"

"Not really, no. Maybe Hermes and Uncle Hades. Everyone else is just kind of annoying. Especially Hera."

"So, anyone need healing?" asked Matthew, moving towards the contingency that had followed Heracles over, while their trainers continued to bicker.

"I could use some," said Lance, who was sporting a swollen lip.

"I could also use a little healing, *por favor*," said Ana Maria, who had a gash over her right eye.

"I'm good," said Sophie. Out of the four, she was the only one who looked completely uninjured.

"I'm fine too," said Johnny, despite the fact that he was cradling his right arm.

"No, you're not," snapped Lance as Matthew got to work healing his injuries. "I heard your arm crack when Heracles threw you."

"It's fine," said Johnny stubbornly.

"The only one who is fine is Sophia," said Ana Maria. "Where did you learn that spinning move by the way?"

"The leg one? I saw it in a movie once, and I had my *sensei* help me figure it out."

"So you already knew martial arts before you started training with Heracles?" asked Matthew as he moved on to Ana Maria.

"Yup. I've been studying martial arts since I was six. I've got black belts in *aikido*, *taekwondo*, *karate*, and *jiu-jitsu*. I've also done some *kung fu* and *tai chi*."

"Remind me not to piss you off," said Andrew as he and the rest of the new gods joined the group, all of them having finished their own training for the day. Matthew, having finished healing Ana Maria, started to walk over towards Johnny.

"I said I'm alright," barked Johnny, limping away from Matthew.

"What is your problem?" asked Sophia. "You clearly have a sprained ankle and a broken arm. You trying to prove how much of a man you are or something?"

"No. I just don't want that fag touching me."

"Excuse me?" asked Sophia, her eyes flashing. "What did you just call him?"

"You heard me. He's a fucking faggot, and I don't want him touching me."

"Okay, listen up asshole," began Sophia but Matthew put a hand on her shoulder to stop her.

"It's okay," he said calmly. "If he doesn't want me to heal him that's fine. Hecate can do it. That's part of why she's here in the first place. Although who knows when these two are going to stop fighting."

"How are you ok with this?" demanded Sophia.

"It's nothing I haven't heard before and nothing I won't hear again. I've made peace with it. I choose to rise above it."

"Well I'm not going to stand for it," said Sophia, turning back to face Johnny. "Just because he's okay with you being a homophobic shit stain doesn't mean I am."

"Why the fuck do you care about some glittery fruitcake?" asked Johnny in derision.

"Because I'm gay too ya jackass!"

"Wait, seriously?" asked Johnny in disbelief. "But you're so hot."

"How does me being *hot* have anything to do with my sexual orientation?"

"Because only ugly girls are gay."

"What kinda fucked up logic is that?"

"Well, they are only gay 'cause they can't get a guy. But you're super hot. You could get any guy you want."

"And what if I don't want a guy."

"Well, maybe you just haven't found the right guy. If you want, you can come to my room later. I'd be happy to help straighten you up if—"

POW! Before anyone could even react, Sophia had punched Johnny full in the face. He fell backward, landing on the ground hard. A second later Sophia was on top of him, repeatedly slamming her fists into his face with great ferocity.

"HEY!" Heracles rushed over and pulled Sophia off of Johnny with one hand.

Sophia, dangling in the air, flailed about wildly, desperately trying to get in a few more shots at Johnny.

"ENOUGH!" bellowed Hecate. A pulse of pale blue light billowed out from her, leaving calm in its wake. Heracles put Sophia, who had stopped struggling, down and went over to inspect Johnny.

"Whoa, Hekkie, you're gonna wanna get to healing him now. She damn near beat him to death."

"I despise it when you call me that," said Hecate coldly as she descended on Johnny, her hands glowing with blue light.

"Training is over for today. All of you, leave. Expect you, Benjamin. I wish to talk to you. I'll send Johnny along after I've finished healing him. And keep him and Sophia apart in the future. We don't want any more incidents."

The group headed towards the only door out of the arena, throwing sidelong glances towards Sophia as they went. For her part, Sophia was resolutely unabashed. She held her head up high and keep on walking, completely unconcerned about the others' scrutiny of her, or by the fact that Johnny's blood was drying on her hand.

Everyone drifted apart as they entered the apartment. Lance plopped down on one of the couches and turned on the T.V. The rest headed off to classes or to their own rooms, except Vincent, who followed Matthew into his. A few minutes later, Irene, unnoticed by anyone, snuck out of the apartment. Interactions between the fourteen roommates were sparse for the rest of the night. This meant that Irene's absence, and subsequent return well past midnight, was overlooked.

The next day, Saturday, found Irene up and in the kitchen making breakfast before anyone else was even awake. By the time Sara, who was usually the second or third person up after Irene, stumbled, half asleep, into the dining room, Irene had made enough eggs, bacon, toast, hash browns, and coffee to feed a platoon of soldiers.

"How do you have time to do all this?" yawned Sara as Irene handed her a plate loaded with food.

Irene merely shrugged as she slid back into the kitchen, skillfully avoiding the question. Slowly the rest of the group started to trickle into the dining room. As they sat down at the large, circular dining table, they were immediately presented with a plate of food specifically tailored to their tastes and appetites, though how Irene knew their preferences they'd long since given up trying to figure out.

Breakfast was a lively affair. Everyone chatted and joked as they tucked into Irene's delicious food. Fortunately, any tension that might have arisen between Sophia and Johnny was averted by their dogged attempts to ignore each other.

After breakfast, the group scattered again, some off to hide in their rooms, some to the arena for exercise, and the rest to the living room to relax, watch T.V., or read a book. The rest of the morning passed by uneventfully until Benjamin came out of his room to get a drink of water. As he passed through the living room the sound of knock reverberated through the room. It seemed to be coming from every direction at once. As the sound of knocking faded a voice spoke out.

"I'm coming up."

A moment later Hades erupted from the ground next to Benjamin. In contrast to their first meeting, Hades' clothes, though still predominantly black, where much more modern in appearance. In fact, were it not for the simple circlet of obsidian upon his brow, Hades could easily have been mistaken for a rock star.

"Nice threads dude," said Sammy.

"Thank you," said Hades with a smile, "and good morning to you all. I hope you are enjoying yourselves." There were nods and expressions of contentment from those in the room.

"If you don't mind me asking, to what do we owe the pleasure?" asked Vincent from his seat on the couch. "I would think the god of the Underworld might be too busy to pay a social call. After all, you much get tons of new arrivals every day."

"You're right, I do tend to get pretty busy. But one of the many perks of being the god of the dead is that I've got a massive labor force. And I never have to worry about working them to death."

"Why's that?" asked Lance.

"They're already dead."

"How very droll," said Vincent. "So, what are you doing here anyway?"

Hades smiled an evil smile, a sinister gleam in his eye.

"I've come for Benjamin, of course. I've come to drag him down to Hell."

# Chapter Six

A dead silence followed Hades' pronouncement. Everyone stared awkwardly around at one another. Finally, Matthew, who had been lying on the couch with his head in Vincent's lap, rose up and looked at Hades.

"You're joking right?"

Hades turned to stare at Matthew, his face cold and unfathomable. Matthew's eyes narrowed in concern. The corners of Hades' mouth twitched and then he succumbed to laughter.

"I'm sorry," said Hades as his mirth subsided. "I couldn't help myself. Ben is coming down to the Underworld yes, but I am making it sound much more serious than it actually is. I'm just taking him down for the day so he can start getting acquainted with his new kingdom. He'll be back later."

"Ah, the delights of dark humor," said Matthew as he leaned back down onto Vincent's lap, "how gauche."

"A bit of dark humor never hurt anyone," said Hades. "Well, okay maybe a few people, but they're already dead so who cares."

"Oh, hello Hades," said Irene, who had just come out of the kitchen. "Can I offer you some refreshments?"

"No, I won't be here much longer. But thank you for the offer. I'm just here to take Benjamin down to the Underworld for a tour."

"How nice. Shall I go get him for you?"

"I'm standing right here," said Ben, waving his hand through the air in irritation.

"Oh, sorry," said Irene in embarrassment.

"It's okay," said Ben in resignation. "I'm used to it."

"So, Benjamin, you ready to go?" asked Hades, quickly defusing the situation.

"Sure, and you can just call me Ben."

"Well then Ben, hold on to your breakfast 'cause here we go."

Hades snapped his fingers and, the next thing Ben knew, he was falling fast through an all-consuming darkness. Before he even had enough time to register what was happening, it was over, and he was standing upright on rocky ground.

In front of him was a wide river, its dark waters rushing by in a furious frenzy. Apart from the river, the area around him was barren and bleak. Fragmented earth stretched as far as the eye could see. Cold, gray light shone through heavy clouds, which hung sullen and still overhead. The entire scene was so lifeless and forlorn that Ben would not have been surprised if he was the first living thing to ever stand upon this barren, cracked ground since the dawn of time.

"I hope the trip didn't freak you out too much." Hades had appeared next to Ben, a warm smile on his face.

"It was . . . an experience. So, where are we?"

"The shores of the River Styx: the border to the Underworld."

"And where is this exactly? Geographically speaking."

"Down."

"Down? The best you can do is down?"

"Pretty much, yeah."

Ben rolled his eyes.

"So now what? Are we gonna try and cross the river? Cause if I knew I'd have to drown myself to get into the

Underworld I would have brought my swimming trunks."

For answer, Hades let a long, shrill whistle, which hung in the air long after he'd stopped. Eventually, the sound faded, leaving a deathly silence in its wake.

"What now?" asked Ben once the silence had grown excruciating.

Hades held up a finger for silence and tapped his ear. At first, Ben couldn't hear anything, but then the soft sound of water sloshing against wood reached his ears. A bank of fog rolled slowly into existence. A second later, from the depths of the fog, emerged a barge of black wood, which glided down the river towards them.

At the head of the barge stood a figure clad in black robes, his face hidden under a hood. He held a long paddle in his hands, which he was using to move the boat effortlessly against the current. Soon the boat reached the shore where Ben and Hades stood. The figure in black docked the barge and tapped the deck with the blade of his paddle. A gangplank, made of the same dark wood as the barge, slid out from a chute on the side of the boat and descended down to the shore.

"All aboard," said Hades as he ascended the gangplank. Ben followed him, the smell of wet wood invading his nostrils.

"This is Charon," said Hades, gesturing towards the pilot of the boat. "He's the ferryman for the dead. He takes them across the River Styx and the River Acheron to the gates of the Underworld. Think of him as a spectral taxi."

"Hi," said Ben, as he extended a hand towards Charon.

Charon turned to face Ben. Even at this distance, Charon's face was completely imperceptible. His hood cast an impermeable veil of shadows over his face, hiding it from view. Several seconds passed as Charon appraised Ben, who continued to stand awkwardly with hand extended. Finally, Charon extended his own bony hand and gripped Ben's in a firm handshake. Ben, unable to help himself, stared down in wonder at Charon's fleshless, skeletal hand.

"What?" asked Hades nonchalantly, "never shook hands with a corpse before?"

"Can't say that I have," said Ben as he and Charon released each other. "I suppose it makes sense for the ferryman of the dead to be... well dead."

"It does add to the authenticity, I'll give you that," said Hades. "But in actuality, his form changes based on the beliefs of the souls he's ferrying. To some he's Saint Peter, to others a warrior woman with wings. It varies. Now Charon, if you would."

Charon nodded and stuck his paddle back into the water. Immediately the barge began to move, turning gracefully in the water. A moment later they were sailing down the river.

"The River Styx is one of five rivers within and around the Underworld," explained Hades, "though it can be considered the most important of the five as it serves as the border between the living world and the Underworld. The goddess Styx also resides within her river. The other four rivers have their own god or goddess as well."

"What is she the goddess of?"

"Well, she's the goddess of her own river, which would make her the goddess of the border between the world of the living and the Underworld, I guess. Her main claim to fame, however, is that she's the goddess of divine oaths. Course, no one's sworn a divine oath in about five thousand years, so now she just the goddess of napping a lot."

"So, besides Archeaon, Archinon. Besides Archi-something, what are the names of the other rivers?

"Acheron. That's the river that flows directly in front of the gates to the Underworld. It's the main river that Charon ferries the dead over. The River Lethe flows mainly within the Underworld, though there is a small tributary here in the living world. Something you should know about the River Lethe; its water causes anyone or anything that touches them to forget who or what they are. I'd suggest avoiding taking a dip in it if I were you. As for the other two, they are the rivers Phlegethon and Cocytus. Phlegethon is a river of fire that leads directly into Tartarus, while Cocytus is a river of ice leads out of Tartarus."

"What's Tartarus?"

"The easiest way to describe Tartarus would be to call it Hell," said Hades bluntly. "It's what awaits those souls that have committed atrocities."

"Sounds unpleasant."

"Comes with the territory I'm afraid. The Underworld exists not only to house the souls of the dead but also to punish their misdeeds. Actions have consequences, if not in this life, then in death. Fortunately, I don't actually have to deal with that. I've got people who handle all the unpleasantness. I just sign the checks, so to speak."

"You are a lot more relaxed than I would have expected for a god, especially after meeting Zeus."

"My dear brother has got a lightning bolt shoved so far up his ass he could probably pull it out of his mouth. Don't judge us all by him. Besides, you and the rest are going to be our replacements. I think that warrants some familiarity, don't you?"

"I guess," said Ben with a shrug.

"Also, it's nice to cut loose sometimes. I tend to be a pretty involved god. Don't get me wrong, I delegate a lot, but there is only so much I can have others do. As it is, I still find myself dealing with disputes between the members of my court or requests to expanding parts of the Underworld or just handling issues from the dead in general. Seriously it's never-ending with them. You'd think that the dead wouldn't have any problems. I mean, come on, they're dead, what the hell could they find to have an issue with? But low and behold they find something. Not enough space in the fourth tier of Asphodel, the sacred spring in the Elysium has a funny taste, some idiot fell into the River Lethe and now can't remember who the hell he is. Sometimes I just wanna yell at them to get a life, but then I remember that ship's already sailed."

Ben chuckled as Hades continued to rant. He wasn't quite sure what Hades was talking about with Asphodel and Elysium, but Hades' informal attitude was, at least, putting Ben at ease.

The barge was now entering a thick bank of gray fog. Despite being surrounded on all sides by heavy clouds of swirling vapor, Ben felt oddly cold, as if the fog was sapping him of heat. Just as Ben started to shiver the fog broke and he caught sight of the gates to the Underworld for the first time.

The colossal gates, one hundred feet long, two hundred feet tall, looked as though it had been carved from a single slab of obsidian. It was so intensely black that Ben's eyes hurt just from looking at it. He quickly turned away, his head spinning wildly.

"That gate is something else," said Ben as he tried to keep himself upright.

"Oh crap," said Hades, "I forgot about that. Here." Hades reached out and tapped Ben on the head with the tip of his index finger. The dizziness vanished immediately. Steeling himself Ben shot a quick glance at the gates. Though they remained the same inexplicable black as before, Ben was able to look upon them without his head spinning.

"If you thought that was bad," said Hades, "wait until you see the Pit of Tartarus."

"I'm looking forward to it," said Ben sarcastically. "What was that just now that you did to me?"

"I jump-started your vision slightly. A minor perk of being the god of the Underworld is that you don't get affected by the more unsavory aspects of the job. Otherwise, you'd probably be talking to some withered old corpse instead of the handsome young man you see before you. Not that there's anything wrong with withered corpses." Hades shot a furtive look at Charon.

Ben rolled his eyes and turned his attention back to the gates. The first thing he noticed was that the gates were free-standing. Apart from a small host of people standing around the gate's base, there was nothing but barren earth as far as the eye could see.

"Who are they?" asked Ben, pointed at the assembled mass.

"They are the gods of death. They govern either causes or side effects of death. They are ruled by Thanatos, the god of death, but I don't see him among them."

"I thought you were the god of death?"

"I am the god of the dead, very different. Whereas I keep the spirit of those who have passed on, Thanatos is, in essence, the reason they passed on in the first place. His being, his existence, is death."

"Oh. So, these death gods, do they just stand there all day?"

"Sometimes yes, sometimes no. They spend a lot more time outside the Underworld than in, roaming around the world and inflecting themselves upon others. Thankfully I don't have to deal with them much."

"Why, don't you like them?"

"Not particularly. Meet them and you'll see why."

The barge bumped gently against the shore as Charon brought it to a stop. With a tap of his paddle, Charon lowered the gangplank for Hades and Ben to disembark. Once they had both stepped onto dry land, Charon shoved off, sailing smoothly and quickly down the murky waters of River Acheron before vanishing into a thick bank of fog.

"If he's the ferryman for the dead, how does he have time to ferry us around?" asked Ben as he gazed at the point where Charon and the ship had vanished. "I mean, isn't the death rate something like one hundred deaths per minute or something?"

"Closer to one hundred and five," corrected Hades, "but that's nitpicking. And, as for your question, what you saw was the main Charon body. You see, back in the olden days, the population wasn't as expansive. Which meant that the death rate was much lower, even with all the wars Ares concocted. So, Charon could pilot his barge by himself with no problem. But, as the population increased, so too did the death rate. Eventual Charon wasn't able to keep up with the demands, at least not in a timely manner. So, I granted him the power to create duplicates of himself. The main body, which is the one that ferried us here, controls a small host of clones that ferry the souls to the gates."

"So, you effectively have an army of spooky, scary skeletons?"

"Pretty much."

"Good to know." Silence fell as Ben looked around, taking in the river and the scenery around him.

"Not ready to meet the gods of death I take it?" asked Hades with a knowing smile.

"What makes you say that?" asked Ben.

"Because you are looking everywhere except for where they are all standing."

"I'm just . . . I'm not sure what I'm supposed to do or how I'm supposed to act. I'm not really a people person."

"Well it's a good thing that they aren't people then isn't it."

"You know what I mean. I'm a loner. People don't listen to me. They ignore me. I'm not complaining. I like being left alone. But now I'm supposed to be the new Lord of the Underworld. I'm going to have a court and people answering to me and subjects to rule over. I didn't realize I'd have so many gods working for me. It's just, not what I expected."

"There are actually more once we get inside the Underworld."

"Not helping."

"Are you regretting your decision?" asked Hades. "I hope not. You can't exactly give the powers back."

"No, I'm not really regretting it. I'm just realizing how big a decision it really was."

"Look," said Hades, putting on arm around Ben's shoulder, "I'm not going to say it's going to be easy 'cause, in all likelihood, it won't be. What I will say is that I have faith in you. It wasn't easy for me when I first became the god of the dead. Actually, come to think of it, since mortals didn't exist yet when I took over the Underworld, I was basically just a glorified prison guard. But that's a whole different story altogether. Anyway, when the Underworld did finally become *the Underworld*, I wasn't sure how to deal with it either. But I figured it out. Sure, it took me about two hundred years, but I have faith that you'll manage it much faster than I did."

"Why?"

"Well I'll be around to help you if you need it for one and, for another, you are a better person than I am."

"How can you be so sure?"

"Because I've watched you all your life, Ben. I know the kind of man you are. You have within you the potential to do great things, if you'd only stop hiding, figurative and literally."

Silence fell again as Ben stared down at the barren, rocky ground in contemplation. Finally, he spoke.

"Can I ask you something?"

"Of course. You're my protégée. You can ask me anything you want."

"Why did you bring me here today?"

Hades cocked an eyebrow. "To show you the place you'll be in command of one day. I thought I said that already?"

"I meant the real reason. I know you didn't just bring me down here just for a tour. There is something else."

A smile of satisfaction played across Hades' face.

"Very perceptive. Yes, there was another reason for this *tour* as you called it. Hecate came to talk to me yesterday after your training. As you might know, she is a member of my court, and she's *concerned* about your progress."

"Concerned?"

"Concerned, incensed, whatever. To be honest, I stopped listening after the first screech. But I did manage to get that you hadn't been training like the others. Is that accurate or is Hecate talking out of her ass? Trust me, it wouldn't be the first time."

"No, she's right. I haven't been training. But it's not because I don't want to. I just don't know what I'm supposed to be doing. I tried to explain that to Hecate yesterday, but she wouldn't let me get a word in."

"If my brother has a lightning bolt up his ass, Hecate has a broomstick. And I get it. The others have more obvious powers. God of light controls light. God of travel is super-fast. God of the hunt apparently kicks ass. But god of the dead, that's a bit trickier. I'm guessing you have some idea about what you can do with your powers but are too hesitant to try it?"

"Yeah," said Ben. "I don't really want to start a zombie apocalypse."

"Well, that's why you are here today. After seeing the Underworld firsthand, hopefully you won't be so skittish about your powers."

"Makes sense, I guess. So now what?"

"Now you meet the gods of death. When you are ready, of course. No rush. It's not like lives are depending on it or anything."

Ben shook his head in exasperation. "Alright, let's do it."

They walked together towards the gate, where the eight gods of death stood. Once they had reached the group, Hades began the introductions. Ben could easily see why Hades wasn't particularly fond of the gods of death. Penthos, the god of grief, was a grim-faced, tearful man who seemed to turn everything into a maudlin production. Oizys, the goddess of anxiety, was a thoroughly nervous creature. Her eyes were constantly darting in every direction and she wrung her hands so fast that they were blurs. Out of all them, Ben felt a touch of pity for Geras, the god of old age. He was a feeble, decrepit old man completely dependent on a cane. What rotten luck he must have to be the only god that actually looked their age. Likewise, Limos, the goddess of hunger, was so thin she was painful to look at.

Ben took an immediate dislike to the god of disease, Nosoi. He exuded a diabolical aura and his smile would scare the daylights out of hardened criminals. Despite his intimidating continence, Phobos, the god of fear, seemed surprisingly affable, though a bit stiff. Aporia, the goddess of guilty joy, looked sweet but there was a wickedness in her eyes that hinted otherwise. But, out of all the death gods, it was the goddess of agony, Algea, that Ben feared the most. He wasn't sure if it was her cruel beauty, her twisted smile, her merciless eyes, or her clawed hands that put him on edge. All he knew was that he never wanted to be on her bad side and that he was having serious doubts about whether she even had a good side.

"On behalf of us all, I would like to say it is a pleasure to meet you," said Geras, in his soft, tremulous voice.

"It's nice to meet you all," said Ben nervously.

"I'm afraid the pleasure is somewhat lost on us," said Penthos gloomily, tears flowing from his bloodshot eyes. "You see, your presence marks the end of an era. It seems like only yesterday when I came to work for Lord Hades. And now our once mighty and majestic leader is leaving us. My heart breaks at the thought."

"I'm retiring, not dying," said Hades reproachfully. "There's no reason to be so dramatic Penthos."

"My-my-my-my L-l-lord Hades do you really th-think this is a g-g-good idea," stammered Oizys as she wrung her frail hands nervously. "I-I-I m-m-mean n-n-n-n-no offffense y-y-young ma-ma-master B-Benjamin but-but-but you-you-you are a-a-a mortal. Not that I'm p-p-prejudiced or anything but you-you-you d-d-don't understand the re-res-responsibilities you are t-t-t-t-taking on. My-My-My Lord wouldn't it be b-bbetter for one of your daughters to-to-to take your pl-place. They understand what-what-what must be d-done."

"The decision has been made Oizys so, unless you want to take your concerns up with all the gods of Olympus, I suggest you drop that matter."

"Of-of-of c-c-c-course, my lord."

"Don't be a spoilsport Oizys," said Algea, her hair turning from black to pink as she spoke. "It'll be so nice to a new face around."

"Especially such a handsome face," added Aporia. She and Algea began to circle Ben, who couldn't help feeling like a cornered deer surrounded by a pack of wolves.

"So, young master Benjamin, why don't you tell Auntie Aporia your deepest desires. After all, we are here to serve you in *any way* we can." Aporia's musical voice was hypnotic.

Ben was having trouble keeping his mind clear.

"Oh yes," chimed in Algea as she traced one of her claws against Ben's collarbone. "We're happy to satisfy any desire you may have, no matter how . . . dark or depraved they might be."

Ben could feel his pulse rising as Algea gently caressed him, her claws playing sensually across his skin.

"That's enough of that," ordered Hades. "If Ben wants your company, he can seek it out on his own time. Today is about him getting to know the Underworld."

Ben breathed a little sigh of relief as Algea and Aporia slid back to join the other gods of death. Had that gone on much longer Ben was sure he would have presented a little more of himself to the death gods than he wanted.

"I hope you are up to the task," said Phobos.

Ben felt himself shrink a little under Phobos' withering stare.

"I'm going to try to be."

"Good," said Nosoi. "But remember, we have ways of making sure you do your duty."

"Nosoi," snapped Hades, a touch of warning in his voice, "behave yourselves."

"We are just making him aware of the situation, our lord. He has a right to know that we will not stand for a lackluster execution of his duties."

"Look I can't guarantee I'll be great at the job right off the bat, but I'm sure I'll be able to handle it eventually."

"Eventually? Eventually is not good enough for us."

"I'm sorry you feel that way but there's not much you can do about it."

"Oh, but there's so much we can do. The options available to us are staggering. Let us ask you, what do you think your mother would look best in? Cancer? Polio? Or how about the Bubonic plague? A classic never goes out of style."

"Are you threatening my family?" asked Ben, his pulse rising again.

"Only if we have to," said Nosoi, a twisted smile creeping across his face.

"That's enough," said Hades, his voice as cold as ice.

The smile immediately faded from Nosoi's face.

"There will be no more of this. Benjamin is my heir, and you will afford him the same respect you give to me or I promise you that I'll hurl you into Tartarus myself. Do we understand each other?"

"Yes, our lord Hades."

Hades sighed and shook his head in exasperation. Something tugged on Ben's sleeve. Turning he found small, withered Limos staring up at him, her sunken eyes gazing at him pleadingly.

"Please forgive them," she said, her voice little more than a harsh croak. "This is a new experience for us all."

"I understand," said Ben, before adding in a whisper, "but I think I'll keep my distance for now. We can talk forgiveness once everyone's had a chance to adjust."

"Of course," whispered Limos in reply.

"I know that my fellows have not done well in endearing themselves to you, my young lord," said Geras, his aged eyes glaring at his fellow death gods with disapproval, "but if there is anything we can help you with please, do not hesitate to ask."

"I will, thank you."

Geras moved aside to allow Ben and Hades to pass. The other gods followed suit, stepping aside and creating a path for Ben and Hades to reach the gate.

"Are you ready to see the Underworld for the first time?" asked Hades.

Ben looked up at the imposing gates in front of him. He couldn't quite get over just how big they were. On top of that, Ben had a strange feeling in his gut that what he was about to do was somehow taboo. Sensing Ben's trepidation Hades leaned down to whisper into his ear.

"There's no reason to be nervous. You are to be the new god of the Underworld. You have every right to cross through these gates whenever you wish."

Ben nodded. Taking a deep, steadying breath he stepped through the gates. For a brief moment, it felt as if the world had disappeared. He couldn't see or hear anything. A bone-chilling coldness gnawed at him, pulling at his soul as if it were trying to drag it from his body. And then, he was through. The chill faded, light and sound returned, and Ben was able to take his first look at the Underworld.

# Chapter Seven

In the back of his mind, Ben had always wondered what the afterlife would be like ever since his great-grandfather Mordecai (or Morty as he liked to be called) had died. Being six at the time, Ben didn't remember much about the man. What he did know was that Great-Grandpa Morty had fled Germany when he was eighteen, had changed the family name from Fintster to Darke to avoid persecution, and had credited his faith in God for getting him through the difficulties of World War II. Obviously, that faith had not translated down to Ben's father, which was why the family was now only culturally Jewish, instead of theologically.

His father's atheism was another reason why Ben hadn't known much about his great-grandfather. Since they didn't see eye to eye on religious matters, they decided it would be easier if they didn't see each other much. According to Ben's great-grandmother, *Bubbe* Sylvia, it was just easier that way. Apparently, their shouting matches had resulted in the police being called on them several times. Despite their animosity, however, Ben's father insisted on paying respect to Great-Grandpa Morty when he'd died. After all, he had been the family patriarch, and it was the acceptable thing to do.

Morty's *shiva* had been an interesting experience for Ben. It was the first time he'd met most of his father's family. He remembered wandering around and asking various relatives what happened after you died. None of them had been able to give him an adequate response. In the end, Ben had put the question out of his mind. He was, after all, only six. But, every once in a while, the question would resurface. Most of the time he'd only give it a moment's thought before shrugging and returning to whatever task was at hand. He did try looking up more information on the internet once but found that that resulted in more questions rather than less, so he stopped looking.

Now, finally, he was going to get an answer to his question and actually see what the afterlife was really like. As he stepped out of the gate and into the world, his mind abuzz with possibility, something happened that he didn't expect. Before he could even take a look around, he was bowled over by something black and furry. Whatever had just slammed into him immediately began to lick him ferociously.

"Cerberus, down!" roared Hades.

The black, furry, licking something on top of Ben moved away at once. Ben raised himself up to see what had been molesting him so exuberantly and found himself almost face to face with a human-sized, three-headed, black dog.

"Sorry about that," said Hades as he reached down to help Ben to his feet. "He usually doesn't warm up to people that fast. He must sense a bit of my power within you."

"You got a towel?" asked Ben as he tried in vain to wipe off the slobber left by Cerberus's overly enthusiastic greeting.

Hades snapped his fingers. All the spit immediately evaporated, leaving Ben feeling refreshed and dry.

"Thanks," said Ben as he turned to take his first, unobstructed, look at the Underworld. The sky seemed to stretch on forever. Innumerable chuck of earth hung, unsupported, in mid-air over a vast, dark pit. The island Ben and Hades were standing on seemed to be part of a ring that stretched around the whole of the Underworld. A path led from the gates to a large temple, out of which a river of fire flowed. The flaming river continued on until it reached the edge of the island, at which point it cascaded down into the pit. The entire scene was bathed in a dull gray light that seemed to emanate from nowhere in particular.

"How big is this place?" asked Ben in awe.

"As big as it needs to be," said Hades. "The Underworld exists within its own space in reality. The entrance may reside within the bowels of the Earth, but the Underworld itself exists outside of space and time. It's an entirely self-sustained pocket of reality. It produces its own light, atmosphere, flora, and fauna."

"That's amazing," said Ben. "So, what's that temple for?"

"That's Hall of Judgment. It's where the judges of the Underworld decided where the souls of the dead are sent."

"And the big black void?" asked Ben.

"That would be Tartarus, which I told you about earlier. Not a nice place. That river of fire is the River Phlegethon. It leads to the very depths of Tartarus."

"No welcoming committee on this side?" asked Ben as he looked around him.

"Well there's Cerberus," said Hades as he patted the large dog. "There used to be all sorts of creatures and monsters that hung around the gates: centaurs, gorgons, chimeras, harpies, a hydra, stuff like that. But it was getting too crowded with so many new arrivals that we had to relocate them. Same with the tree that used to be here. Now it's up there."

Hades pointed up at an island high above their heads. "It was smack dab in the middle of this road. With the number of souls coming in increasing every year, the tree was slowing things down. So, we moved it to better advantage."

"Now that you mention it, where are all the dead people?" asked Ben as Cerberus gamboled away, bored from the lack of attention. "I kinda expected there to be more dead people in the land of the dead."

"They're here. You just can't see them yet."

"Well how do I start seeing them?" asked Ben.

"Stop looking for them," replied Hades cryptically.

Ben rolled his eyes. "Just my luck, I get Confucius as my mentor."

They stood there, in front of the gates to the Underworld, for several minutes as Ben tried everything he could think of to see the spirits of the dead. Nothing worked.

"This isn't working," said Ben grumpily. "Can I get a little bit more to go on please?"

"It's not a matter of wanting to see them," said Hades after a moment's thought. "It's more a matter of believing you can see them." Ben's brow furrowed as he thought about what Hades had just said. Closing his eyes, Ben focused his mind on the single salient thought that he would see the spirits of the dead around him. With no trace of doubt in his mind, Ben opened his eyes. A line of colorless, transparent spirits stretched out in front of him, all headed towards the Hall of Judgment.

"Whoa," said Ben in awe. The line of spirits completely ignored Ben and Hades as they trudged along the path in complete silence, their faces devoid of any kind of expression.

"No offense, but this soul train of yours is a bit depressing."

"It's the Underworld. Depressing kind of comes with the territory. Shall we?" Hades gestured towards the path leading down to the Hall of Judgment. Ben nodded and started walking forward, his attention fixated on the spirits around him. His fascination was such that he didn't notice the wall of the temple until he walked into it.

"You could have warned me," snapped Ben as he rubbed his forehead.

"It's not my fault you weren't watching where you were going. Next time you'll remember to pay attention."

Ben glared at Hades, who simply smiled back. Together they entered the Hall of Judgment, the interior of which was much larger than the exterior. Hundreds of chairs stood scattered throughout the room, most of them filled with the waiting spirits of the dead. The line of the dead they'd followed in was queued up in front of a small reception desk, behind which sat a ghostly woman. On the far wall were three doors. The right door was made of stone, black and forbidding, with the name Minos engraved above the lintel. The middle door was made of wood, plain and unassuming, with the name Aeacus above it. The left door was golden, splendid, and inviting. The name carved above it was Rhadamanthus.

"If you'll have a seat, Judge Aeacus will be with you momentarily," said the woman at the reception desk as she took a ticket from the spirit of a young man. As he shuffled away to find a seat the next soul in line, this one of a teenage girl, stepped forward.

"Ticket please," said the receptionist. The girl handed over her ticket. "Thank you. If you'll have a seat, Judge Aeacus will be with you momentarily."

"You know, I've always heard people saying that the DMV is Hell," said Ben. "I just never thought they meant it literally."

"Approximately a hundred and fifty-one thousand people die every day on average. This is the fastest way we've come up to get people on with their afterlife. Before this, it took about a month to go from crossing the gates to receiving your judgment. Now it's a lot faster."

"So how does it work?" asked Ben as he watched another soul take their seat.

"When you die your soul is transported to the banks of either the River Acheron or Styx by Hermes. There you meet Charon. Once you pay him, he'll give you a ticket and ferry you over the river to the gates. From the gates, you come here, hand the ticket over to the receptionist (I think her name is Janet), and she'll direct you from there."

"What do they pay Charon with exactly? Bitcoin?"

"There was a time when you had to pay him with real money, but the practice of burying the dead with a coin under their tongue has long since died out so now Charon just converts your life experiences into money. He uses those as the basis for which ticket to give you. The judges get the final say, but for the most part, the system works."

"How does it work?" asked Ben.

"Well, the simple way to explain it is that every major event in your life is given a numerical value. Most things are only worth one gold piece. Heroic feats, however, are worth more. And, conversely, dastardly deeds subtract gold."

"So, is it possible to get negative money? And how much is a gold piece worth?"

"Each gold piece is equivalent to one hundred of whatever the current strongest currency is. Right now, I believe that is the Cayman Islands dollar but you'd have to check with Hermes to be sure. And no, you can't go negative. The gold pieces you get for being born and for dying are permanent."

"How does Charon change life experiences into money?"

"He sings the money song from the musical *Cabaret*."

"Really?"

"Of course not," said Hades. "He just waves his hand over them."

"So, after the souls give their tickets to Janet, what happens then?"

"They are judged according to the recommendation upon their ticket."

"And I'm guessing the judges are Minos, Aeacus, and Radalamadingdong?"

"Rhadamanthus," said Hades. "And yes. Minos judges those who are bound to Tartarus, Rhadamanthus those brave souls to be sent to Elysium, and Aeacus judges where in the Asphodel Meadows to stick everyone else."

"Sounds like he's got the worst job."

"Yes, he does go through more cases than the other two combined. And speaking of the proverbial devil, here we go." The door marked as Aeacus had opened.

"Amelia Merridew," said Janet.

An elderly woman rose up from her chair and shuffled towards the open door. Hades beckoned Ben forward, and they both followed the soul of Amelia through the doors to Judge Aeacus' courtroom. The room they entered was small. In the center of the room was a dais for the soul being judged to stand. The judge's bench rested against the back wall of the room. Seated behind the bench was Aeacus. Unlike the spirit he was judging, Aeacus was completely corporeal. He had tanned skin, brown hair, brown eyes, and wore a simple bronze crown upon his brow.

"Amelia Merridew," said Aeacus is a strong, clear voice. "You have lived a decent life. Though devoid of any great heroism or notoriety, you have strived to do good where you can. Within your social circle, you were much beloved. For these reasons, I sentence you to eternity upon the fifth tier of the Asphodel Meadows, also known as the Tranquil Township. If you so desire, you may choose to reject this sentence and opt for reincarnation instead. By doing so, your soul will be stripped of all memories and then sent back to the living world to begin life again. If you achieve more in your second lifetime, you will be granted a better eternity. What is your decision."

"The Tranquil Township," said Amelia is a croaking voice.

"So be it," said Aeacus. He raised his gavel and tapped it against the sounding block. Amelia vanished.

"So, what do you think?" said Hades asked Hades as the door to the courtroom opened again.

"About what?" asked Ben.

"About how the judgment process works," replied Hades as the spirit of a young man drifted into the room.

"Seems alright, I guess. Can they appeal their judgment or is it final?"

"Yes," said Hades. "If they don't like where they are placed, they do have the option of appealing directly to me."

"How come Aeacus didn't mention that as an option?"

"Because it's not his place to do so. Don't worry, they are given the information when they arrive at whatever afterlife they've been assigned. That way they can see what eternity has in store for them."

"How often do people appeal to you?"

"Not terribly often. Most of the time people are content with where they are placed. It's those that are placed in tiers one through three that I hear from the most but, on average, people end up in tier four or five more often than not so I only have to hear an appeal every thousand souls or so."

"How often do you change their... sentence? That doesn't sound right."

"And yet, it's the only word that seems to fit," said Hades. "And to answer your question, not often. Aeacus, Minos, and Rhadamanthus are fair and decent judges. Well, maybe not Minos so much."

"He's the one who judges the evil souls right?"

"That's one way of putting it yes," said Hades.

"How bad do you have to be to get sent to . . . what was it, Tartar sauce?"

"Tartarus. And pretty bad. Tartarus was originally created to be a prison for the enemies of the gods. Now, it also holds the souls of those who have committed acts of true depravity and immorality."

"Is Tartarus really necessary?" asked Ben. "I mean, Aeacus said that there was reincarnation option. Why not have them do that?"

"It was decided that one's actions in life should have some sort of consequence in death," said Hades. "Sort of like an incentive for humanity to do better. And, for the most part, it works. Now, if you disagree with this method, that's fine. You can always change it after you gain control of the Underworld. But, a warning, it might not be easy. But, then again, when are major upheavals to the world order ever easy? So, shall we continue on or do you want to see a few more judgments?"

"I think I've got the gist of things," said Ben.

"Onward we go then," said Hades as he walked across the room, Ben following close behind.

"Hey why isn't anyone looking at us?" asked Ben. "We've been standing there talking for like five minutes. Aren't you like the king of this place or something? Shouldn't there be bowing and scraping?

"Normally, yes. But I've made us invisible to them so as to avoid all that."

"You have? How?"

"Well, negating the fact that I'm a *god*, my crown grants me the power of true invisibility. No one can see me, hear me, smell me, taste me, touch me, or sense me if I don't want them to. And I can project that to others as well."

"Your crown can do all that?" asked Ben, looking up at the simple ring of obsidian around Hades brow.

"Never be fooled by appearances," said Hades. "My crown used to be known as the Helm of Darkness, but it got too ostentatious for everyday wear, so I turned it into a crown."

They had now reached the back wall, though there was no door to be seen. Before Ben could mention this, however, Hades stepped right through the stone wall and out of sight. Ben hesitated for a moment, and then he poked the wall with his finger. It remained completely solid.

"You coming or not?" asked Hades, sticking his head back through the wall.

"I don't think I can walk through walls," said Ben.

"Well not with that attitude you can't," said Hades. "Close your eyes and pretend the wall's not there." Ben closed his eyes, took a deep breath, stepped forward, and smacked his head against the very solid stone wall.

"Ow," grumbled Ben, messaging his forehead.

"Focus," said Hades. "Concentrate. Try again."

Ben closed his eyes again but, this time, instead of trying to step through the wall, he placed his hand against it instead and pushed.

"Fine, go the safe way," muttered Hades.

Ben ignored him, focusing his attention instead upon trying to pretend the wall wasn't there, a difficult feat considering the fact that he was now in contact with it.

*There is no wall*, he thought to himself. *There is no wall. There is no wall. There is no*— Ben fell forward, landing painfully upon the rocky ground outside of the Hall of Judgment.

"Very good," said Hades. "You did it. Mostly."

"Mostly?" asked Ben as he tried to stand up, only to find that his right foot wouldn't move. Looking behind him, he found that his foot was stuck in the wall.

"Oh." Ben closed his eyes again, took another deep breath, and then pulled his foot out of the wall. Hades clapped.

"There's no need to mock," said Ben.

"I wasn't mocking," said Hades.

Ben shot him a disbelieving look.

"Okay, maybe I was mocking a little."

Ben rolled his eyes and looked around. Now he was on the other side of the temple he could better see the River Phlegethon. It truly was a river of fire. Flames flowed like water along a channel of scorched and cracked earth. Walking along the side of the river, Ben could feel their intense heat. He followed the flames until he came to the pit that was Tartarus. Once the flames passed the edge of the pit they vanished, engulfed entirely by the all-consuming darkness that seemed to permeate the entirety of Tartarus. No light could be seen within the vast emptiness that stretched out before him.

"Don't fall in," said Hades as he came over to stand next to Ben. "You wouldn't survive."

"And I was just about to jump too," said Ben in sarcastic disappointment.

Ben was just about to turn away from Tartarus when three large, winged creatures soared up out of the darkness. They were dark and horrible, with deadly claws and mouths full of fangs. The creatures circled Hades and Ben three times before landing, their leathery wings folding to cloaks and their monstrous appearance melting away.

Three women now stood in front of Hades and Ben, each with a face contorted in malice. The first had hair the color of dried blood and a face twisted in utter rage. The second had hair as black as ink, and her face was distorted by displeasure. The final woman had poisonous green hair and a face full of discontent.

"Ben, these are the Erinyes. They are also known as the Furies. They used to relentlessly chase after living criminals and reprobates but we've since had them reassigned. Now they punish those who have committed crimes against their fellow man down in Tartarus. Personally, I think they rather enjoy the promotion. Alecto, the fury of anger, punishes those who have committed moral crimes such as assault or rape. Tisiphone, the fury of vengeance, punishes murderers. Megaera, the fury of jealousy, punishes those who've been unfaithful."

"Unfaithful?" asked Ben. "As in cheating?"

"That is one interpretation, yes. Though it does take a rather heinous offense to get them sent down to Tartarus. It does happen though."

"So, this is the boy who will be replacing you?" asked Alecto, her indignant red eyes flashing in Ben's direction.

"Yes," said Hades. "This is Ben. He will be the new Lord of the Underworld."

"Nice to meet you," said Ben, even though it wasn't. "I hope I won't be a disappointment."

"We shall see," said Alecto coldly. Without another word, she and her sisters transformed back into their hideous, monstrous forms and took to the skies. They circled Ben one last time before plunging back into the depths of Tartarus.

"I don't think they like me," said Ben.

"Don't take it personally," said Hades. "They don't like anyone. I'm surprised they even came up here at all. Guess they wanted to size you up personally."

"Seems to be the theme of the day."

"After thousands of years with me at the helm, it's not surprising that some of the gods are concerned about the situation. I know I would be. Gods don't react well to change."

"So where to now?"

"My palace, I think. You can meet my daughters and the rest of my court. Then I can give you a quick tour of the different afterlives. After that, I'll send you back up. You've got to get back to studying for that geology test after all."

"How did you—" began Ben but he was interrupted by a scream.

Both he and Hades turned to see a spirit streaking back up the path towards the gates back to the mortal world.

"What the…?" asked Ben.

"He's trying to escape," said Hades.

"How do you know it's a he?"

"You mean besides his rather throaty scream, my divine eyesight, and the fact that I have knowledge of every spirit that crosses into my domain? Lucky guess."

"Oh right. Well is anyone going to stop him?" asked Ben.

A second later he got his answer. As the man was just about to reach the gates, Cerberus appeared out of thin air. Unlike before, however, he wasn't just large, he was gargantuan. Whereas before Cerberus had been roughly the same size as Hades, now he was at least as large as three-story building. In a single, swift motion the middle head of Cerberus swooped down and swallowed the man whole.

"Oh," said Ben, a little taken aback. "I guess that makes sense."

Cerberus turned and bound down the path, the earth trembling under the weight of his enormous paws. He jumped over the Hall of Judgment and landed in front of Hades and Ben with a monstrous thud that would have sent Ben backward over the edge of the pit had Hades not reached out a hand to stop him.

"Release him," ordered Hades. Cerberus opened his mouth and deposited the would-be escapee at Hades' feet. The spirit looked up at Hades in abject terror. Hades, in turn, looked down at the man with regal detachment.

"Once the dead have entered my kingdom, they are not allowed to leave lest by my say," proclaimed Hades. As he spoke, he began to grow in size so that he towered even more so over the man at his feet. "Why did you attempt to leave?"

"I-I-I-I," stammered the man, who seemed incapable of stringing together a cohesive thought. Hades fixed him with a stern and penetrating stare. The man immediately fell silent.

"You have been sentenced to Tartarus for your sins," declared Hades. "I find myself in agreement with Minos. Your sentence stands."

"Please," cried the man, tears streaming down his colorless face. "I repent. I didn't mean any of it. Please don't send me there. Have mercy. Have mercy!"

He grabbed at Hades' leg, prostrating himself pityingly upon Hades' mercy. Hades reached down, took the man about the collar, lifted him to eye level, and stared him straight in the face.

"No."

## Heir to the Underworld

With one fluid gesture, he tossed the man into the flaming river. A tongue of flames leaped up to greet the condemned spirit, who gave one last horrified scream before he was consumed totally by the blazing river. Ben gazed at Hades, taken aback by the sudden change in character. Where only a few moments ago he had been jovial and relaxed, he was now stern and imposing, the true picture of a death god. Hades closed his eyes and let out a deep breath as he shrunk back down to a more natural size.

"What did he do," asked Ben hesitantly, not sure now how he should feel about this side of Hades' personality.

"He was a pedophile," said Hades gravely. "To date, he has victimized over twenty little boys and girls. He died in a police shootout. He tried to use his latest victim as a hostage. Fortunately, they were able to save her."

"I hope he rots down there," said Ben in disgust as Hades' actions became clear.

"You're not too far off," said Hades. "Alecto trends towards poetic justice. I'm sure he'll regret his possession of certain body parts before long."

Hades gave the monstrous hound a pat on the rump and Cerberus bounded off back towards the gates before vanishing into thin air.

"I can't say I'm sympathetic," said Ben, looking down into the darkness of Tartarus. "What's it like down there?"

"The term Hellish comes to mind," said Hades with a sly smile. "Like the Underworld above it, Tartarus is ever-expanding. Also like the Underworld, a vast majority of Tartarus is empty space. There are, however, an innumerable amount of, what I suppose you could call, cells that float about, rather like the rocks you see up here. Inside each of these cells is a prisoner. Now, I should point out that those *cells* aren't exactly your generic six by eight prison cells. They are more like small worldlets, pocket dimensions if you will, that have been created by Tartarus to keep the horrors sentenced to his realm at bay."

"His?"

"Tartarus is both a place and a god. He is the protogenoi, primordial god, of the pit. Actually, he was the protogenoi for the entire Underworld, but I managed to get the top half for myself in the divorce settlement. Just kidding. But I did convince him to let me have half the Underworld for the souls of the dead. Anyway, he is both a god *and* a place."

"That's a little confusing."

"Get used to it. Tartarus is not the only primordial, trust me."

"I'm guessing that he didn't make any happy worldlets full of rainbows, sunshine, and unicorns," said Ben.

"Not really, no," chuckled Hades. "Although, all of those do appear in different worldlets separately."

"Unicorns? Really?"

"Have you ever been gored continuously by a unicorn's horn?"

"No," said Ben, a little taken aback.

"Well, neither have I," said Hades. "But, if the screams are any indication, it hurts quite a lot."

"What do you have to do in life to end up a pincushion for a unicorn?" asked Ben.

"Trust me," said Hades, "you really don't want to know."

"Right. Moving on then—"

"That is what we do best around here," said Hades, smiling wickedly at the look of exasperation Ben shot him.

"What is the Asphodel Meadows like? You and Aeacus kept mentioning tiers."

"The Asphodel Meadows used to be just one large, flat plain where the souls of the dead stood about, frozen in time. Now it's been broken up into several tiers. The first tier still remains the same as it originally was, full of the standing dead, but as you move up the tier the quality of life improves. Or would it be un-life? You know, I've never had to really explain all of this to anyone before. I should have prepared better."

"Isn't that kind of cruel?" asked Ben. "Just having the souls stand there, unmoving all the time."

"I just threw a pedophile into a river of fire so that he can be tortured for all of eternity and you are calling standing in one place, completely oblivious to the world around you, cruel?"

"There isn't a monopoly on cruelty," countered Ben. "Just because Tartarus is cruel doesn't mean that the first tier isn't cruel as well. It's not like they did anything wrong."

"They didn't do anything at all," retorted Hades. "That's why they're there. Tartarus is for whose lives were deemed abhorrent. The Elysium is for those whose lives were deemed heroic. And the Asphodel Meadows are for those whose lives were deemed undistinguished."

"So just because you weren't a hero you get the second-rate afterlife?" demanded Ben. "That's not fair to them."

Hades smiled. "That's exactly what my wife said when she came down here for the first time."

"You're married?"

"Don't sound so surprised," said Hades. "And yes, I'm married to one of the kindest goddesses alive. She's the reason that the Asphodel Meadows have a tier system. She didn't like the old way any more than you."

"I think I'm gonna like your wife. Is she at the palace too?"

"Everyone likes my wife. And no she's in the world above right now. She's only around for half the year. The other half she's helping her mother Demeter with her work."

"Well that's nice of her," said Ben.

"She's the goddess of spring growth. It's kind of her duty."

"What's her name?"

"Persephone, my beautiful spring flower."

"If I ever meet her, do I have to call her *my beautiful spring flower* too?" asked Ben with a smile.

"Keep it up and I'll sic the Furies on you," said Hades haughtily. "Now come this way."

He waved his hand and created a path of winding earth over Tartarus. "After you."

Ben stepped onto the path and was immediately sent rushing forward. The Underworld whooshed past him in a blur as he sailed along, his feet firmly glued to the ground beneath him. After a few seconds, he was deposited in front of Hades' palace.

# Chapter Eight

Hades' palace, which was built to resemble a gothic cathedral, was made of the same black stone as the gates to the Underworld. A large stain glass window, depicting the various exploits of Hades, was featured above two large doors of black wood. As Ben's eyes flitted from turret to turret, Hades stepped off the path to stand beside him.

"It's subtle," said Ben. "If I didn't know any better, I'd think Mother Teresa lived here."

"I had her over for dinner once," said Hades. "She was a horrible guest. Never really got over the *God doesn't exist* thing."

"Well, when you've dedicated your life to an apparently fictional deity it might take some time to adjust to their non-existence."

"She was screaming at me to accept the light of God or spend all eternity in Hell all night. Apparently, irony is lost on the dead."

"Guess she wasn't feeling very *humerus*."

"Glad to know that I'll be passing on the mantle of King of the Underworld to someone in possession of such a *killer* wit."

"At least I won't have to worry about anyone *dying* of laughter."

"Which is a good thing 'cause this place could use some cheering up. It's so *grim*."

"That joke *paled* in comparison to your other ones."

"I can see I've made a *grave* mistake keeping this going. Let's go inside before these jokes get any worse."

They walked forward towards the doors, which swung open as they approached. Ben stepped into the palace's entrance hall and froze; taken aback by the room he'd just entered.

The exterior gloom of Hades' palace belied its interior brightness. The floors, walls, and ceilings were made of white marble, polished mirror bright, and glowing with a soft, warm, sunny light. Large-scale paintings and portraits, in every conceivable style, decorated the walls, each resting within its own golden frame. The room was littered with French antiques, extravagant candelabras, and exquisite vases. Marble columns, carved to resemble angels, rose up to a vaulted ceiling from which multiple large, crystal chandeliers hung. The beauty and elegance of the palace was marred, however, by the presence of several dead plants. Each of the angelic columns had withered vines snaked around them and every vase was full to bursting with wilted flowers.

"Okay, not what I was expecting," said Ben, his eyes darting around the room.

"Persephone's doing. She redecorates every few years. It's been this way for two years now. Before this, it was English colonial. And before that, it was Asian influence."

"Who are these paintings by?"

"Everyone: Da Vinci, Michelangelo, Raphael, Picasso, van Gogh. Name a dead artist and their works are probably on our walls. Same with the furnishings, antiques straight from the original craftsmen and designers. Although I don't know if you can actually call them antiques when they were made within the last five years."

"I guess art never truly dies."

"Don't start with the jokes again. We'll be here all day."

"Well, we do have an eternity."

Hades rolled his eyes while trying to suppress a smile.

"So, ghosts can paint?" asked Ben.

"Oh yes. There's an entire tier for artisans in the Asphodel Meadows."

"But how? Aren't they, you know, incorporeal?"

"This is the land of the dead. Things such as corporeal and incorporeal don't matter quite as much. After all, if a soul can be tortured in the pits of Tartarus, I see no reason why a soul can't hold a paintbrush in the Artisan's Abode."

"Where do they get the materials?"

"I did mention that the Underworld creates its own resources, didn't I?"

"Like these dead plants you mean?" asked Ben, gesturing towards a nearby pillar as they started walking down the entrance hall towards another pair of double doors.

"Living things don't really flourish in the Underworld so without Persephone' presence, they wilt and die. When she comes back, however, they return to life."

"Aren't the Asphodel Meadows... well, meadows? Are all the plants there dead too?"

"Plants of the Underworld are different. These plants here are from the living world."

They had reached the second set of double doors by now. Like the doors into the palace, these doors also opened of their own accord, leading them into a cavernous throne room. Several banners, half of them pale green and half of them pitch black, hung from the ceiling. The black banners were emblazoned with the image of a skull wearing a black crown, while the green banner depicted a bouquet of spring flowers bound together with a black circlet. At the far end of the room was a dais, upon which stood two beautiful carved thrones of marble, one black and the other green.

Six people stood in the room. Five of them Ben didn't know, but the sixth one was, much to Ben displeasure, Hecate. She was dressed in a black, formal gown with a long train, held up by several fluttering bats.

"You already know Hecate, of course," said Hades as they walked forward toward the assembled group, "but this is the rest of my court. Or, at least, these are the ones that I could gather up to meet you."

"Who's missing?" asked Ben.

"Well Persephone, of course," began Hades, ticking off those who weren't present on in his fingers. "Tartarus isn't much of a people person, so he refused. For whatever reason Nyx, the primordial goddess of the night, is only around when night falls in Greece. Yes, she's another one of those two-in-one gods. In this case, she is both the goddess of the night *and* the actual night sky. Just don't think about it, it's easier that way. Where was I? Oh yes, Thanatos comes and goes as he pleases. Eris, goddess of discord, is likewise engaged. I believe she said something about causing some ruckus regarding a politician and their emails. Polemos, he's a war god, is on loan to Ares. Every time Ares wants to start some conflict or another, he borrows him. Honestly, at this point, he's more a part of Ares' court than mine. Styx is, of course, continuing with her prolonged slumber. I think she's been napping for some fifty years or so, give or take a decade. And I haven't a clue where Ascalaphus, my custodian, is."

"There was a small disagreement between two flights of harpies," said Hecate. "He went to sort it out."

"Ah," said Hades. "Well, that answers that. Now then everyone, I would like to introduce Ben, my heir. Everyone if you could introduce yourselves, I'd appreciate it. I feel as if I've been talking nonstop all day."

The only male in the group stepped forward immediately.

"I am Hypnos, god of sleep." His voice was soft and calming. He had a gentle, handsome face, long blue hair, and deep purple eyes. He was draped in an extremely long, shimmering shawl of the deepest blue Ben had ever seen. As Hypnos reached out to shake hands, Ben caught a delicate flora scent wafting from the god of sleep. As he took Hypnos' offered hand, Ben could feel his eyes growing heavy. Without meaning to, he let out a wide yawn.

"So sorry," said Hypnos, backing away from Ben. "My presence tends to cause mortals to fall into a stupor. I'd hoped that the divinity you received from Hades would be enough to protect you from my soporific effects, but I'm afraid you're not yet there."

"It's fine," said Ben as he tried to stifle another yawn. "No harm done. Although I wouldn't say no to a cup of coffee."

Hypnos chuckled softly.

"If you need a pick me up, I've got a brew for you," said one of the goddesses. She had wide hips and was dressed all in black. A shadowy veil fell over her face and her long, black hair hung about her in a twisting braid.

"What kind of brew?" asked Ben, not sure if he trusted her.

"It's my own special kind of coffee," said the goddess. "It's guaranteed to keep you awake for hours."

"I think I'll save it for next time," said Ben. "I'm not that tired."

"Good choice," said Hades. "This is Achlys, goddess of misery. That brew she was talking about, it's called insomnia. As in actual insomnia. One sip and you'll be unable to sleep for days."

"What a clever boy you brought, Hades," said Achlys bitterly. "I was so hoping to try out my new recipe on him. Ah well. I'll just have to find another guinea pig. Now if you all will excuse me; I left a pot of troubles on the fire. Can't let that boil-over. We don't want another Pompeii, do we?"

"Pot of troubles?" asked Ben curiously.

"I'm the goddess of misery, darling," said Achlys. "It's my job to bring pain and sorrow to the mortal world. I cook up misfortunes in my pot and then unleash it upon the world. And now, if you'll excuse me, I have work to do." Without another word, Achlys disappeared in a puff of black smoke.

"Does she actually cook them up?" asked Ben. "Like a cake or something?"

"Yes," said Hades, chuckling slightly at the look on Ben's face. "If you don't mind a little sadness, her teardrop soup is actually quite tasty. You'll probably be crying for days, but it does taste good."

"God, I hope you're joking," muttered Ben.

"Not even a little," said Hades with a wide smile.

"Am I next?" asked one of the remaining goddesses. Her hair was as white as fresh snow, her skin was pale as chalk, and her eyes were a pair of milky pearls. She wore a cascading white dress that fell about her thin frame like a waterfall.

"If you want to be," said Hades.

"I'm Lethe, goddess of forgetfulness." Lethe smiled at Ben. "It's nice to see meet you. I'd shake your hand but, if I did, you'd forget who you were."

"I'll keep that in mind," said Ben. "And it's nice to meet you too."

"You can shake my hand without any complications."

The goddess who had spoken was very different from anyone else Ben had met so far. She was noble, bold, and radiant, with tumbling locks of golden hair and twinkling green eyes. She wore a simple white gown of shimmering light and a golden crown entwined with flowers in full bloom.

"Good to know," said Ben, taking the goddess proffered hand. "And you are?"

"Macaria, goddess of blessed death." Her voice was as clear and strong as a trumpet.

"Blessed death?" asked Ben as he let go of Macaria's hand.

"Let's just say a hero's death."

"Got it," said Ben. He turned to face the final goddess.

"That is my sister Melinoë, goddess of madness."

Melinoë was nothing like her sister. She was timid, wispy, and morose. Her black hair was so dry and ratty that it resembled a tumbleweed, and unlike Macaria's dress of woven light, Melinoë's dress looked to be made of flecks of gray ash that had been stitched together. Melinoë too wore a golden crown, though hers was wreathed in thorny briars. Slowly, tentatively, she extended a nail-bitten hand, her eyes cast downwards instead of at Ben.

"It is a pleasure to meet you Melinoë," said Ben kindly.

"Pleasure," muttered Melinoë quietly.

"My sister is... shy," said Macaria apologetically.

"Nothing wrong with that," said Ben. "I can be shy too. If you aren't comfortable around me yet that is fine. No need to rush."

Slowly Melinoë looked up at Ben and their eyes locked for the first time.

The world around him fell away, leaving a crushing, hopeless darkness in its wake. Ben felt as though he was falling down through endless abyss of sorrow and misery. There was no light. There was no hope. There was no escape. There was only the gnawing pain of depression and the nagging fear of isolation.

Color and light suddenly returned. Ben blinked several times as the throne room came back into focus. Someone's hand was on his shoulder. Turning, Ben saw that it was Hades'.

"There are many dangers in the Underworld that you are not yet capable of handling," said Hades. "And my daughters are perhaps the top of the list, even if it is inadvertent."

Something warm and wet trickled down Ben's face. He reached up to wipe it off and found that he was crying. When had that happened?

"Please forgive my sister," said Macaria apologetically. "As with Lethe and Hypnos, her presence can cause adverse effects on mortals."

"Sorry," muttered Melinoë, her eyes downcast again.

"It's fine," said Ben. "It was an interesting experience."

"A rather kind response," said Hades with a smile.

"It's not her fault if her powers are a bit erratic," said Ben. He turned to look at Melinoë, who continued to avoid his gaze.

"I'm not upset," he told her calmly. "I promise."

"You chose well, Lord Hades," said Hypnos. "The boy seems more than capable of adjusting to the many *complications* of the Underworld."

"Yes," said Hades. "It would seem so."

"I hope you'll be happy here Ben," said Lethe with a kind smile. "As many dangers as there are in the Underworld, there are just as many wonders, if you know where to look. The memories I've seen. I cou— oh darn it all."

"What's the matter?" asked Hypnos.

"I just remembered, I was supposed to reincarnate several souls yesterday and I completely forgot."

"Do people ask to be reincarnated a lot?" asked Ben.

"It used to be a more common practice," said Hypnos, "but the number of souls who request it has waned over centuries. Now, only about one in every one-thousand souls elects to be reincarnated."

"And it's only for souls that are bounded for the Asphodel Meadows or the Elysium, which helps to keep the numbers low as well," chimed in Macaria. "Souls headed for Tartarus are not allowed to apply."

"Why would you want to be reincarnated if you are already headed to paradise?"

"Because within the Elysium there is an area called the Isle of the Blessed," explained Hades. "Only heroic souls that have been reincarnated three times can enter it. You might call it paradise plus."

"But even fewer people elect for that," noted Hecate. "I don't think we've had anyone actually enter the Isle of the Blessed in what, two hundred years?"

"Something like that," said Hades thoughtfully. "I think it was George Washington, wasn't it?"

"Yes," said Macaria. "He reincarnated as William H. Stewart. And before he was Washington, he was King Frederick IV of Denmark."

"Sorry to interrupt but I really must get to those poor souls," cut in Lethe. "I've left them hanging for far too long. It was a pleasure meeting you Ben."

"I can help you if you'd like," said Hypnos. "I have nothing better to do. Pasithea is off with her sisters blessing health spas and it's rather boring at home without her."

"Thank you," said Lethe. "I could use a hand. Just make sure you don't dip it in the river."

"I'll be careful," Hypnos. He turned to Hades. "If you will excuse us, my lord, it seems Lethe and I have work to attend to."

"Of course," said Hades. "Thank you for your presence in greeting my heir."

Hypnos and Lethe both nodded before vanishing from sight: Hypnos in a swirl of glittering blue smoke and Lethe in a flash of white light.

"Are he and Lethe an item?" asked Ben.

"No," said Hades. "Hypnos is married to Pasithea, goddess of relaxation."

"They seem kinda chummy. Are they having an affair?"

"I don't think so," said Hades thoughtful. "But who knows. Hypnos and Lethe do live right next to each other so he could just be being neighborly. Then again his wife Pasithea is gone a lot so there are plenty of opportunities I suppose."

"Father, such speculations are beneath you," chided Macaria.

"I'm King of the Underworld Macaria, nothing is beneath me. Literally."

Macaria rolled her eyes.

"Besides, it's just a little harmless conjecture."

"You are the god of the dead, not the god of scurrilous gossip."

"Yeah Hades," chimed in Ben, a wicked smile spreading across his face, "don't be such a *yenta*."

"Boy, I will sic the dog on you," said Hades in mock indignity. "And Macaria, there's nothing wrong with having a little fun. I'd tell you to lighten up, but you are already the brightest thing in the Underworld."

"Your jokes do not amuse me, father."

"You see what I have to deal with?" asked Hades, turning to Ben in resignation. "I work all day ruling the Underworld. Then, when I've finished my day's work and finally get to relax, I have to come home and deal with two full-grown children who just won't move out. I mean, what's god to do?"

"Retire, apparently," said Ben.

"Yes well, that's a good point," said Hades with a smile. "Ah, retirement. I can't wait. I can finally enjoy my immortality. And, best of all, I can be as undignified as I want."

As Hades gazed off into the distant, clearly imaging a life devoid of decency, Ben turned to face Macaria and Melinoë

"Can I ask you two something?"

"Of course," said Macaria, taking her disapproving eyes off her father. Melinoë nodded her assent, her eyes still downcast.

"How do you two feel about your dad giving me control of the Underworld? I mean, if he's the king, wouldn't that make you the princesses? I'm guessing you expected to inherit eventually."

"What makes you ask that?" asked Macaria.

"It was something Ozzy… Oozy—"

"Oizys," said Macaria helpfully.

"Yeah, her. She said something about how I didn't know what I was getting into and how either you or your sister might be a better choice since at least you've had some experience with Underworld related stuff."

"Well, if truth be told, I'm actually relieved," said Macaria. "I don't want to be Queen of the Underworld. Much too much work. I'm currently the one in charge of the Elysium, where all the fallen heroes reside. Why would I want to give that up to deal with the endless onslaught of problems, complaints, and annoyances that my father has to deal with on a daily basis?"

"I guess that makes sense, although it's making me regret my decision to take his place. How about you Melinoë?"

"I like to be left alone," said Melinoë quietly. "Father's work would be, unpleasant."

"Yep, definitely regretting my decision."

"I hope we didn't put you off," said Macaria.

"No, I'm just joking," said Ben with a laugh. "Well, maybe I'm feeling a little bit of regret but mostly I'm just joking."

"Are you sure?" asked Macaria.

"It's mostly just nerves. Don't worry about it. Besides, it's not like there's any way out of it now."

"That's not quite true." A new voice, soft and cold, resounded through the throne room.

"Who was that?" asked Ben, his eyes darting around the room.

"Thanatos," whispered Hades.

A thick column of swirling gray mist billowed up around the black throne, obscuring it completely from sight. A few seconds later the column broke and the mist faded away. Sitting upon the throne was a man who bore a striking resemblance to Hypnos, save for a few key differences. His hair was black not blue, his eyes were gray not purple, and his face was hauntingly gaunt instead of a gently handsome. He wore black and gray robes that swirled about his thin frame like a dark mist.

"I believe introductions are in order," said the newcomer.

"Ben, may I present Thanatos, god of death. Thanatos, this is my heir apparent, Benjamin Darke." Hades' relaxed air had been replaced with stiff formality.

"I see you have picked a suitable replacement," said Thanatos, his eyes still focused unblinkingly at Ben. "How nice."

"What did you mean before," asked Ben. "About how it's not true that there is no way out of being a god."

Ben wasn't sure why but Thanatos unnerved him, more so than anything else he'd seen that day. It wasn't anything overt, his mere presence just seemed to put Ben on edge.

"Only that there is *one* way out of your commitment."

"What's that?"

A smile crept across Thanatos' face. He rose up from the throne to glide through the air towards Ben. Once they were face to face, Thanatos reached out and took Ben's face in his hand, forcing Ben to look him straight in the eye. The metal claws that he wore on his fingers pressed sharply into Ben's skin. There was something strange behind Thanatos' cold, penetrating stare that made Ben feel uncomfortable, though he wasn't sure why.

"Death," said Thanatos softly.

Ben, in spite of himself, gulped, audibly.

"Thanatos," chided Hades warningly.

"He has a right to know," said Thanatos, his eyes still boring into Ben's.

"I thought a god couldn't die," said Ben, desperately trying to keep his voice from cracking.

"A god may be immortal, but *you* are not a god." Thanatos took his hand from Ben's face. "At least, not yet."

"Hades?"

"He speaks the truth," said Hades. "Until you, all of you, have fully acclimated to your powers you are still mortal and, as such, still susceptible to death."

"That would have been nice to know," snapped Ben, yanking Thanatos' hand from his face and rounding on Hades. "Why didn't you tell us?"

"We didn't think it was relevant."

"Not relevant? You've got us training with Hecate and Heracles every day. Combat training no less. There are swords, spears, axes, and other sharp, pointy weapons of various sizes and shapes involved. Gavin's been running face-first into a wall for the past week, Vincent's drinking himself to early liver damage, Lance is literally playing with fire, Andrew's been trying to learn how to fly with disastrous results, and who knows when Sophia is finally gonna snap and beat Johnny to death with a rainbow flag. And do you know why everyone is okay with all of this? It's because they think they're immortal. Bruises, cuts, burns, whatever, as long as Matthew's around to heal us up who cares. It's not like we can die. Except now, you're telling me we can."

"It's not like we kept it from you on purpose," said Hades. "It just didn't cross our minds as something important. And, if you remember, I warned you about falling into Tartarus. I did say you wouldn't survive."

"I thought that was a joke," said Ben.

"Well, it wasn't. You can die. All of you can die. But that's what Hecate and Heracles are there for, to make sure you don't die."

"Do you fear death, little godling?" asked Thanatos, cutting off Ben as he opened his mouth.

"I'm not anxious to meet it, but it wouldn't say I'm afraid of it."

"Even now after you have met death face to face? Now that you see it manifested before your eyes? Do you still not fear death?"

"Well you are kinda creepy, but I wouldn't say I'm afraid of you."

"Then you don't understand me at all." Thanatos' robe swirled upwards, enveloping him in whirling gray mist.

"I am death, in all its forms." Thanatos' voice issued out from the billowing vortex of mist like a creeping frost, filling the room with the cold chill of a frozen winter's evening.

"I came for the old."

The swirling mist cleared. Standing where Thanatos had been was an old man, his skin wrinkled, his hair gone, his limbs trembling. He reached out a shaking hand towards Ben, gazing at him with tired eyes, before he was consumed by gray fog.

"I came for the young."

This time the mist parted to reveal a young boy, his eyes sparkling with hope and energy. He turned to Ben and smiled, a wide, carefree smile. And then he was gone, swallowed up by the gray fog as the old man had been.

"I came for the rich."

The mist parted to reveal a handsome man, dressed in an expensive suit, a haughty look of satisfaction upon on his face. And then the fog closed upon him too.

"I come for the poor."

The mist opened and closed upon a filthy, emaciated man, his body weak and frail, his eyes hollow and forlorn."

"I come for everyone and everything, for all mortal life must, eventually, end."

The mist didn't part this time. Instead, it began to grow and darken, rising upward towards the ceiling, building itself up into a towering pillar of swirling darkness.

"Death is inevitable. Death is inescapable. Death is eternal."

The pillar of black mist had now reached the ceiling. From its depths came a rumble like thunder, an ominous roar that made the hairs on the back of Ben's neck stand on end. Suddenly the revolving pillar of mist surged down towards Ben. A gap opened at its head, a vast yawning maw ready to consume him, body and soul. Ben instinctively threw up his arms even though, in the back of his mind, he knew that there was no defense against what was coming towards him. The mist was now inches away from Ben's face.

"ENOUGH!" roared Hades.

The mist ricocheted backward into itself and turned into a massive, churning cloud of black mist. For a few moments, it hung there, a seething eddy of dark vapor completely devoid of substance, of light, and of color. And then the mist settled, and Thanatos was once again standing before them.

"If you are to be the god of the dead you must learn something, and learn it well," said Thanatos, his gray eyes fixing Ben with the same penetrating look as before. "Death is not some triviality that you can ignore. If you do become the god of the Underworld, your greatest responsibility will be to maintain the balance between the living and the dead. The dead have had their time. It may not be fair, it may not be pleasant, but it is the way of the universe."

Thanatos' robes dissolved into mist once more, whirling up around him to form a pair of large, feathery, gray wings.

"Goodbye, little godling," said Thanatos with a slight bow of the head. "Until we meet again."

With one powerful downward stroke, he shot up into the air and out of the palace, passing through the ceiling as though it didn't even exist.

"Yup, totally regretting my decision."

# Chapter Nine

Despite their training with Heracles and Hecate, it was their classes at M.O.U. that took up much of the new gods' time. Though most of them had similar course loads, there were some (Ana Maria, Lance, and Gavin specifically) who had to stay up late into the night studying. Ana Maria, in particular, was very strident about her need to study.

"Why bother?" Johnny had asked one day at breakfast. "It's not like it matters."

"I have an academic scholarship," replied Ana Maria as she shifted through the mountain of notes she had brought out with her. "I have to maintain a certain GPA."

"Your scholarship isn't based on your grades," said Johnny, "it's based on the fact that you are going to be a god. Lighten up." Ana Maria looked up from her notes to glare at him.

"My family is expecting me to do well, and I will not let them down. Furthermore, Hermes stated that we still need to do well even if we are going to be gods. If you want to coast through life, that is your business. I, on the other hand, intend to make sure that I learn as much as I possibly can. Just being a god doesn't mean I'll automatically have all the answers."

"You're crazy lady," said Johnny.

"*Y eres el culo de un burro,*" muttered Ana Maria under her breath. Vincent, who overheard her, choked on his orange juice.

"What's so funny?" demanded Johnny.

"Nothing," said Vincent, coughing softly to clear his throat. "Don't worry about it."

Johnny looked suspiciously between Vincent and Ana Maria.

"You two are weird, even for a fag and a nerd."

"Are we really going to get into this again?" snapped Sara. "You are on the wrong side of history mate."

"Don't blame me," said Johnny. "He's the one living an alternative and immoral lifestyle."

"I'd drop the subject if I were you," said Lance. "You don't want Sophia to come in here and hear you."

Johnny blushed.

"She got a lucky shot," said Johnny. "No way a chick could do that to me in a fair fight."

"Homophobic and misogynistic," muttered Sara. "Boy did we hit the jackass jackpot with you."

"It's a scientific fact that guys are better than girls," said Johnny. "And if God had wanted men to be with men, he would have made created Adam and Steve instead of Adam and Eve."

"Really?" asked Lance in incredulity. "You're gonna talk about God? I think that argument went out the window the minute Hermes turned up."

"You think he's smart enough to figure that out?" asked Vincent. "You give him too much credit."

"Shut up!" yelled Johnny. "Y'all can make whatever excuses you want. All I know is that two guys together ain't natural. So, if you wanna encourage this disgusting display, that's your business. But you will never convince me that they ain't pervs."

Without another word, Johnny stormed out of the dining room.

"I'm so glad I met him," said Vincent as he poured some of the contents of his flask into his glass of orange juice. "He gives me a reason to be drunk at nine o'clock in the morning."

"Where is Matthew today anyway?" asked Sara.

"He got himself elected as an officer for the school's GSA," said Vincent. "So he's off helping them with some event or another."

"You two seem to be getting close," said Lance.

"Seems that way doesn't it," said Vincent noncommittally. "If you'll excuse me, I have to get to class. Grub was as good as always Irene."

As Vincent left Irene swept up his and Johnny's plates from the table and took them back to the kitchen for cleaning.

"You don't have to serve us you know," said Lance. "You aren't our maid."

"I know," called back Irene.

"But she's gonna do it anyway," muttered Lance.

"I've tried to talk to her," said Sara. "So have Matthew and Reneé. Nothing. She just keeps at it."

"It makes me feel uncomfortable," said Lance.

"Me too," said Sara.

"What are you two talking about?" asked Ana Maria distractedly without looking up from her notes.

"Irene waiting on us all," said Sara.

"Has she been? I hadn't noticed."

"How did you not notice?" asked Sara.

"Because she's been too busy studying," said Lance. "She barely noticed who is in the room, let alone what people are doing while in it. Can you pass me the juice, Sara?"

As Sara stretched out a hand for the juice Ben, who was closer, reached and pushed it down towards Lance.

"When did you get here?" asked Sara.

"I was here before you two," said Ben.

"Really?" asked Lance and Sara in unison.

"Really," repeated Ben.

*"Supongo que no soy el único que no presta atención,"* muttered Ana Maria smugly to herself.

"You mean we've been ignoring this whole time?" asked Sara.

"Yup," said Ben. "But don't worry about it. I'm used to it."

"Dude I'm—" began Lance but Ben cut him off.

"It's fine," said Ben as he stood up from the table.

"Are you mad?" asked Sara tentatively. "I bet you're mad."

"I'm not mad," said Ben, picking up his plate. "I just have to go to class. And, about Irene waiting on us, I don't think she should either but, I also don't find it as uncomfortable as you all do."

"Why's that," asked Lance.

"Because, like the rest of you, she forgets I exist." And, without another word, Ben carried his plate into the kitchen himself.

Ana Maria wasn't the only one with a lot on her plate. As a Theatre Arts and Music major, Matthew was required to participate in at least one play a year and sing in the school choir. Part of Sophia's veterinary degree required her to volunteer time at an animal shelter. Sammy and Andrew, who were both on athletic scholarships, were required to not only join the swimming and football teams, but also attend team workouts.

Out of the two, Sammy had an easier time of it. It was off-season, so the focus was not on competitions but on building up the swimmers' abilities. In Andrew's case, however, football season was in full swing. Between classes, team practices, team workouts, god training sessions, and homework, Andrew was almost as overworked as Ana Maria. But he didn't seem to mind. In fact, it seemed like he almost enjoyed it. When asked, he simply said that he liked being busy. He was so busy, in fact, that he was almost never seen outside of training by any of the other new gods. And then, three weeks into the term, he popped his head into the dining room while everyone was eating dinner.

"Hey everyone," said Andrew.

"Hey," was the chorused reply.

"I just thought I'd let you know that the first JV game of the year will be this Friday in case any of you wanted to come watch."

"Will you be playing?" asked Vincent pointedly.

"Yup, I'm the JV first-string QB."

"JV?" asked Reneé. "I do not know zis word."

"It means junior varsity," explained Gavin automatically. "It's the team of lesser significance." Gavin looked up at Andrew in embarrassment. "Sorry, I didn't mean—"

"Nah, don't worry about it, dude," said Andrew, waving away Gavin's concerns. "JV isn't as important as varsity. It just a fact."

"I thought you were supposed to be good," said Vincent. "Why are you only on the JV?"

"You're not helping," muttered Matthew so that only Vincent could hear him.

"The college doesn't let freshmen on the varsity team," explained Andrew. "No matter how good they are."

"Ah," said Vincent. "Well, I'll be there. We gods have to be supportive of each other after all." He winked slyly at Andrew, who just rolled his eyes.

"I'll go too," said Johnny. "It'll be nice to see a little bit of America in the place, even if I have to be around the fruitcakes."

"To football," said Vincent, lifting his glass of wine into the air in a toast. "Bring the world closer together one bigot at a time."

The others quickly expressed their interest in attending, cutting Johnny off before he could respond to Vincent's insult.

"Great," said Andrew. "I'll see you all there."

"Do we have to buy tickets?" asked Lance as Andrew turned to leave.

"Oh right," said Andrew, turning back around, "forgot about that. Yeah, you have to get tickets. They are like twenty-five bucks, I mean euros. You can get them online or at the stadium. Anyway, got to get to practice. See ya."

"Maybe I won't go," said Johnny ruefully.

"Why's that?" asked Lance.

"I don't think I have twenty-five euro," said Johnny.

"Come to think of it," said Lance. "I'm a little short on cash myself."

"I'll cover it," said Vincent. "I'll pay for everyone."

"What?" asked Lance. "Really?"

"Sure, why not."

"Even for the donkey?" asked Sophia.

"Even for the donkey."

"Will you stop calling me *the donkey*?" snapped Johnny.

"We will as soon as you stop calling Matthew and Vincent fags," retorted Sophia.

"Thank you for the offer but no," said Ana Maria as Sophia and Johnny started bickering. "My father wouldn't like me accepting charity."

"Is your father here?" asked Vincent. "Besides, it's not really charity. My father gives money to this school. I'm sure I can get the tickets for nothing."

"Really?" asked Ana Maria. "Or are you lying to me just to get me to come?"

"Why would I lie about something as pointless as a football ticket?" asked Vincent. "But, if you don't believe me, you can come with me when I go to get the tickets if you want."

"Very well. If they are actually free, then I will go."

"Good. Any other objections?" No one spoke up. "Thank the gods for that."

When Friday night came, the new gods gathered in the living room and headed to the game together. Ben was almost left behind because no one thought to knock on his door. Fortunately, since his room was closest to the front door, he was able to hear them leaving. Grabbing his wallet and phone, he ran after them, only managing to catch up to them because they had to wait for the elevator.

Heracles Stadium was not as spectacular as the one belonging to its namesake. In fact, the only thing that set it apart from American football stadiums was its carved arches and marble columns. There were a lot of marble columns at Mt. Olympus University. Once they had arrived at the stadium, Vincent took the lead and presented their tickets to the attendant.

"Where are our seats anyway?" asked Lance as the group filed into the stadium. Vincent had refused to let them see their tickets.

"You'll see in a minute," said Vincent. As it turned out, their tickets were for a special VIP box.

"You're kidding right?" asked Sara as Vincent opened the door to the box and motioned for them to all step inside.

"My father paid for this stadium," said Vincent. "And about a fourth of the buildings on campus. I see no reason why we shouldn't benefit from his generosity. Although, I doubt he was actually being generous."

"Why has he given so much money to this place?" asked Johnny. "Couldn't get in any other way?"

"That's rich, coming from the jackass with less brains than roadkill," muttered Sophia coldly.

"My dad went to this school," said Vincent. "He's one of their most successful alumni. Now, I'd suggest you get in before I decide to call security, and have you escorted out."

Grudgingly, Johnny followed the others into the VIP box.

"Does anyone know who we are playing?" asked Gavin.

"Some French team," said Johnny dismissively. "They'll probably give up before the first quarter's over."

"*Âne*," spat Reneé.

"*Qu'il est,*" said Vincent.

"I didn't even know Europeans played football," said Sammy. "At least not American football. Isn't it all soccer on this side of the sea?"

"It is ze more common," said Reneé.

"In Australia, it's rugby that's more common than either version of football," said Sara.

"So why is there a football team here then?" asked Gavin.

"'Cause they've realized that our version of football is better than any other sport," said Johnny smugly.

"Because the school wants a reputation for excellence in everything," corrected Vincent. "Be it engineering, medicine, arts, or sports. So it started a program in the 1990s to make the sports program the best in the world. Now it's the top school that recruiters look at for pretty much every sport, even American football."

"Dude, how do you know all this?" asked Sammy.

"Like I said, my dad went to this school. He pretty much drummed all of its history into me. Or, at least, he told my tutors to."

"Well I'm excited," said Reneé as she and the others took their seats. "I 'ave never seen a game of Amewican football before."

"You're about to get your chance," said Johnny. "Games about to start."

Everyone looked out the window to see both teams of players lining up opposite each other.

"Which one is Andrew?" asked Reneé.

"That one behind the guy in the middle," said Johnny, pointing towards one of the players in a blue jersey.

"Number six," said Ashley.

"Oh look, 'e 'as ze ball," said Reneé. "And now 'e's thwown it. 'E 'as got a great arm. Now zat guy 'as caught it. Oh, zat must 'ave 'urt."

"Is the play by play really necessary?" asked Johnny.

"Agreed," said Ashley. "It's very annoying."

"Give her a break," said Lance. "Like she said, she's never seen a football game before."

The game proceeded onwards. Before the first quarter had finished, the Mt. Olympus Demigods had scored three touchdowns, all thanks to Andrew's excellent passes. During the second quarter, the Paris Institute Profiteers managed to break through the Demigods' defenses and score a touchdown. By the time half time came around, the score was thirty-five to seven.

"I think we can figure out how this game is going to go," said Johnny as he popped a chip into his mouth.

The VIP box had come with a refrigerator loaded with drinks (both alcoholic and non) and a table laden down with various snack foods. The new gods had been gorging themselves all game.

"A victory for M.O.U.," said Ashley.

"And all zanks to Andrew," added Reneé. "'E is playing very well, is 'e not?"

"Yes, he is," said Vincent. "I guess he does have some talent after all. Though it probably helps that all the other schools don't put much stock into their football programs. I think M.O.U. has won the European Championship for the last ten years running now?"

"Don't be a spoilsport," whispered Matthew reprovingly.

"Just stating facts here," said Vincent innocently.

"Ooo, cheerleaders," said Johnny, pressing himself against the glass of the booth. "Too bad we aren't closer."

"There's no rule that says you can't go down there to take a closer look," said Vincent.

"Good point," said Johnny. Getting up from his seat, he headed for the door.

"Quick," said Sophia as the door closed, "someone lock him out."

Everyone laughed. No one actually got up to lock the door, however, and eventually Johnny returned in time to watch the last two quarters. By the time the game was over, the score was seventy to twenty in M.O.U.'s favor. The new gods all headed down to the field to congratulate Andrew.

"You were amazing, *mon ami*," said Reneé, kissing Andrew on both cheeks in congratulations.

"Thanks," said Andrew. "I didn't think you all had actually come until I saw Johnny during half time. Where were you?"

"VIP box," said Vincent. "Good job, by the way. I could see you actually have a future in this sport, if it weren't for our *divine* calling."

"That was the big plan," said Andrew. "Dad's been training me for the NFL since I was seven. I don't want to know how he'll react when he finds out that it won't be happening."

"I thought you were still going to play anyway?" inquired Matthew.

"I want to, but I'm starting to question how practical it will be. I would think being a god would be kind of time-consuming."

"I hope it works out for you," piped up Gavin. "You're really good."

"Thanks, little buddy," said Andrew with a smile.

Gavin blushed.

"Hey, St. Cloud, you comin'!" One of Andrew's teammates was calling to him from the entrance to the locker rooms.

"Yeah, I'll be there in a sec!" called back Andrew.

He turned back towards the new gods. "The team's going out to celebrate our first win, so I'll see you all back home later."

"Enjoy," said Matthew.

"Don't do anything I wouldn't do," said Vincent.

"Well that's a short list," muttered Ashley.

"See ya," said Andrew, waving goodbye to the group and heading towards the locker room.

"I guess we should go back to the apartment now," said Lance. "Unless there's something else you all want to do."

"I want to study," said Ana Maria.

"What a surprise," muttered Ashley.

"You might consider it," retorted Ana Maria. "I saw what you made on that test we had in English."

Ashley glared at Ana Maria coldly.

"I think I'd like to go back to the apartment too," said Matthew. "That football game got me all . . . excited." He looked suggestively at Vincent.

"Oh?" asked Vincent. "Excited? I like excited."

"Disgusting," grumbled Johnny.

"I guess that's a no on you joining us?" asked Vincent.

"Fuck off, faggot," snapped Johnny. "I'd rather eat dirt."

"Now there's a thought," said Sophia and she shoved Johnny over the edge of the stands. He landed face-first on the field.

"Enjoy your meal," said Sophia as she and the others headed home. Johnny, red-faced and angry, picked himself up off the ground and stomped after them.

# Chapter Ten

"Anyone want to go on a sailing trip?" asked Vincent.

Everyone in the room turned to look at him. It was dinner time and, and for the first time in weeks, all fourteen new gods were in the same room.

"Like on a boat?" asked Johnny.

"No, on a kite," snapped Sophia. "Of course, he means on a boat."

"Well actually, it's a yacht," said Vincent, "but same difference really."

"You have a yacht?" asked Ashley as she turned her attention away from Andrew and towards Vincent.

"My father does. Since he's an alumnus he keeps a vacation house nearby, just in case. It's got all kinds of stuff: yachts, cars, planes, etcetera."

"You don't say?" asked Ashley, her eyes fixed adoringly on Vincent.

"*Elle est sur la rôder,*" muttered Matthew in exasperation.

"Can you shut up?" snapped Ashely. "I'm trying to have a conversation over here."

Vincent, however, seemed completely uninterested in talking to Ashley. He just stared, glassy-eyed, at the wall as she continued to chatter on.

"*La pute est en colère,*" said Matthew, causing Reneé to chortle softly.

"Why do I have the feeling I was just insulted," said Ashley, her eyes flashing.

"Not at all," said Matthew with an innocent smile that fooled no one.

"If your dad has a place here, why don't you stay there?" asked Andrew as Ashley and Matthew continued to bicker. "I mean this place is nice and all but it sounds like you'd have it made over there."

"There are certain fringe benefits to this place," said Vincent with a smile, his eyes darting over to Matthew for a split second. "But the yacht is there, sad and lonely, with no one to play with. I thought it might be fun to take it out. Thankfully this school is near the coast."

"Can you pilot a ship?" asked Ana Maria.

"No, but there is an on-call pilot or captain or helmsman or whatever they are called."

"I can do that," said Sammy. "My gramps taught me when I was younger."

"Your grandfather has a yacht too?" asked Ashley, cutting her tirade short as she turned her full attention on Sammy.

"No. He worked at a yacht club. Every once in a while, he had to take a yacht out to make sure it was still in working order. He'd bring me along sometimes."

"Oh," said Ashley, obviously disappointed. With both Vincent and Sammy a bust, she turned her attention back towards Andrew.

"That works out well. Means we can use our powers without issue. So, who's in?" asked Vincent.

The group was unanimous in their interest.

"Great. I'll set everything up. Saturday good for everyone?"

*****

The day of the yachting expedition dawned bright and warm. The sky was clear, and a cool, a strong breeze blew through the harbor as the fourteen new gods headed towards the yacht. Upon reaching the correct berth, there were expressions of shock, admiration, and even envy. The yacht was at least three hundred feet long and included such amenities as a pool, a fully stocked kitchen, eight staterooms, an elegantly decorated dining room, and a helideck (which was currently unoccupied).

"I never got the point of a pool on a yacht," said Vincent as they all gather around the lido deck. "What's the point of being out on the ocean if you are just going to hop in the pool instead."

Soon enough they were on their way, Sammy having disappeared into the helm. They sailed around for an hour, relaxing and enjoying the sea breeze as they marveled at the beauty of the Grecian coastline. Eventually, they moved further out to sea, far away from the mainland, and anchored the boat in open water.

"This a good spot?" asked Sammy, coming out of the helm to join the others.

"You're the future god of the sea," said Vincent. "You tell us."

"I'm not really sure. I guess since it was my instinct to stop here it's probably okay."

"Hey, fish boy," called out Johnny from the edge of the deck. "Can you tell if there are sharks in these waters?"

"Not a clue."

"You are useless," grumbled Johnny as he stared apprehensively down at the waters below.

"You're scared of sharks?" asked Lance. "You're built like a brick house, and you're a god to be. What have you got to be scared of?"

"Hey, it never hurts to be sure. We aren't immortal anymore remember." Ben had made sure to mention the fact that the gods had neglected to tell them that they were still mortal when he had returned from the

Underworld, though it had taken several attempts to get everyone's attention.

"We never were," said Ana Maria.

"Whatever. I'd still like to know for sure."

"Well I can't tell you for sure," said Sammy. "At least not from up here. And probably not from down there either. Unless, of course, a shark pokes their head up out of the water and says hello."

"That's not funny," snapped Johnny.

"Oh, for Heaven's sake," said Sophia as she stripped down to her swimsuit. "I'll reassure the big baby."

She took a running dive over the edge of the deck and into the clear blue waters below. The others rushed to the side of the ship, peering down to see if she was alright. After a few seconds, she surfaced, bobbing slightly with the waves.

"Y'all coming in or what?"

"Totally," said Sammy, pulling off his hoodie and diving in with a gleeful yell.

He was quickly followed by Andrew, Johnny, Lance, Sara, Ben, Vincent, and Matthew. The other five chose to remain on the ship: Ashley and Reneé to tan, Ana Maria to read, Irene to fix lunch, and Gavin to wander off and hide. He managed to find a secluded corner in the main cabin of the yacht, its many windows offering him a spectacular view of the ocean around him. There he hid for the next hour until his solitude was interrupted.

"What are you hiding in here for?" Gavin, who had been lost in thought, nearly jumped out of his skin. He turned to find Matthew standing in the doorway of the cabin, water still trickling down his well-toned body.

"Nothing," said Gavin, his cheeks flushing and his temperature rising. "Just getting out of the heat."

"It's not that hot," said Matthew.

"I'm sensitive to the heat," said Gavin, determinedly look anywhere but at Matthew. Matthew sighed softly. "You'll eat lunch with us at least?"

"Uhh, sure," said Gavin. "Just let me know when it's ready."

Matthew turned a walked away, leaving Gavin alone to stare at his retreating back, a sad expression in his eyes. Back on the lido deck, Matthew made his way over to sit next to Reneé.

"*Est-ce qu'il va nous rejoindre?*" asked Reneé.

"*Pour le déjeuner,*" replied Matthew.

"*Encore avec les Français?*" asked Vincent, sitting down next to Matthew.

"You didn't tell us you could speak French," said Matthew reproachfully.

"You never asked," replied Vincent. "So, what are you both talking about anyway?"

"Ze little one," said Reneé.

"Ah," said Vincent. "I take it he's now taken to literally hiding?"

"Yes," said Matthew sadly. "Poor thing."

"He'll come out and join us when he's ready," said Vincent as he lay down across Matthew's lap. "Until then there's no point in pushing him."

"What are you three talking about?" asked Ashley as she primly readjusted her position.

"Nothing," said Reneé.

"You know," said Ashley. "This secret little club of yours hurts morale. You should be more open and honest with the rest of us."

"Like you?" asked Vincent.

"Yes," said Ashley. "Exactly."

"Very well," said Vincent. "Then, in the spirit of honesty, I have a question for you, why are you wearing so much make-up on a yacht trip with your... I'm not sure if friends is the right word here, but let's just go with it for now?"

"My mother taught me to always look presentable, no matter what," said Ashley.

"You don't need to wear make-up to be pwezentible," said Reneé. "I'm sure you look very beautiful without it."

"Thank you," said Ashley. "But at this point it just part of my routine. Now shush, I want to relax before lunch and your negative attitude is stressing me out."

"Our negative attitude," snapped Vincent. "I'll give you a neg—"

In an attempt to shut him up, Matthew leaned over and kissed Vincent. It worked.

"'Ere we go again," muttered Reneé to herself as she watched Matthew and Vincent make out. With a sigh, she leaned back onto her lounge chair and closed her eyes.

"Lunch is ready," called out Irene thirty minutes later as she came up from the lower decks. Floating along behind her were trays of sandwiches, bowls of chips, pitchers of water and juice, several cups and plates, and a table for it all to sit on.

"Looks good," said Andrew as the plates arranged themselves on the table. "Someone go get Gavin."

Once Gavin had joined them, the group dug into the sandwiches and chips ravenously. After lunch, they relaxed by the pool.

"Anyone got any good music to play?" asked Johnny after several peaceful minutes of silence had passed. "It's too quiet."

"We came out here to relax, and you're complaining it's too quiet?" asked Lance.

"I can only do tranquil for so long," said Johnny. "I'm a city boy. I'm used to action and noise."

"I've got a playlist of show tunes if you're interested," suggested Matthew.

"I'd rather drown."

"That can be arranged," muttered Sophia.

"What was that shortie?" demanded Johnny.

"Hey, hey, hey," said Lance, "no fighting. Here, check out what I've learned to do."

Holding out his hands, palms up, Lance created several small balls of fire, which he then proceeded to juggle.

"Big whoop," said Johnny, unimpressed.

"Ooo, can I have a turn?" asked Sammy.

"Sure," said Lance.

He hurled his fireballs off the edge of the yacht and into the waters below. Sammy pulled out his phone. He fiddled with it for a moment before handing it to Gavin.

"Hit play when I say so okay."

Gavin nodded. Sammy stretched out his arms in front of him, steadied himself, and then nodded to Gavin. As the first notes of a piano concerto sounded, Sammy's fingers twitched. A small jet of water sprang up out of the pool, followed by another and then another. At Sammy's conduction, the water began to jump up in time to the music. After the song had ended there was a round of applause.

"Thank you, thank you," said Sammy bowing several times. "Anyone else wanna show off?" There were a few seconds of silence as everyone looked around at each other. Then Matthew stood up.

"I guess I can," said Matthew.

Switching places with Sammy, Matthew held his hands up, palms forwards, before clasping them together. Bring his hands down he opened them, cupped together as though holding water. Resting within his cupped hands was a small, golden ball of light. For a moment it floated there, tiny, soft, and comforting. And then Matthew threw his arms wide.

Several streaks of light darted out from the tiny ball, curving and twisting through the air in shimmering, graceful arcs. The others watched in wonder as Matthew guided the gleaming ribbons of light through the skies. The air around them began to shine. Slowly the light grew more and more intense, molding itself at Matthew's command. Within seconds a towering dragon, composed entirely of golden light, hovered above the awed spectators.

The dragon opened its maw and let loose a cacophonous roar, before taking wing and soaring out over the sea. The luminous construct circled the yacht several times before stopping to hover several feet above them all. It opened its maw again, this time releasing of powerful, roaring stream of fire directly at the assembled group. There were several cries of shock as the audience ducked to avoid the flames, which swirled around above their heads before exploding into glimmering droplets of light that rained down gently upon them all. Matthew lowered his hands. The streaks of light, the glittering rain, and the golden dragon all faded away. After a moment of stunned silence, there was an uproarious round of applause.

"Quite the finale," said Vincent as Matthew sat down next to him. "You deserve a prize."

"What did you have in mind?" asked Matthew coyly.

Vincent leaned in and kissed him.

"Uggh," grumbled Johnny, turning away from the sight of Vincent and Matthew. "Here we go again."

"Oh, shut up," snapped Sophia.

As Johnny and Sophia began to argue, Sara sat down next to Ben.

"Hey," said Ben.

Sara jumped. "Oh, hi. I didn't see ya there."

"Story of my life," muttered Ben.

"I'm sorry."

"Don't worry about it. I'm used to it."

"You say that a lot," said Sara. "It doesn't really make any of us feel better."

"It's the truth whether it makes you feel better or not," said Ben with a shrug. "If this is making you uncomfortable, we can change the subject. How'd you like the show?"

"Matthew was impressive," said Sara. "It's amazing how fast he's mastered his powers."

"It really is," said Ben ruefully.

"What's wrong?"

"What do you mean?"

"Just because I can't notice you from across a room doesn't mean I can't tell when something is bothering you when you are right in front of me."

"You'd be surprised," countered Ben.

"Are you jealous of Matthew?" asked Sara.

"I wouldn't go that far," mused Ben. "But it does seem like everything comes easier to him."

"I wouldn't worry about it. You'll get the hang of your powers soon enough."

As Ben was about to reply, a shadow fell over the group, though there hadn't been a single cloud in the sky all day. They all turned to see what was blocking the sun, only for their faces to turn pale at the sight before them. The monstrous head of a giant sea serpent was glaring down at them. Fear and shock rooted every last one of them in place, keeping them from moving or even uttering a sound. The monster opened its massive jaws, revealing rows of pointed fangs, and hissed.

"Maybe if we don't move, it won't see us," said Johnny as quietly as possible.

The serpent let out another furious hiss as it slammed heavily into the yacht. The boat pitched violent, sending those on deck flying to the floor.

"So much for that idea," snapped Ashley.

"Is everyone alright?" asked Andrew.

"Where's Ben?" asked Sara eyes scanning the group.

"I'm right next to you," said Ben calmly.

"Oh, sorry."

"Wait a second," said Matthew as he too surveyed the group. "Where's Gavin?"

Looks of horror spread across the group as everyone scrambled to their feet and scampered towards the edge of the yacht. There, thirty feet below them, was Gavin, bubbling about in the waves.

"Oh god," gasped Ana Maria and Sara in unison.

"Get up the ladder now!" order Andrew.

Water dripped down on top of their heads. Looking up they saw the massive body of the sea serpent stretching over them as it arched down towards Gavin, its mouth opened wide.

"Sammy, do something!" shrieked Sophia.

Sammy raised his hands in front of him, his eyes fixed on the head of the monstrous snake. Just as the monster was about to close its jaws around Gavin, Sammy gave a great sweep of his arms. The water around Gavin shifted, dragging him out of the way of the savage beast. With another wave of his hand, Sammy caused the water to rise up and push Gavin up out of the ocean and onto the deck of the ship.

"Are you okay?" asked Sara, pulling Gavin into a tight embrace.

"I'm fine," gasped Gavin, his body shaking with fear.

Before anyone could do anything else, the colossal serpent exploded out of the water. It hissed menacingly as it reared back its head, poised the strike. As the monster thrust forward its head, a dome of gray energy erupted into existence around the new gods. The serpent slammed into the barrier and ricocheted off.

"Everyone stay in the barrier," ordered Ana Maria, her hands raised in the air.

"How long can you keep this up?" asked Andrew.

"I don't know," said Ana Maria. "I'm just hoping it gives itself a concussion before I have to find out."

At that moment the sea serpent slammed into the barrier again, only to be rebounded as before. Shaking its head, the monster hissed in annoyance. A new shadow passed over the group inside the dome of energy. Turning, they saw the creature's tail rising fifty, sixty, seventy feet into the air. And then the tail was falling, its immense bulk on a collision course for the unprotected deck of the yacht.

"NO!" cried Ana Maria as she thrust her arms wide.

Her barrier of energy expanded, enveloping the length of the ship under its protection. The tail slammed heavily into the dome and ricocheted backward, just like the monster's head. Ana Maria let out a groan of pain.

"What's wrong?" asked Matthew in concern.

"I've spread the barrier too thin," replied Ana Maria through gritted teeth, as the tail lashed again. "I think I can safely say that I won't be able to hold it for long. At least not like this. We need to come up with a plan to get out of here."

"Sammy, get to the helm," order Andrew.

"Aye, aye captain," said Sammy.

As Sammy turned to leave the sea serpent let out a terrible hiss. It's opened is massive jaws and released a torrent of water at the dome. The water struck the dome just as the monstrous tail lashed against it. Ana Maria let out another cry of pain and sank to one knee. Her barrier was beginning to crack.

"I can't hold back both attacks," said Ana Maria, sweat trickling down her face.

Sammy shoved his hands forward, pushing the spray of water away from the barrier. It was slow work at first but eventually, he managed to move the water a few inches away from Ana Maria's crumbling defenses.

"This is as far as I can push it back," said Sammy as he strained against the onslaught of water. "But I can't do this and pilot the yacht."

"Anyone got any ideas?" asked Andrew.

"I've got one," said Ben.

"Maybe we can reason with it."

"Reason with a giant sea serpent? What kinda hippie-dippie idea is that?"

"Now is not the time for insults."

"Let's see if this works."

"I don't think fire is going to do much against the giant sea monster."

"I don't see you trying anything."

"Hey guys, I have an idea," said Ben.

"Can you stop trying to blast it? You are just annoying it."

"Here, let me have a go."

"Where the hell did you get a sword?"

"Umm guys."

"Just get out of my way."

"Well, that was a bust."

"Please don't do that again."

"Don't tell me what to do!"

"Well next time try thinking so we won't have to."

"Anyone else got any ideas?"

"Seriously guys, I think I know what to do."

"Anyone at all?"

"*Monsieur* monstare, could you please go a-way."

"That's not going to work."

"Well, no one else 'ad anyzing better."

"HEY GUYS!" yelled Ben, frustrated.

They all turned to look at him, startled by his sudden outburst.

"What?"

"I have a plan. But I need the name of someone dead who can pilot a boat, preferably someone who wouldn't be freaked out by seeing a giant sea serpent."

"And who would that be?" asked Vincent. "Angus T. Serpent-killer?

"I don't know," snapped Ben. "If the Greek gods are real maybe the myths are too. Problem is I can't remember any, so anyone got a name for me?"

"Jason," said Gavin as the tail lashed again. "He was the captain of the Argo in Greek myth." Ben nodded and closed his eyes. He concentrated all his energy on the thought of a Jason, captain of the Argo.

"We are waiting," demanded Ashley.

"Shut up and let him concentrate," snapped Sophia.

Ben ignored them both, desperately trying to clear his mind of all distractions. There was no monster, there was no panicked group of people beside him, and there was no looming threat of death. It was only him, Ben, the future King of the Underworld, calling on one of his future subjects to get his ass out of the Underworld and help him.

"How in the name of Hades did I get up here?" Ben opened his eyes.

Standing in front of him was a handsome young man with curly brown hair and a sailor's tan.

"Jason?" asked Ben hesitantly.

"Yes, I am Jason. And who, might I ask, is – holy Hera!" Jason had caught sight of the sea monster. "Who decided to aggravate a Cetus?"

"I am Benjamin Darke," proclaimed Ben, "future king of the Underworld and future god of the dead. I command you, Jason of the Argos, to pilot this ship and get us away from the sea monster. NOW!" Ben's attempts at forcefulness were lost completely on Jason

"You and I are going to have to have a conversation later," said Jason. "But, seeing as I'd prefer not to be fish food, I suppose I could give you a hand, just this once. Where's the helm?"

Ben pointed.

"Right, on it." Jason ran off towards the helm and out of sight.

For several tense minutes, the group waited, hoping against hope that Ana Maria and Sammy could hold out long enough for Jason to get the boat started.

"How much longer can you hold out?" asked Andrew.

Before Ana Maria could answer the tail lashed again, shattering her barrier. As her protection crumbled around her, Ana Maria collapsed heavily to the floor. She didn't get back up.

"You just had to ask, didn't you?" snapped Ashley.

The monster pulled back its tail again, a look of savage triumph in its gleaming eyes. Just as the tail began to fall, the yacht shot forwards, racing quickly away from the monstrous creature. There was a loud splash as the creature's tail slammed into empty water. The enraged serpent let out a murderous hiss as it chased after the speeding yacht. It was clear that the yacht was the faster of the two.

In a desperate attempt to slow their pace, the furious sea serpent began to shoot jets of water at the speeding ship. Fortunately, Sammy was able to keep the boat safe by deflecting the water blasts. Soon enough they had left the vicious serpent behind. A relieved silence fell on the group as they sailed onwards back toward the Grecian coastline. With the immediate danger behind them, Matthew bent down to tend to the unconscious Ana Maria.

"Now I see why there's a pool," said Vincent, dropping heavily into one of the lounge chairs and pulling a large bottle of vodka out of thin air. "Anyone want a drink, or twelve?"

Once they had docked the boat, Jason came out to bid his farewells to the group.

"I'm not sure how to send you back," said Ben sheepishly. "Give me a sec."

"Not a problem. I have all of eternity to wait."

"While he figures that out, I have a question for you," said Andrew. "How do you know how to pilot a yacht? You've been dead for centuries."

"Why are you under the impression that we do not have yachts in the Underworld? Remember, everyone who has ever died is down there. We have everything you all have up here and more. As it so happens, I've won the annual Elysium Cup Yacht Race for the last ten years."

"Lucky us," said Matthew as he helped a still groggy Ana Maria to a chair.

"When you have eternity ahead of you, you have to fill your time somehow."

"So, have the dead come up with anything cool?" asked Lance.

"As a matter of fact, yes. The man who invented the radio and the man who founded the cell phone company that was named after a fruit have come up with a new wireless communication system. It works by—"

Before he could say anything more, Jason suddenly vanished into thin air.

"Hey, I did it," said Ben delightedly.

# Chapter Eleven

The attack of the sea monster, or Cetus as Jason called it, garnered mixed responses from the gods of Olympus. Poseidon took time out of his incredibly busy schedule to personally pay a visit to the apartment, where he apologized profusely for the unfortunate incident and reassured them that an investigation as to how a Cetus was able to attack them without his knowledge was underway.

Some of the gods were apoplectic. They fussed and worried over their protégés for a week. They probably would have continued to pester the new gods for longer than that had it not been for Zeus coming down and ordering them away. Zeus himself, as well as a few other gods, considered the incident little more than a growing experience. In Zeus' own words, "You're still alive so quit complaining."

Only three of the gods chose to give no opinion on the subject at all. Both Dionysus and Hephaestus had not been in contact with either of their protégés since their initial meeting and, of course, none of them had ever heard from, or even seen, Hestia.

As for the new gods, their reactions were just as mixed. Some agreed that the experience should be used as a growing point and they redoubled their efforts in training, working harder than ever to master their new abilities. Others considered it a non-issue. They continued on as if nothing had happened. Out of the whole group, Gavin had taken the attack the worst. His nervousness had been elevated to full-blown paranoia. Matthew and Sara were working overtime trying to calm him, though they didn't seem to be making much progress.

Gavin was not the only one adversely affected by the attack. Vincent, though fine during the day, had taken to sleeping in his own room recently so as not to alert Matthew to the fact that he was having terrifying nightmares. Ashley had become far more imperious, ordering everyone around so that she didn't have to lift a finger. In reality, however, her actions were not caused by her sense of entitlement. The truth was that her hands trembled so much that she couldn't pick up anything without immediately dropping it. As for Johnny, he had grown far more vicious and temperamental in the last couple of weeks. In training, he fought to cause severe and intentional harm to his opponents and his attitude towards Sophia, Matthew, and Vincent had, if possible, gotten worse.

It was fortunate that the new gods had school to distract them. The normalcy of classes was helping to take their minds off their troubles. It proved that, no matter what horrors they may face, life still went on. Though it was not the most comforting thought, it helped to demonstrate to the new gods that dwelling on the past would not help them in the future. With this in mind, the new gods continued on with life. They attended classes, went to meetings, studied, and went (as a group) to every one of Andrew's home games. After a few weeks, the cloud of fear and panic that had set in around the apartment began to fade.

One of the few positive effects of the attack was a boost in confidence for Ben. Having successfully summoned the spirit of Jason, Ben was much less trepidatious about his power over the dead. Unfortunately, every attempt that he'd made to summon a spirit since had ended in failure. But he wasn't concerned. Having done it once, he knew, eventually, he'd be able to do it again. It would just take time to get in the right headspace again. So, whenever he had the opportunity, Ben would practice trying to summon a spirit. On one particular night, his concentration was interrupted by a phone call from his parents.

"Hello?" asked Ben as he answered the phone.

"Happy birthday!" chorused his parents in two-part harmony.

Surprised, Ben looked at the time on this phone. It was, indeed, 12 A.M. on the 17th of September. He was now, officially, nineteen years old.

"Thanks," said Ben.

"I hope you have a good birthday," said his mother. "I've sent you a present. Make sure to let me know when you get it."

"Sure Ma, no problem. How's everything going with you two? How's the museum, Ma? Pops, how's the library?" His mother was the curator of an art museum and his father was the town's head librarian.

"Everything is fine," said his mother happily. "We just opened a new exhibit on Degas."

"Sondra, don't let him change the subject like he always does," remonstrated his father. "It's his birthday. You got anything planned for today son? Those new friends of yours throwing you a party?"

"Yeah Pops," said Ben. "They tried to keep it a surprise, but I found out about it anyway."

"Good for you son," said his father proudly. "You were always the smartest kid around in my opinion."

"Thanks, Pops," said Ben, blushing a little. "You still haven't told me how the library's doing."

"It's doing okay," said his father. "Mostly people are coming in to use the computers instead of to check out books, but I guess that's what *in* right now."

"Jake," chided Ben's mother, "need I remind you that it's Ben birthday. Don't bring him down."

"You're right," said Ben's dad. "So, you enjoying classes?"

"Yeah, they are great. I'm learning loads."

"That's good dear," said his mother.

"You dating any cute girls?" asked his father. "Or guys, if you're into that, no judgment."

"No Pops," said Ben with a little laugh. "I'm not dating anyone, male or female."

"You do know we're okay with either, right?" asked his father.

"I know," said Ben, "and if I ever decide that I want to date a guy you'll be the first ones to know."

"Just make sure to practice safe sex."

"Jake!" snapped his mother. "That's enough of that. I'm sure Ben doesn't want to talk about his sex life with his parents."

"I just want to make sure he's safe," countered his dad. "I think one awkward conversation is worth that."

"It's fine Ma," said Ben. "I don't mind, really."

"See Sondra, he gets it. Hey kiddo, we're going to let you go now. Get a good night's sleep. Just because it's your birthday doesn't mean you should stay up all night."

"Will do Pops."

"Love you," chorused his parents.

"Love you too," replied Ben.

As he ended the call, he felt a pang of sadness. With everything that had happened since he'd arrived at M.O.U., he hadn't realized how much he missed his mom and dad. They had been his only friends. On top of that, he had just lied to them. Truth was that his friends weren't planning any kind of party. Ben doubted they even knew that it was his birthday. He'd mentioned it several times during the past week, but no one seemed to hear him. After his ninth attempt had fallen on deaf ears, Ben had just given up. But he couldn't tell his parents that. He knew they missed him just as much as he missed them, and he saw no point in making them feel worse.

"Happy birthday to me," sang Ben to himself. "Happy birthday to me. Happy birthday, happy birthday. Happy birthday to me."

"Are you trying to depress me?" asked a voice behind him.

Ben whipped around to find Hades sitting on his desk chair.

"What are you doing here?" asked Ben.

"I came to wish you a happy birthday, obviously. And to deliver these." Hades snapped his fingers and a pile of presents appeared next to Ben.

"Are these all from you?" asked Ben in surprise.

"Only that one is," said Hades, pointing to a large package. "The others are from various members of my court. A warning, there's one from Hecate. If I were you, I'd find a way to open that one from a few hundred feet away, just to be safe."

"Tell them all thank you from me," said Ben.

"My pleasure," said Hades. "Now, if you don't mind my asking, why are you singing happy birthday to yourself alone in your room?"

Ben shrugged. "Mom and Dad already wished me happy birthday and I didn't really expect anyone else to."

"I'm insulted," said Hades. "What made you think that I wouldn't know when your birthday was?"

"No one else does," said Ben. "And when I told them, they didn't even hear me."

"Well, I'm not your roommates," said Hades. "I hope you will remember that in future. And I hope that, if you are ever feeling depressed or anxious or need to talk, you'll come to me."

"I'll keep that in mind," said Ben. "Though I'm not really sure how to contact you."

Hades pointed at Ben's phone.

"I just gave you my phone number."

"You have a cell phone?"

"I've had a cell phone since the eighteenth century," said Hades. "The amount of misconceptions you have about me is astonishing. Just because I'm a god doesn't mean I live in the past."

"Sorry," said Ben with a smile. "I'll try to be more open-minded in future."

"See that you are," said Hades sternly, before winking slyly at Ben. "I have to get back to the Underworld, but I hope that, even if you roommates are ignorant of it, you have a good birthday."

"Thank you," said Ben.

Hades smiled one last smile at his protégée before dropping out of sight. Ben turned his attention to his pile of presents. Picking up Hades' first, he unwrapped it to find a large, velvet bag that contained a collection of precious gemstones.

"Holy hell," muttered Ben in wonder as he picked through the various stones. "Where did he get all of these?" Spotting a note at the bottom of the box, Ben picked it up and read it.

*Dear Ben,*

*As a geology major, I thought you might appreciate these. I got as many variations as I could think of. Enjoy.*

*Hades*

Ben smiled. If he showed his classmates these, he would be the envy of the geology department. Assuming, of course, they even noticed him in the first place.

The next present he opened was from Macaria. It was a large, heavy, leather bound book. Like Hades, Macaria had included a note

*To Ben,*

*This book is an index of all the heroic souls currently in the Elysium. I hope that you can use it in your training. Sometimes having a face to focus on can help. The book will update itself as souls enter or leave the Elysium. Happy birthday.*

*Best wishes,*
*Macaria*

Ben flipped through the book. Each page was dedicated to a specific hero. There was a picture of the spirit in question, as well as a short biography. Ben had a feeling that this book would make his attempt to summon a spirit much easier.

The next present he opened was from Melinoë. It turned out to be a small flower with white petals. Like the other two presents, there was an accompanying note.

*To Benjamin,*

*This flower absorbs odors so as to keep your room fresh smelling. Not to imply that your room smells bad. I just thought it would be nice.*

*Wishing you a pleasant birthday,*
*Melinoë*

Ben smiled to himself as he set the flower on a shelf. Besides being functional, it was very pretty. He just hoped he remembered to water it.

Returning to his presents, he picked up Hypnos'. Inside was a blue velvet eye mask with stars stitched into it. And, as with the others, there was an accompanying note.

*Ben,*

*If you are ever in need of sleep, this mask will help you. All you have to do is put it on and say how many hours of sleep you want. And it's bad dream free.*

*Pleasant tidings on your birthday,*
*Hypnos*

Out of all of the gifts so far, this was probably the most helpful. There were times, especially nowadays, when he just couldn't turn off his mind.

Lethe's present, a tiny vial of opaque water, was the smallest by far. Ben read Lethe's noted without even bother to try and figure out that the vial was supposed to be.

*Dear Bartholomew,*

*This is diluted water from the River Lethe. One drop will erase one hour's worth of memories. Use it sparingly.*

*Merry Christmas,*
*Lethe*

Ben chuckled to himself at the contents of Lethe's letter. Not only had she forgotten his name, but it seemed that she'd forgot this was supposed to be a birthday present.

The last two gifts were from Thanatos and Hecate. Unsure which one scared him more, Ben chose to open Thanatos' gift first. He figured that Thanatos would provide a quicker, and less painful, death than Hecate. Inside the box was a single gray feather and a note. Ben picked up the note.

*Benjamin,*

*This is one of my feathers. If you ever have need of my assistance, wave it in the air three times and I'll appear.*

*Try to stay alive,*
*Thanatos*

Ben wasn't sure how he felt about this gift. While having a way to summon the god of death had its obvious benefits, Ben got a strange feeling around Thanatos that he couldn't quite explain. It was a strange mixture of fear and excitement.

Putting the note back in the box, Ben turned his attention to the last of his presents. Gingerly he unwrapped it and looked inside. The only thing with the box was a leather bracelet with a triquetra charm attached to it. There was no explanatory note.

"Of course," muttered Ben. "Why would Hecate make it easy on me?"

Ben placed the bracelet on his right wrist and tightened it. Nothing happened. Shrugging, he gathered up the boxes and wrapping paper from his bed and head out of his room. The garbage can in the kitchen was much bigger than his. After he had finished dumping his boxes he turned to head back to his room, only to literally bump into Sammy.

"Sorry dude," said Sammy. "Didn't see ya."

"It's not a problem," said Ben. He couldn't exactly blame Sammy since he hadn't exactly been looking where he was going either.

"What you up and about for?" asked Sammy.

"Throwing away boxes and wrapping paper from my birthday presents," said Ben.

He knew immediately that he shouldn't have said that. Sammy's eyes widen, his nostrils flare, and his mouth dropped.

"It's your birthday?" demanded Sammy indignantly.

"Yes," said Ben hesitantly. He knew where this was going to go.

"Dude, why did you say anything?"

"Umm," said Ben, trying to find a tactful way to answer Sammy's question. Fortunately, he didn't have to.

"You did tell us, didn't you?" asked Sammy. "We just didn't hear you right?"

"Pretty much," said Ben. "But don't worry about. I'm used to it."

"I wish you wouldn't say that," said Sammy. "It makes us all feel worse."

"Sorry," said Ben.

"Don't apologize," snapped Sammy. "We are the ones who should be apologizing to you. How many times did you try to tell us? Actually, don't tell me. Knowing will probably make me feel worse."

"Okay," chuckled Ben.

"Well we need to get a party planned pronto," said Sammy. "I wonder if Irene is still awake."

"No don't," said Ben. "You don't need to throw me a party or anything."

"But dude, it's your birthday."

"I know. But I don't want to make a big fuss about it. It'll just make everyone feel bad and I don't want that on my birthday."

"Okay, I get ya," said Sammy. He pulled out his phone. "But here's what I'm gonna do. I'm gonna set up some reminders for myself for next year. That way I'll make sure to remember it's your birthday."

"You really don't have to," said Ben, though the thought Sammy might actually do it did make him happy inside.

"Already done," said Sammy, showing Ben a week's worth of reminders.

"Thanks," said Ben.

"No problem, buddy."

Without anything else to say on the subject, they went their separate ways. Ben had just reached his door when someone tapped him on the shoulder. Turning around he found himself face to face with Sammy again.

"What's up?" asked Ben.

Sammy spread his arms wide and pulled Ben into a tight hug. Ben could smell the persistent scent of chlorine and sun that clung to Sammy.

"I forgot to wish you happy birthday," said Sammy. "So happy birthday and here's a birthday hug. Best I could do on short notice."

Ben, who had been initially taken aback by the sudden show of affection, slowly wrapped his arms around Sammy. He'd never been hugged by anyone outside of his family before. He had to say, he rather liked the experience. Ben wasn't sure how long they stood there in each other's arms, but he did know that he felt very comfortable and very happy. Eventually, they separated.

"Thanks, Sam," said Ben, a single tear rolling down his cheek.

"No problem Benny," said Sammy with a wide smile.

As Sammy turned around and headed back to the kitchen, Ben slipped back into his room and closed the door. Suddenly, he didn't care that the other didn't know that today was his birthday. Picking up the eye mask he'd gotten from Hypnos, Ben got into bed and put on the mask.

"Eight hours," said Ben. He immediately fell asleep.

# Chapter Twelve

Towards the end of September, a new distraction came along to help lift the new gods' spirits. It was late in the evening and several of them had gathered in the living room to watch a movie. Just as it was about to reach the climax, however, the television flickered off.

"What the?" complained Lance as he fiddled with the remote. "We blow a fuse or something?"

"I don't think so," said Gavin. "Everything else seems to be working."

"Then what happened?" demanded Johnny.

"Me."

Gavin let out a yelp and fell out of his seat as everyone whipped their heads around to find Hermes, dressed like paperboy from the 1800s, floating in mid-air.

"Still as jumpy as ever, ehh kiddo?" asked Hermes with a mischievous grin.

"Dude, couldn't you have picked a better time?" grumbled Sammy. "It was just getting good. Now the flow's gonna be all messed up."

"I'm sure you'll recover from the pain of it," said Hermes. "I've got something to tell you all, and I wanted to wait for everyone to be in the apartment before I did."

"We've all been here since the end of dinner," said Andrew.

"Not quite," said Hermes. "Give it three, two, one."

Right on cue the sound of the front door opening and closing could be heard.

"Who the hell is that?" asked Lance.

"Ben," said Hermes. "He had a late class. Didn't you notice he wasn't at dinner? Don't bother answering. I already know you didn't."

"Hermes, what are you doing here?" asked Ben as he walked into the living room.

"I'm marveling at your roommates' lack of observational skills. And I've got a message for you all. But before that, we need everyone else."

With a flourish, Hermes pulled his winged staff out of thin air. As he raised the staff to his lips, it turned itself into a herald's trumpet. Taking a deep breath, Hermes let loose a powerful blast of sound, causing everyone in the room to plug their ears.

"Who the hell is making all that racket?" bellowed Ashley as she stormed out of her room.

"Really?" demanded Vincent as he and Matthew entered the room together, both in a state of partial undress. "You have the worst timing."

"I have perfect timing," said Hermes smugly, his staff returning to its original form as he twirled it through his fingers. Vincent glared at him.

"Can I offer you some refreshments Hermes?" asked Irene, sticking her head out of the dining room.

"It's kind of you to offer, but I'm just here to deliver my message and then be on my way."

"Well get on with it," snapped Vincent as he sat down on the arm of a couch.

"That attitude of yours is gonna get you into trouble one day," said Hermes.

"Who says it hasn't already," replied Vincent.

"Not that I don't love the verbal banner," said Matthew, "but can we move this show along a bit, please. Vincent isn't the only one who's a little *frustrated* right now."

"Right," said Hermes. He let go of his staff, leaving it to hang unsupported in mid-air, and reached inside his messenger's bag to pull out a scroll of black parchment. Unfurling it he began to read, his voice shifted from his usually quick, excited patter to Hades' calm and cool delivery.

*To the new gods of Olympus,*

*As some of you may be aware, the autumnal equinox is fast approaching. While not auspicious for most people, to me it marks the day that my beauteous wife, Persephone, returns to the Underworld for the fall and winter months. Every year, in honor of her return, I host a party in celebration. As such, I wish to formally invite you to join in the festivities, which will be held on September the 22nd. To RSVP simply inform Hermes of your intentions. Formal wear is required. Dinner will start at 6:00 p.m., so please be at the linen closet door no later than 5:50 p.m.*

*Hope to see you,*

*Hades*
*God of the riches of the earth, Lord of the dead, King of the Underworld*

Hermes rolled up the scroll and stuck it back into his satchel.

"So, who's interested?" he asked, his voice returning to normal.

"I'm always down for a party," said Vincent.

"I have to study," said Ana Maria. "That yacht trip put me behind."

"Really?" asked Ashley derisively. "*You* have to study? Our English professor spent an entire class period talking about the last paper you wrote. You can take a night off to have some fun."

"I came to this college to learn. Just because I have chosen to become a god does not change that fact. What am I going to learn at a dinner in the Underworld?"

"Well, geography and history for a start," chimed in Hermes.

"What?"

"Just thinking out loud here but, Hades is a very accommodating host. If you ask for a tour of the Underworld, he'd probably be able to arrange it. And, again just guessing here, while on this tour you'd probably learn some things about the history and geography of the Underworld, which you can't learn anywhere else. It's not like it has a traveler's guide. Although, that might not be a bad idea. I'll have to look into that."

There was a moment of silence as Ana Maria considered Hermes' argument.

"Okay, I might be able to go if I shuffle some things around."

"Uhh-mm," said Ashley, rolling her eyes. "Anyone else got a lame excuse they wanna try out?"

The rest were all for attending the party.

"Good," said Hermes. "Well, I'll let you get back to your movie and your *other* endeavors." As Hermes grabbed his staff, he gave the group a friendly salute, and then disappeared in a puff of vivid green smoke. The movie immediately started playing again.

"Ah man," complained Sammy, "rewind it. I wanna see whose head just got blown off."

The days leading up to Hades' party were packed with anticipation. Everyone was looking forward not only to the celebration but also to the chance to see the Underworld, especially since Ben hadn't been able to satisfactorily answer their questions. There was one small issue though, several of the new gods lacked formal wear.

"How is this a problem?" asked Vincent when Sammy mentioned his lack of appropriate attire the day before the party. "You can have one of my old suits. Let me see what

I've got in my closet. Anyone else need something well I'm looking?"

"Me," said Johnny.

"I do too," said Lance. "But I doubt anything you have will fit us. Johnny and I are both much bigger than you, and Sammy is considerably taller."

"I can get them altered," said Vincent as he headed towards his bedroom, waving his hand unconcernedly.

"Why do zat?" asked Reneé. "Bwing zem to me and I'll see what I can do."

"Cool."

"Reneé, can I ask a favor?" asked Sara as Vincent disappeared into his room.

"Of course. What is it."

"I don't really have anything formal either, and I was wondering if—"

"You could bawo somezing fwom me?"

"If you don't mind."

"Certainly. I know e-xactly which dwess would be per-fect for you. Let me go get it."

Reneé disappeared into her room, returning at the same time as Vincent. They each had three garment bags in hand.

"Here you go," said Vincent handing a bag to Sammy, Lance, and Johnny. "Try these on so Reneé can see what needs to be done."

"Cool, thanks," said Sammy as he stripped off his hoodie. Lance too started to undress, but Johnny turned around and walked towards his bedroom.

"Where you goin'?" asked Sammy as he slipped into Vincent's collar shirt.

"To change," said Johnny.

"Dude, no reason to be shy," said Lance as he tried to pull Vincent's pant up past his thighs. "Just change out here."

"I'm not shy," said Johnny as he opened his bedroom door. "But if you think I'm going to get naked around that drunken fag, you're nuts."

With that, Johnny slammed his door shut and locked it.

"Charming as always, zat one," muttered Reneé. She handed one of the garment bags over to Sara.

"Thanks. So ah, who are the other ones for?"

"'Ave you seen Ana Maria and Irene's clozing? Something tells me zat zey don't 'ave formal wear. Zese are for zem."

"Well that's nice of you," said Sara as she unzipped the garment to take a look at the dress. "Hey, this is really aces mate."

"Twy it on," said Reneé. "In case I need to alter it."

"Okie doke," said Sara, pulling off her blouse.

"I see someone isn't shy," said Lance.

"If you guys can change in front of me, there's no reason I can't change in front of you," said Sara.

"You go, girl," commented Lance.

"What are you doing?" asked Vincent as Sammy scuttled around to the other side of the nearest couch and crouched down.

"Changing my pants," said Sammy.

"Oh, come on," demanded Sara. "Not you too."

"What?" asked Sammy. "Oh! No, no, no. Has nothing to do with Vincent. I'm just not wearing any underwear and I didn't want to give you all a peep show that you didn't ask for."

"I'm always game for a peep show," said Vincent, his eyes twinkling wickedly.

"Maybe when we're alone," teased Sammy as he straightened up. "So, how do I look?"

"Like a scarecrow," said Vincent. The dark blue suit that Vincent had picked out for him was far too short. Several inches of bare leg and arm were left exposed.

"Well I'm not much better," said Lance. The gray suit he'd been given was hugging him in all the wrong ways. He hadn't even been able to zip up the zipper.

"Look everyone," said Vincent. "It's a package of Canadian sausage."

"Haha," said Lance as he adjusted his clothing uncomfortably. "How'd you know I was Canadian anyway?"

"I finally figured out your accent," said Vincent. "Quebec?" Lance nodded before complaining,

"Can I take this off now? It's really tight."

"No," said Reneé as she held up her hands. "Just stay zhere and don't move."

She twiddled her fingers. Both suits began to adjust themselves until they fit Sammy and Lance perfectly.

"Well that's handy," said Vincent.

"Ya might wanna send some of your mojo over here, mate," said Sara.

The dress that Reneé had picked out for her was a beautiful green number, laced with a delicate floral pattern. Unfortunately, the effect was marred by the fact that the dress was simply too long and too tight for Sara.

"Yes, zat will need a bit of fitting," said Reneé as she twiddled her fingers in Sara's direction. The dress immediately began to adjust itself until it fit Sara like a glove.

"Thanks again," said Sara admiring the dress.

"No pwoblem," said Reneé. "In fact, if you want, you can keep the dwess."

"Really? Are ya sure?"

"Of course. It suitz you better zan me."

"Ok, I don't think this is gonna work." Johnny had come out of his room, his hands covering his nether regions.

If Lance's suit had been tight, it was nothing compared to Johnny's. The pants were stuck halfway up his thighs, only three of the dress shirt buttons had been fastened, the maroon vest had been left completely unfastened, and the blazer was ripped.

"Oh my," said Reneé as everyone else cackled with laughter at the sight of him.

"Can you fix it or not?" asked Johnny irritably.

"Of course," said Reneé. "Spwead your arms so I can see what I'm working with."

"Tell him to turn around," demanded Johnny, nodding at Vincent.

"Oh, come on," snapped Lance. "Dude he's lending you a suit to wear. Are you really gonna be an ass right now?"

"Giving actually," Vincent. "You all can keep the suits if you want them."

"Just 'cause he's giving me a suit, doesn't mean I'm gonna give him a look at the goods," said Johnny stubbornly.

"I'm far too sober for this," muttered Vincent as he turned to face the opposite wall.

Reneé twiddled her fingers again. The pants slid up the rest of the way, buttoning and zipping themselves as they went. The shirt and vest expanded as their buttons fastened themselves shut. Likewise, the jacket grew larger as the seams repaired themselves.

"Can I turn around now?" asked Vincent.

"Yes, ze ape is covered."

Vincent turned back to face Johnny and gave him an appraising look.

"It's amazing what a five-thousand-dollar suit can do. It turned this ass into a gentleman."

"Yeah, yeah, yeah," said Johnny as he looked himself over. "Whatever, fruitcake." Johnny turned around and disappeared back into his room.

"You could have at least said thank you," yelled Lance.

"Why are you giving him your suit man?" asked Sammy as he changed back into his own clothes. "He's being a total jerk to you."

"Ehh, I don't really care," said Vincent, flopping down on the couch. "Besides, I was gonna give that suit to charity anyway, and I can't think of anyone more unfortunate than that jackass."

Everyone chuckled at this.

"So, what are you planning on wearing, Reneé," asked Sara as she slipped back into her own clothes.

"Oh, I 'ave a fabulous little number in shades of pink and fuchsia."

"You can't wear that," said Vincent. "That's what I'm planning on going in."

Everyone laughed again.

"What are really gonna wear?" asked Lance.

"Oh, I've got something planned that will really stand out," said Vincent lazily.

"I'd believe it," muttered Sara. "So, what kinda dresses did you pull out for Ana Maria and Irene."

"Ze one I got for Irene is a vewy simple white dress. It is elegant but not over zhe top. I zink she will appweciate zat. As for Ana Maria, I pulled out a little bwown number that would go wonderfully with 'er skin. Now I just have to talk 'er into doing somezing with 'er 'air. I swear et gets rattier and rattier evewy time I see it."

"If you think her hair is bad, wait until you see Melinoë's."

They all jumped with shock and turned around to find Ben, sitting on a chair in the corner of the room reading a book.

"How long have you been there?" asked Lance.

"I've been here for about an hour," replied Ben as he flipped to a new page. "I was here before any of you."

"And you didn't say anything?" asked Sara.

"I did," said Ben. "You just didn't hear me."

"And thus continues the unseen adventures of Invisi-boy, the world's only visible, invisible man," said Vincent. "Tune in next week to see who ignores him next."

"Dude, like make a sound next time or something," said Sammy. "Also, sorry for the strip-tease."

"I didn't care," said Ben. "And it'd probably be easier if I don't make a sound at all. Then you'd never noticed me, and we wouldn't have to have this conversation."

"I'm sorry we did not see you," apologized Reneé.

"Don't worry about it. I'm used to it."

"Actually, it's good that you are here," said Sara. "Can we talk? In private."

"Lover's tryst?" teased Vincent.

"Personal conversation," replied Sara coolly.

"Sure," said Ben as he closed his book and stood up. "Your room or mine?"

"Yours if you don't mind. It's the furthest from the living room."

"Sure. No problem."

They headed off towards the door to Ben's room.

"Use protection!" said Vincent with a wicked smile.

Sara raised her middle finger at Vincent over her shoulder.

"Is that an invitation?" asked Vincent, his smile widening.

The duo simply shut the door to Ben's room in response.

Ben's room was very tidy, well ordered, and bare. His books were alphabetized by subject and author, his desk was meticulously organized, and there didn't seem to be a speck of dust on any surface. There were no posters up on the wall or knickknacks on his desk. In fact, had it not been for a large, velvet bag and a small, white flower on one of his shelves, there would not have been anything decorative at all in the room.

"Didn't come to school with a lot of stuff did ya?" asked Sara.

"I'm not really one for *tchotchkes*," replied Ben. "So, what did you want to talk about?"

"Right," said Sara as she turned to look at Ben. "I was wondering if you could do me a favor."

"Depends on what the favor is."

Sara bit her lip slightly.

"What? Is it illegal or something?"

"No, it's just kinda... personal."

"Personal how?"

"It's... well... I was wondering if..." Sara stammered before finally blurting out, "Can you bring my dad back to life?"

An awkward silence filled the room as Sara stared determinedly at the floor and Ben tried to figure out how to respond to her, somewhat unexpected, request.

"Umm, I don't think I'm allowed to bring the dead back to life," said Ben. "And even if I am, I don't know how."

"Oh," said Sara sadly.

"How did he die?" asked Ben before he could stop himself. "Sorry. That was insensitive."

"Nah, it's fine," said Sara. "I don't have a problem talking about it. He was a farmer. This one year, we were having a hot summer and he was out every day working the land, trying to make sure our crops didn't burn up. Eventually, the heat just got too much for him. I was five when it happened."

"I'm sorry," said Ben quietly.

"Don't be. It happened a long time ago. And it was selfish for me to ask you to bring him back I know. I just thought—"

"I get it," said Ben. "You miss him. But I can't bring him back to life. But I think I can call up his spirit like I did with Jason so you can see him again. If you want."

"Really?" asked Sara, her eyes wide with joy.

"I think so," said Ben. "Might take me a minute though."

Closing his eyes, Ben tried to recreate the feeling he had had on the yacht, all the while thinking *'Sara's dad, Sara's dad'*. A minute passed and nothing happened.

"Well this isn't working," said Ben as he opened his eyes. "Maybe I'm not being specific enough."

"I got a picture of him, if you think that will help."

"Worth a try," said Ben.

Sara took a worn, folded picture out of her pocket and handed it to Ben. Unfolding it, Ben found himself staring down at a smiling family of seven. Sara's father was the only man in the picture. He was ruggedly handsome, with tanned skin and curly brown hair. He had one of his large, muscular arms draped around a petite woman with straight blonde hair and skin the color of milk. Gathered around them were Sara and, assumedly, her four sisters. The oldest looked to be about nine, while the youngest looked to be little older than one.

"All girls?" asked Ben.

"Yup," said Sara with a smile. "Those are my sisters: Sasha, Sabrina, Susan, and Serena. I'm the middle child."

"I hope I get to meet them one day," said Ben.

Looking back down at the photo, Ben concentrated on the smiling man. A soft, cold breeze seemed to blow through the room, which Ben took as a sign that the picture had helped. Slowly, the form of Sara's father materialized out of thin air.

"Where am I?" asked Sara's dad in confusion, his eyes darting around the room.

"D-d-daddelion?" asked Sara, her voice quavering as tears streamed down her face. Sara's father turned to face her. His eyes widened in shock.

"Rose?" he whispered.

For a moment the two stared at each other, as if not quite sure the other was real. And then they were hugging each other tightly, both of them crying fat tears of joy. Ben slowly inched towards the door, opened it, slipped out of the room, and then closed it as quietly as he could. It seemed to him that Sara and her dad could use some time alone.

# Chapter Thirteen

"That was fast," said Vincent as Ben sat down next to him on the sofa. "Bit of a minute man, I take it?"

"We didn't have sex," said Ben in exasperation. "She just asked me to summon up the spirit of her dead father."

"And did you?" asked Lance as he came out of the kitchen, a sandwich in his hand.

"I managed to, yes," said Ben. "I needed a picture to do it, but I did manage it."

"Zat vas very kind of you," said Reneé, smiling at Ben as she sat down next to him.

The others agreed.

"Thanks," said Ben as he picked up the remote. "Anyone want to watch anything in particular?"

No one did so, for the rest of the day Ben channel surfed while he waited for Sara and her father to finish reconnecting. His fellow roommates came and went at their leisure. Some joined him if they liked what was on at the time, while others simply hid in their rooms.

Eventually night fell. He and some of the others had dinner and then returned to the living room to watch a movie; it was Gavin's turn to pick. After they'd finished *Duck Soup*, they decided to watch another. Matthew suggested *The Phantom of the Opera*. Johnny, uninterested in a "girly musical", went to bed early but everyone else stuck around, enjoying themselves immensely as they sang along to the music.

They enjoyed themselves so much in fact that, after *Phantom*, they decided to watch two more musicals. By the time they had finished *Rent*, it was near midnight and everyone was starting to get sleepy. Ben silently opened the door to his room and poked his head inside. Sara and her father were both asleep on his bed, Sara's head resting comfortably on her father's chest. Both of them wore contented expressions on their faces. Ben closed the door as quietly as he could and head back to the living room. The only people in the room were Reneé, Matthew, and Vincent. They sat, huddled together, on one of the sofas. As always, they were engaged in a clandestine conversation in French.

*"Est-ce que quelqu'un l'a vue depuis le dîner?"*

*"Non. Elle s'est échappée pendant que nous regardions tous* Duck Soup, *je pense."*

*"Je me demande où elle est allée."*

They all shot a look toward Irene's room.

*"Et pourquoi elle revient toujours si tard. Je l'ai vue revenir en même temps que moi. Et parfois il est environ trois ou quatre heures du matin."* A wicked smile crossed Vincent's face.

*"Et que fais-tu à quatre heures du matin?"*

*"Nous ne pouvons pas tous trouver un partenarire dans l'appartement."*

*"Je suis sûr que tu pourrais si tu voulais. Que cherchez-vous?"*

*"Je m'en fous,"* said Reneé with a shrug.

*"Eh bien, Sophia, si vous voulez une fille. Lance est votre meilleur pari pour un garçon. Je suppose que Sammy et Ben pourraient être une option aussi. Andrew est attrayant, mais quelque chose me dit que les yeux d'Ashley sont sur lui."*

"I think they are talking about us," said Sammy, coming out of the dining room with a glass of water in his hand.

"Only a little," said Vincent. "But don't worry. We aren't saying anything bad."

"And do we get to know what you're saying about us?" asked Sammy.

"Zey are just giving me options on 'o I could date," said Reneé. "Are either of you intewested?"

"Or perhaps both of you at the same time," suggested Vincent wickedly.

"Don't put them on the spot," chided Matthew. "You not going to bed yet Ben?"

"Sara and her dad are asleep in my room," said Ben. "I didn't want to disturb them. I'll just sleep out here on the couch. Although I'm not sure I can sleep in my jeans."

"You can always join me or Matthew," offered Vincent. "No clothing required. In fact, if you choose to sleep with me, I insist on no clothes at all."

Ben snorted with laughter.

"I'll keep that in mind," he said.

"That's enough of that," said Matthew, jabbing his elbow into Vincent side. "If you want, you can use my room, Ben. I can spend the night with Vincent."

"Don't I get a vote in all of this?" asked Vincent.

"No," said Matthew pointedly.

"Good to know."

"Or, ya sleep in my room," suggested Sammy. "I know that it would be more comfortable in Matt's room by yourself, but it would be cool to have a sleepover for once."

"Thanks for the offers guys," said Ben, "but they really aren't necessary. The couch is just fine."

"Don't be a martyr," said Vincent. "Just accept our love. You know you want to. We'll be gentle. I promise."

"That's enough out of you," said Matthew, placing a finger delicately on Vincent's lips. Vincent opened his mouth and bit Matthew's finger lightly.

"Save that for when we are alone," said Matthew, removing his finger from Vincent's mouth and flicking him gently on the nose.

"I zink you should sleep with Sammy," said Reneé.

"What?" asked Ben. "Why?"

"It is an opportunity for you to get closer to each other," said Reneé.

"In more ways than one," murmured Vincent.

"I zink it will be good for you," said Reneé, ignoring Vincent's comment. "Unless, you 'ave a pwoblem sharing a bed with another man."

"I couldn't care less about that," said Ben.

"Zen you might as well do it," said Reneé.

"I can lend some more comfortable clothes if you like," said Sammy. "But I can't help you with underwear."

"Why's that?" asked Ben. "As long as it's clean I don't really care."

"Because I don't own any," said Sammy.

"None at all?" asked Vincent, his interest piqued. He would have probably said something racy, but Matthew clamped a hand over Vincent's mouth.

"Just because you have a thought doesn't mean you have to voice it," chided Matthew.

"Mrrmph hmmph phemma pher," said Vincent through Matthew's obstructing hand.

"Behave," said Matthew, removing his hand from Vincent's mouth.

"What is it zat you normally wear?" asked Reneé. "Zat black shirt with the gway pants?"

"Yeah," said Ben. "How did you know?"

"I've seen you in zem in ze mornings before you've changed," replied Reneé. "Now, dwop your pants."

"What?" asked Ben in surprise.

"I need to see your underwear," said Reneé.

"But why—"

"Just do it."

Utterly confused, Ben unzipped and lowered his pants. Vincent whistled rakishly, which caused Matthew to elbow him in the ribs again.

"Happy?" he asked.

"Do you 'ave more zan one like zat?" asked Reneé.

"Yes," said Ben, zipping up his pants again. "Is there a point in all of this?"

For answer, Reneé held out her hands. A second later Ben's pajamas and a pair of fresh underwear had appeared in a swirl of pink sparkles.

"When did ya learn to do that?" asked Sammy in amazement.

"Just now," said Reneé. "I zought zat, if I could change the size of clozing, zen I might be able to summon it to me as well."

"Thanks," said Ben, taking his clothes from Reneé. "I don't suppose you could do the same with my toothbrush could you?"

"I don't zink so," said Reneé.

"I have a spare one ya can borrow," said Matthew. He disappeared into his room for a few seconds. When he returned, he was carrying a green toothbrush.

"Thanks, "said Ben as Matthew hand him the brush.

"No problem," said Matthew with a smile.

"Zere you go," said Reneé. "Now off to bed with you." She started pushing towards the door to Sammy's room again.

"Why are you so interested in us sleeping together?" asked Ben.

"'Ave you ever 'ad a sleepover?" asked Reneé.

"No," said Ben.

"Well, zere is your answer and 'ere is your chance," said Reneé. "You are eighteen years behind scheduwala. Dwastic measures must be taken."

"Nineteen," said Ben before he could stop himself.

"Nineteen?" asked Matthew. "When was your birthday?"

"The seventeenth," said Ben sheepishly.

Matthew and Vincent exchanged discontented looks.

"We'll go shopping tomorrow," declared Vincent.

"Will we have time?" asked Matthew.

"Day after then."

"Shopping for what?" asked Ben, though he had a sinking suspicion he already knew the answer.

"Your present," said Matthew and Vincent in unison.

"You don't have to—"

"We are both buying you a present each," snapped Vincent forcefully. "Deal with it. Reneé, you want to join us?"

"I am about to give 'im ze best pwesent I can," said Reneé and she started shoving Ben towards Sammy's bedroom. "But yes, I will join you."

"Alright already," said Ben as Sammy hurriedly opened his bedroom door. "I'll sleep in Sammy's room. Now stop pushing."

"'Ave a pleasant night," said Reneé with a wide smile.

"You too," said Ben, walking into Sammy's room.

"Night," said Sammy happily as he closed the door.

"The hell is up with her?" asked Ben.

Sammy shrugged. "Not a clue, dude."

Ben rolled his eyes in exasperation and then took a look around Sammy's room. It was a bit of a mess. Books, shorts, and hoodies were strewn all over the floor. His desk was hidden under piles of papers, DVDs, and empty glasses. A collection of towels and swimming trunks hung on the pull-up bar that had been set up in his closet doorway and his sheets and pillows were in a crumpled pile at the foot of his bed.

"Sorry about the mess," said Sammy. "I wasn't expecting company."

"Doesn't really bother me," lied Ben politely.

In truth, he was somewhat taken aback by the chaos around him. Ben had always been uncomfortable with untidiness and disorder. That was why his books were always organized, his desk was always clear of excess clutter, his bed was always made, and his dirty clothes always filed away in the laundry basket he kept in his closet. But, Ben reasoned to himself, the mess didn't really matter. After all, the room seemed to be mostly dust-free.

"Ya wanna use the bathroom first?" Sammy.

"Sure," said Ben. "Thanks."

Unlike his room, Sammy's bathroom was pristine, which made Ben feel considerably better.

"Is it alright if I use your shower?" asked Ben.

"Go ahead," said Sammy. "Just let me get you a clean towel." He reached into his closet and pulled out a fresh, folded towel, which he handed to Ben.

"Thanks," said Ben.

"No problem."

Ben closed the bathroom door, turned on the shower, stripped, hopped in, and quickly bathed himself. Once done, Ben dried himself off, changed into his pajamas, brushed his teeth, and stepped out into Sammy's bedroom. Sammy was sitting at his desk, absentmindedly playing a game on his phone.

"Done?" he asked.

"Yes," said Ben.

Sammy got up, set his phone down, headed into the bathroom, and closed the door. Ben, unsure of what to do, stood awkwardly in a corner of the room, his clothes clutched to his chest, until Sammy had finished.

"You can get into the bed," said Sammy once he'd stepped back into the room. He patted the bed lightly. It jiggled.

"You have a waterbed?" asked Ben. "I guess I shouldn't be surprised."

"Yeah," said Sammy. "I always wan'd one but mom could never afford it. Is that'n issue? Ya can still sleep on the couch if ya wanna," said Sammy. "Reneé's probably in'er room by now so she won't bother ya. I won't be insulted."

"I'll give it a try," said Ben. If he could stand the mess around him, he should be able to deal with a jiggling bed.

"Cool," said Sammy. He started to strip off his hoodie but stopped and looked over at Ben. "I normally sleep topless. If that makes ya uncomfortable I can keep it on."

"I saw you change early," said Ben. "If that didn't make me uncomfortable, why would this?"

"Some guys have issues sleeping next to a shirtless dude," he said. "They think it'll make them gay or something stupid like that."

"Really?" asked Ben. "That's nuts."

"Agreed," said Sammy as he started to lift his shirt again. "So, all good?"

"You do whatever makes you comfortable," said Ben. "I don't want to be an imposition."

"Cool," said Sammy, pulling off his hoodie and dropped it on the floor.

Ben grimaced slightly but Sammy didn't notice as he hopped onto the bed, which jiggle violently.

"Do you own anything besides hoodies and shorts?" asked Ben, his eyes scanning the various articles of clothing littered the room.

"I gotta a few other things," said Sammy. "But shorts and hoodies are more convenient. So, ya joinin' me or not?"

"Um, where can I put my clothes?" asked Ben.

"You can just drop them anywhere," said Sammy. "Or," he added after seeing the expression on Ben's face, "you can put them on my chair."

Ben set his clothes on Sammy's desk chair and then gingerly climbed onto the bed, which sloshed about with his every movement.

"Thank god I don't get seasick," said Ben as he laid down next to Sammy.

"Ya good?" asked Sammy.

"Let me get into a good position," said Ben. He shifted around until he was comfortable. "Ok, I'm good."

"Cool," said Sammy. He reached up to the light switch that was above his bed, turned off the lights, and settled in for the night.

Ben closed his eyes and tried to get to sleep but it wasn't easy. If he'd been in his own room, he would have simply used the eye mask that Hypnos had given him to get to sleep but, unfortunately, that wasn't an option right now. He should have asked Reneé if she could summon it like she had his pajamas. He was sure that, on a normal bed, he'd eventually be able to fall asleep. However, every movement he or Sammy made sent ripples through the waterbed, which kept him from drifting off properly. After ten restless minutes, just as Ben had decided that he would spend the night on the couch, Sammy spoke.

"You awake?"

"Yes," said Ben.

"Do ya mind if I ask ya a kinda personal question?"

"Go ahead." Ben was rocked by waves as Sammy turned over.

"How are ya so okay with everythin'?"

"I'm sorry?" asked Ben, rolling over so that he and Sammy were now face-to-face.

They could just make each other out by the small bit of moonlight coming through the window blinds.

"Like, being ignored by everyone," clarified Sammy.

"Oh. Well, I've been ignored by people my whole life so, like I keep saying, I'm used to it. The only people who don't ignore me are my mom and dad."

"That sucks dude," said Sammy.

"It does," said Ben. "But, it's not like people do it on purpose. It just happens. And I'm sure I don't help the situation either. I'm quiet, I wear dark clothes, and I tend to hang out in dark corners, so it's not surprising that I get overlooked."

"But don't ya ever feel... I don't know, left out?" asked Sammy.

"Sometimes," said Ben. "I mean, do I want people to notice me more? Yeah sure, why not. But do I think it's going to happen? No, not really. If history has taught me anything it's to not get my hopes up."

"That's depressing as fuck, dude," said Sammy.

"I'm used to it," said Ben.

Sammy moved closer to Ben and pulled him into a one-armed hug. Once again, Ben breath in the smell of chlorine and sun.

"I hope ya know," said Sammy into Ben's shoulder, "that, even if I or the others ignore ya, you're still our friend."

"I know," said Ben, trying to keep the skepticism out of his voice. He obviously didn't do a good enough job.

"I mean it," said Sammy, looking squarely into Ben's dark eyes with his blue ones. "Whether you want to admit it or not, you have friends." There was nothing but sincerity in Sammy's gaze.

"Thank you," whispered Ben, a warm feeling spreading through him.

Sammy smiled, squeezing Ben even tighter. He rather liked the fact that Sammy was a hugger. When Sammy eventually loosened his grip and back off, Ben felt a touch of disappointment. He could have happily stayed like that all night.

"I'm not making ya uncomfortable, am I?" asked Sammy.

"Not at all," said Ben. "In fact, I was rather enjoying myself. Why would you think I was uncomfortable?"

"Some guys don't like being touched by other dudes," said Sammy. "Let alone being hugged by one."

Ben stretched out his arm and pulled Sammy back towards him. "I don't mind in the least. I was never taught that there was anything wrong with guys showing affection to one another. So, as long as it makes me feel good on the inside, I'm all for it."

Sammy chuckled lightly. "My mom would love you."

"Is she the reason you're so affectionate?"

"Pretty much. She was a social justice warrior long before it became popular. She's been fighting against social, racial, and sexual inequalities for years. She's probably the most liberally progressive person I know. With a mother like that, there was no way I was goin' be anything but a big, old softy."

"Is your dad the same way?" asked Ben.

Sammy's face fell. "I wouldn't know. He ran off before I was born. We haven't seen him since."

"I'm sorry," said Ben, mentally kicking himself.

Sure he'd ruined everything, Ben tried to pull away. Sammy, however, tightened his hold on Ben in response.

"I'm not upset," he said. "And I'm over it. Well mostly over it. I know I can't do anything about it except try to be a better man than he was. And I think I've done a good job of that so far."

"I agree," said Ben.

Sammy smiled at Ben, who smiled back. For several seconds they looked happily into each other's eyes.

"So . . . you want to make out?" joked Ben

"I'm game if you're game," said Sammy, jovially playing along.

They gazed intently into each other's eyes for a few more seconds before they both started to laugh.

"Maybe another time," said Ben. "Like when Johnny is around."

Sammy laughed even harder at that. "I'd love to see his reaction. He'd probably blow a blood vessel."

They both started laughing again as they pictured Johnny's reaction to another pair of men making out in front of him. The next few hours were spent talking about everything and nothing. Finally, exhausted, they fell asleep, Ben's head resting on Sammy's chest and Sammy's arm draped around Ben's shoulder.

# Chapter Fourteen

"You two enjoy yourselves last night?" asked Vincent as Sammy and Ben entered the dining room for breakfast the next morning. As always, the table was laden down with enough food to feed a small army. There were platters of sausages, plates of bacon, chafing dishes of scrambled eggs, large bowls of oatmeal, tins of cereal, mounds of bread, cartons of milk, and jugs of orange juice. Vincent, Matthew, Irene, Reneé, Ashley, Gavin, Lance, and Johnny had all already started eating.

"It was fun," said Sammy.

"Yeah, I'd do it again," said Ben.

"What'd you two do?" asked Lance.

"Yes," said Vincent slyly, "do tell. What *did* you do? Go ahead, don't be shy. Tell us. And don't leave anything out."

"Ben spent the night in my room," said Sammy, taking a seat at the table and ignoring Vincent, "since Sara's using his."

"Why?" asked Gavin.

"She asked me to summon the spirit of her father up from the Underworld," answered Ben taking a seat next to Sammy. "They ended up falling asleep on my bed and I didn't want to bother them."

"I didn't think ghosts needed sleep," commented Ashley.

Johnny, on the other hand, had a different concern. "You tellin' me you two slept in the same bed?" he demanded.

"Yeah, we did," said Ben.

"Somethin' wrong with that?" asked Sammy.

"I'd never sleep in the same bed as another dude," said Johnny aggressively.

"Surprise, surprise," muttered Vincent.

"You got something to say, fruitcake?" snapped Johnny.

"There is nothing wrong with two men sleeping in the same bed," said Vincent.

"It's fucking gay," retorted Johnny.

"Only if they were in some way intimate," snapped Vincent. He turned to look at Sammy and Ben. "Were you?"

"No, not really," said Ben.

"We hadda pretty personal conversation," said Sammy. "But nothin' sexual happened."

"See," said Vincent. "Nothing gay about it. Unless talking to a guy somehow makes you a fag now."

"It's still weird," complained Johnny.

"Please," begged Lance as Vincent opened his mouth to say something insulting, "can we table this fight for now. It's too early for all this negativity."

"Besides," said Sammy, "it's not like I'd only have a sleepover with a dude. If anyone wants to camp out in my room, I'm open to it."

"Just give him a heads up so he can clean his room beforehand," said Ben.

Sammy stuck his tongue out at Ben before applying himself to the plate of bacon and eggs that Irene had set down in front of him. As usual, she was acting as server for the group. To Ben's surprise, Irene put a plate of food in front of him too. He usually had to help himself.

"Thanks," said Ben, "but you don't have to serve me you know."

"I know," said Irene, smiling as she returned to her seat. "But I like being helpful."

"Has anyone seen Sara this morning?" asked Ben. "I want to get back into my room before classes today."

"No," said Matthew. "At least not since I've been up."

"Which was dawn," muttered Vincent.

"What can I say," said Matthew, "I'm an early riser."

"I hope she wakes up soon," said Ben. "I feel like I should get her father's spirit back to the Underworld sooner rather than later."

"Why?" asked Sammy. "It's not like a spirit's a library book. There's no late fee."

"I just don't want anyone thinking that I'm trying to resurrect the dead," said Ben. "Thanatos was very clear that I shouldn't do that."

"Obviously, not clear enough."

Everyone whipped around. Thanatos was standing in the entrance to the dining room, his eyes fixed intently on Ben.

"Who the hell are you?" demanded Johnny, raising up from his seat at the table.

Thanatos turned his cold eyes on Johnny, who gulped and sat down again. Ashley, however, seemed to be made of sterner stuff.

"Unless you are the god of silence stares, that's not an answer," she snapped coolly.

Thanatos turned to face Ashley, who looked back at him with regal disdain. After several seconds of tense silence, Thanatos spoke.

"I am Thanatos, god of death."

Everyone, except for Ben and Ashley, instinctively shifted away from Thanatos.

"Good for you," said Ashley snobbishly. "But that does not give you the right to enter our home without knocking first."

Everyone turned to stare at Ashley in astonishment. Ben, however, kept his eyes on Thanatos, unsure of how the god of death would react. To Ben's utter surprise, he saw a corner of Thanatos's mouth twitch. A pillar of thick gray smoke whipped around Thanatos. When it cleared an instant later, he had gone. Suddenly, there came a series of knocks on the front door.

"Ben," said Ashley, returning to her bowl of oatmeal, "I think that's for you."

"Right," said Ben, a newfound respect for Ashley growing inside him. He got up from the table and headed to the front door. Opening it, he found Thanatos standing on the threshold.

"May I come in?" asked Thanatos, a note sarcasm in his voice.

"Yes," said Ben and he moved out of the way so Thanatos could step into the apartment. Together they walked back into the dining room.

"Welcome," said Ashley coolly. "And thank you for knocking."

"Thank you," said the god of death calmly. "And my apologies for my lapse in manners."

"That's quite alright," said Ashley. "Just don't let it happen again." Picking up her plate, Ashley reached over to hand it to Irene who, like the others, was staring at Ashley in stunned silence.

"Ahem," coughed Ashley.

Irene snapped out of her daze, took Ashley's plate from her, and took it into the kitchen. With that done, Ashley turned back to Thanatos.

"So, what are you doing here?"

"I've come to reclaim the soul that was removed from the Underworld," said Thanatos, rounding on Ben. "I thought I expressly warned you not to bring the dead back to life."

"I didn't," said Ben. "At least, I wasn't intending to. I just wanted to summon the spirit of Sara's dad like I did with Jason."

"Spirits are, by nature, transparent and intangible," said Thanatos. "What you did with Jason and with

Leonard Gardener was not summoning but resurrection. Now, let me be clear, summoning or resurrecting a soul to help you or advise you in a dire situation is fully within your rights as the future god of the dead. In fact, I encourage you to do so. But, resurrecting a soul, or even summoning one, for no other reason than to have a little chat is irresponsible and dangerous. The dead must remain in the Underworld."

"Why?" asked a voice from behind Thanatos. Sara and her father had finally left Ben's room.

"Because this is no longer their world," explained Thanatos calmly. "Their life, their time has come to an end. It is the fate of all mortal things and that must be respected."

"It's not fair!" shouted Sara.

"Rose, it's alright," said Sara's father but Sara continued on anyway.

"My father died when he was twenty-six. Twenty-six! How can you say that he's lived his life?"

"I may be the god of death," said Thanatos, "but it is not my place to decide the fates of mortals. I am merely one thread in a tapestry. My job, my duty, is to ensure that those who are destined to die do so. I care not about who, what, why, or how. I only care about when."

He turned to glare at Ben. "And it is your duty to make sure that those who have died remain dead."

"I was going to send him back," said Ben. "I just wanted to give them some time together."

"What if I don't want him to go back?" asked Sara, placing herself squarely between Thanatos and her father. "What if I want him to stay?"

"Rosie, don't do this," whispered Sara's dad, his face full of fear.

"That is not my concern," said Thanatos emotionlessly. "If you wish to rail against fate, I wish you all the luck in the universe. But, that doesn't not change my position." Thanatos waved his hands and Sara's father immediately faded away.

# Heir to the Underworld

"NO!" screamed Sara. She hurled herself at Thanatos, pummeling him repeatedly with her fists. "Bring him back! Bring him back! Bring him back!"

Reneé, Matthew, and Lance jumped up from their chairs and dashed over to Sara. Matthew and Reneé each grabbed one of Sara's flailing arms, while Lance wrapped his large arms around her waist and pulled her away from Thanatos.

"No!" screamed Sara, struggling against her captors as she tried to get back to Thanatos. "Let me go! LET ME GO!"

All the chairs in the room began to rattle and shake. Those that weren't occupied rose up into the air and flung themselves at Thanatos, who raised a hand and froze them in midair. Now the dining room table was beginning to tremble. As the table started rising up into the air Ashley got up from her seat, marched over to Sara, and slapped her hard across the face. Time seemed to stop. Everyone stared from Ashley to Sara, breathless with anticipation about what would happen next.

"Enough," order Ashley sternly.

Though it when unnoticed by the others, Ashley's eyes momentarily flashed purple. Immediately the furniture stopped wobbling. The table and chairs all dropped down to the floor with a clatter. Sara blinked once, twice, three times and then began to cry. Matthew, Reneé, and Lance released their hold on Sara as she sank down to the ground, sobbing uncontrollably. Reneé, her face full of concern, knelt down and put her arms around Sara, who collapsed completely into her embrace.

"Honorable as your intentions may have been, Benjamin, that does not excuse you of the pain you've caused," said Thanatos as he looked down at Sara, pity in his normally cold eyes. "Because of you, she has lost her father twice."

"It was what she wanted," said Ben. "I thought it would make her happy."

"So rarely do those two things coincide," said Thanatos. "Everyone always says that all they want is five more minutes. Five more minutes to say whatever was left unsaid in life. And yet, no one ever really considers what will happen after those five minutes are up. You have been granted a great power, Benjamin. A power far greater than you are yet able to comprehend. You must learn to use it responsibly or this will not be the last time you cause someone unwanted pain." A pillar of gray smoke swirled around Thanatos and he was gone.

It took Reneé and Matthew several hours, but they eventually managed to calm Sara down. The first thing she did, once she'd regained her composure, was tell Ben that she didn't blame him in the slightest. Ben, who'd been feeling incredible pangs of guilt since breakfast, was slightly comforted by this. Whatever Sara might say to the contrary, he still felt responsible for causing her distress. Any discussion that the new gods might have normally had after such an incident was forgone, however, because, once their classes were over for the day, they all had to start getting ready for their dinner with Hades.

At the appointed hour the new gods gathered in front of the door to the linen closet, all of them dressed for the occasion. Ashley was wearing a glittering blue dress of silk and tulle. Sophia sported a white and peach off-the-shoulder number that left the group speechless. It was the first time any of them had seen her in anything that could be considered even remotely dressy. Reneé's pink and fuchsia gown was as fabulous as she had promised, though Reneé was so beautiful she could have worn a paper bag and still turned every head in the room. Sara, Ana Maria, and Irene all looked wonderful in the dresses Reneé had given them, though Reneé hadn't managed to succeed in convincing Ana Maria to comb her hair.

As for the boys, Ben's basic black suit made him look as though he was going to attend a funeral. Andrew, Gavin, and Matthew were all in sleek, tailor-made, three-piece suits in shades of black, brown, and tan respectively. Johnny, Sammy, and Lance were all quite dapper in the suits they'd been given. Vincent, however, was another matter. He had come out in a suit of the deepest purple any of them had ever seen.

"You look like an eggplant," snickered Andrew as they all tried, and failed, to contain their laughter.

"But a sexy eggplant," said Matthew as he leaned in and kissed Vincent on the cheek.

"Uggh," retched Johnny. "Don't start. You'll make me lose my appetite."

"Don't talk," ordered Sophia. "You'll make me lose my appetite."

Before Johnny could respond there was a soft click as the closet door opened of its own accord.

"Guess it's time to go," said Andrew.

The group stepped through the door and found themselves in the entrance hall of Hades' palace. Those who had never seen the palace before oohed and ahhed at the architecture and commented on the beautiful vases of flowers and the exotic vines of ivy, all of which were in full bloom.

"Welcome young masters."

Perched upon one of the angelic wings of a pillar was a large owl, his black and white feathers patterned to resemble a tuxedo.

"A talking owl," commented Vincent. "Well can't say I saw that coming."

"I am Ascalaphus, the custodian of this palace. If you will all follow me, I shall lead you to the dining room."

Ascalaphus took flight, soaring down the entrance hall with the new gods following after him on foot. He led them through a series of doors until they finally reached the dining room. They all let out gasps of astonishment.

The dining room had been decorated to resemble an autumnal forest. In place of pillars, there were large, golden trees, their many leaves and branches spreading out across the ceiling. Fall foliage littered the ground, and a soft autumn light bathed the room in shades of red and yellow. The table was carved to resemble an expanse of woodland, and each of the chairs looked to be small recreations of great trees. On top of the table was an assortment of food, their intoxicating aromas filling the air.

A mature woman was walking around the table. She wore an elegant gown of autumn colors. Her light coppery hair was pinned to resemble a cornucopia, similar to the one she carried in her arms. Upon her head, she wore a crown made of fall leaves, ears of corn, and stalks of wheat. As she made her way around the table, she pulled out plates of cooked vegetables from her cornucopia and added them to the already assembled feast in front of her.

"It's good that you all have come," said the woman as she set down a dish of green bean casserole. "My dear daughter has been most anxious to meet you all."

"Who is your daughter?" asked Sara.

"Persephone, of course."

"And who are you?" The woman looked up to stare at Sara in disapproval.

"You mean to tell me you don't recognize me?"

There was a moment's silence.

"Demeter?" asked Sara hesitantly.

Demeter inclined her head in acknowledgment.

"You got old," said Ashley.

Demeter turned her bright green eyes on Ashley, who stared back at the aged goddess unashamedly.

"My form shifts with the changing seasons," explained Demeter, still appraising Ashley in cold rebuke as she pulled more plates of vegetables from her cornucopia. "In spring I am a young sprig brimming with potential. In summer I am a mighty stalk in its prime. In autumn I am a ripe harvest full of life's bounty. In winter I am a wither husk in need of rest."

"Will I change with the seasons too?" asked Sara.

Demeter turned her gaze to Sara. "I do not know. I was born a goddess, so my form is not as set as yours. It remains to be seen how your divinity will affect you. Perhaps you will remain the same, perhaps you will not."

"Are you stuck looking like that or can you still change forms?" asked Ana Maria.

As Demeter turned her attention to Ana Maria, her hair darkened and let loose from its pins to flow freely about her shoulders. The lines on her face faded away. Her autumnal gown became a dress of red and gold and the crown upon her head was now the same one she had worn when they had first met her. For a moment she stood before them: young, beautiful, and full of life. And then her youthful splendor faded, and she was a woman in the autumn of her years once more.

"I can still take what form I will, as is true for all gods, but I see no reason to do so. Unlike my fellow goddesses, I am not overly vain. I am the goddess of the seasons; I see no reason why my form should not reflect that."

A door opened off to the side of the room and Hades, dressed in white tie, entered. He was accompanied by Macaria, Melinoë, Hecate, Hypnos, Lethe, and a beautiful young woman that could only be Persephone. She was tall and willowy, with pale blonde hair and warm, smiling face flecked with freckles. Her eyes were the same bright green color Demeter's were. She wore a dress of the purest white with a green sash tied about her waist. Upon her head was a gleaming tiara of silver flowers.

Macaria and Melinoë had both dressed to match their mother. They wore simple white dresses with sashes tied around their waists, gold for Macaria and blue for Melinoë. Unfortunately, whereas Macaria looked regal and graceful in her dress, Melinoë more closely resembled a corpse in repose. She had, however, managed to tame her turbulent mess of hair.

Hecate, Lethe, and Hypnos too had dressed for the occasion. Hypnos wore ceremonial robes of deep blue that glittered with moving stars. Lethe wore a gauzy dress of hazy gray that seemed to swim around her lithe body. As for Hecate, she wore an impossibly tight, snake-skin dress in vivid green, complete with a live boa constrictor boa. She had also braided and styled her hair to resemble snakes, which writhed and undulated about in a memorizing fashion. Hades introduced each member of this court to the new gods, making sure to leave Persephone for last.

"And finally, may I present my dear wife, Persephone." Reaching down, Hades took Persephone's hand and brought it to his lips.

Persephone smiled warmly at her husband before planting a kiss of her own on his cheek. Delicately, she slid her hand out of his grasp and gracefully swept over to the group gathered around the table.

"I'm so happy to meet each and everyone one of you," said Persephone warmly.

She then proceeded to hug every last one of them. Her voice was sweet and gentle, like the first rays of dawn on a beautiful spring day. As her arms wrapped around them, all their worries and cares seemed to fade away.

# Chapter Fifteen

"Please, sit," said Hades as Persephone gave out her last embrace. "Some of the greatest cooks that have ever lived have been working on this meal all day."

"Sara, beside me please," commanded Demeter.

As they all took their seats, everyone tried to avoid sitting next to Hecate. In the end, Sophia bit the proverbial bullet and seated herself next to Hecate and her snake.

"A toast," said Hades, raising his glass of wine. "To my lovely wife Persephone, whose very presence brings me untold joy. She is the apple of my eye. She is my world, my goddess, my love. She is a bright light in a sea of darkness. To Persephone, my beautiful spring flower."

"To Persephone," chorused the table as they all lifted a glass in her honor.

Persephone, her cheeks a furious shade of red, leaned over and gave her husband a passionate kiss on the lips.

"Thank you, my dark king," she said sweetly. "My light would be but a candle were you not in my life."

"This lovey-dovey stuff is making me sick," muttered Johnny.

Andrew, who was sitting to his left, nodded in agreement. At a sign from Hades, they all began to dig into the feast in front of them. The food tasted as good as it smelled.

"So, Hades, how'd you bag such a hottie?" asked Johnny.

Several of the others groaned.

"He kidnapped her," said Demeter.

"What!" exclaimed Ana Maria, Sara, Sammy, Lance, Gavin, and Sophia.

"It's not as bad as it sounds," said Hades.

"It was at the time," teased Persephone.

"Why did you kidnap her?" demanded Ana Maria.

"Just to be clear, it was only a kidnapping because she didn't know about it beforehand," said Hades. "I'd asked Zeus for Persephone's hand in marriage and he'd agreed. How was I supposed to know that he didn't tell her ahead of time that I was coming?"

"In truth, it was probably a good thing that he didn't say anything to me," said Persephone. "Since Mother would not have approved at the time. As a matter-of-fact, it took her some thousand years before she finally did approve."

"I just wanted to make sure you found a good husband," sniffed Demeter. "You are my favorite child after all."

"And as much as I appreciate your love and devotion, even you have to admit that you were smothering me."

"Heavens forbid a mother love her child," said Demeter testily. "I was only doing what I thought was best."

"Must we start up this old conflict again?" asked Hades. "I thought we settled this ages ago."

"I'm not starting anything," said Demeter. "Who's starting anything? You are a wonderful husband. I just wish things could have been handled differently."

"It's not like you gave us much of a choice, dear sister."

"Sister!" exclaimed Lance. "Wait, you two are brother and sister?"

"Yes," said Hades and Demeter in unison.

"But if you two are siblings, wouldn't that make Persephone your niece?" asked Sammy

"Correct," said Persephone. "In fact, I'm Hades' niece twice over since Zeus is my father."

"What does that have to do with anything?" asked Sara.

"Zeus is our youngest brother," said Hades, gesturing towards himself and Demeter.

"So you married your niece?" ask Johnny. "That's gross."

Hades cocked an eyebrow. "Incest is a human construct," he said coolly. "It was created out of necessity because it caused issues with your genetic materials. We gods, as being of divine energy, are not subject to such concerns."

"But—"

"Persephone and I have a deep and profound love for each other. I think that should be sufficient for everyone at this table, don't you?" There was a finality in his voice that made it perfectly clear that this particular conversation was over.

"Ben," said Persephone, clearly trying to steer the conversation in another direction, "I want to thank you for agreeing to take over my husband's duties. It will be so nice to have more free time."

"No problem," said Ben. "What will you guys do once I take over?"

"I was thinking a trip around the world," said Persephone. "Since Hades will no longer be the King of the Underworld, he'll finally have the time."

"What about you, aren't you the Queen?" asked Sophia.

"I'm only queen because Hades is king. Once Ben takes over, I'll be free."

"For half the year," muttered Demeter.

"Drop it mother, please," said Persephone.

"Does that mean that I have to marry Andrew to be Queen of the gods?" asked Ashley. She shot Andrew a quick look. "Not that I'm complaining, mind you. I just want to know how it works."

"Thanks, I guess," said Andrew bemused.

"There was considerable discussion about that subjected," said Hades. "Eventually it was decided that you would be granted the title and powers of Queen of the gods without there being any need for marriage. Most of us felt it was the fairer path."

"Good to know," said Ashley.

"So, how are you all enjoying your classes?" asked Persephone.

It took a few minutes but eventually conversation began to flow freely. Persephone was very interested in the lives of the new gods before they had been drafted into their new roles and spent most of the meal chatting with the more candid members of the group. Demeter spent almost all her time talking with Sara, conversing about various horticultural and agricultural processes and giving Sara sacks of seeds from her cornucopia. Macaria and Ana Maria entered into a long discussion about the First World War, while Melinoë, rather uncharacteristically, got drawn into a conversation between Lance and Vincent about the causes of alcoholism. Hypnos and Matthew were conversing glibly about dreams (nightmares specifically), while Lethe chatted about memories with Irene and Gavin. Hecate dominated most of Hades' attention, updating him on various issues within the Underworld. Beside her, Sophia had made friends with the boa constrictor boa. She was now feeding the large snake scraps from her own plate.

"Hades, can I ask you something?" asked Ben, taking advantage of a lull in Hecate's sermon.

"Of course," said Hades, shooting a warning glance at Hecate who'd just opened her mouth to complain about the interruption.

"Why wasn't the rest of your court invited?"

"Because they don't make very good dining companions," answered Hecate testily.

"Simple, but accurate," said Hades, with another pointed glare at Hecate. "Dinner with Eris or Polemos always turns into a catastrophe, and Achlys would have just brought down the whole evening. It's not yet night here so Nyx couldn't attend. Charon doesn't eat, Styx is still napping, Tartarus flat out refused – which is to be expected – and the Erinyes would rather work than join in the festivities. As for those at the gates: Penthos would have had us all crying to our soup by now, Algea would have had us screaming, Aporia's idea of polite dinner conversation would have made Caligula blush, Oizys is nervous around new people, Limos can't be around Demeter, and anyone sitting next to Nosoi would have probably contracted botulism. Only Geras and Phobos would have been welcome to eat here, but Phobos is helping his father Ares with something, and Geras isn't a party person."

"Why can't Limos be around Demeter?" asked Sara.

"She is the goddess of hunger and I the goddess of the harvest," explained Demeter. "We are fundamentally opposites."

"So, you don't get along?" asked Sophia as she popped another piece of meat into the snake's mouth.

"We have no animosity towards each other," said Demeter. "But when opposites in divine power meet, the effect may be disastrous."

"What about Thanatos?" asked Ben. "He not invited either?"

"My brother chose to remain at home tonight," said Hypnos. "He felt his presence would be unsettling."

"Good," muttered Sara, her grip on her cutlery tightening. "He's horrible."

Hypnos, who had been about to take a sip of wine, lowered his glass. "Would you care to explain what is so horrible about my brother?" he asked, turning narrowed eyes on Sara.

"He took my father from me," said Sara. "Twice."

"Thanatos no more dictates who dies than Phanes dictates who lives," said Hypnos delicately. "As for his reacquisition of your father's soul, would you blame a policeman for reclaiming an escaped prisoner?"

"My father was not an escaped prisoner!" shouted Sara.

"Perhaps not in the most literal sense but the principle it is still the same," said Hypnos. "Whether you like it or not, your father belongs here in the Underworld. My brother was merely returning him to his rightful place."

"He didn't have to take him in the first place!" snapped Sara.

"Thanatos does not *take* anyone," said Hypnos, "unless they are of particular significance. I can assure you, however much your father means to you, he was not significant enough to garner my brother's attention."

"Your brother—"

"My brother was not responsible for your father's death," said Hypnos flatly. "He is the embodiment of death, not its cause. If you are looking for someone to blame, might I suggest the goddess sitting to your left."

"What does Demeter have to do with anything?" demanded Sara.

"If she had blessed your farm with a better harvest, than your father would not have had to work so hard," said Hypnos. "Or perhaps you would prefer to blame the sun? Had Helios not shone so hotly that day your father might still be with you. Or, if not Helios, might I suggest Achlys or Algea. After all, they spread their misery and agony indiscriminately. Maybe you'd rather go after Limos for withering your crops, the Horae for including a dry spell in that year's seasonal schedule, Hermes for transporting your father's soul to the banks of the River Styx, or Charon for taking him across the River Acheron to the Gates of the Underworld.

"Or, perhaps you'd rather aim for those higher up the rung. Iapetus, the titan of mortality, was the one who decided that all non-divine creatures should be mortals. And it was his sons Prometheus and Epimetheus who enacted this idea. Why not blame them? And, if even they are not enough for you, there is always the Fates, or even Ananke, the goddess of inevitable."

"Eighteen. That's eighteen beings of power who had more to do with your father's death than my brother ever did. And yet, you choose to curse him. You choose to consider him horrible, when all he has ever done is fulfill the duty that he's been burdened with since time immemorial. Do not blame my brother for your pain Miss Gardener. It's not his fault. It was Iapetus who created the concept of mortality, not Thanatos. It was just his misfortune that he was selected to be the god of death."

"But does he have to be so cold about it?" demanded Sara.

"There are those of us whose domains are more curse than gift," said Hypnos, his eyes momentarily flickering to Melinoë. "Thanatos feels everything when someone dies. He feels their pain, their sorrow, their fear. Occasionally he feels their relief but that is a rarity. So, let me ask you, if it were you, how would you deal with what my brother feels on a daily basis? Can you honestly tell me that, after eons of pain and sorrow, you wouldn't grow cold?"

Sara and Hypnos locked eyes. A tense silence fell over the table.

After a minute's silence, Sara spoke. "I'm sorry. I didn't think about it like that."

"That's quite alright," said Hypnos.

"What's so wrong with the dead coming back to life?" asked Johnny.

"It goes against the cosmic order," said Hades. "The living world actively rejects the dead, just as the Underworld actively rejects the living. It is a fundamental law of nature. As Lord of the dead, I must follow that law."

"So, you've never brought anyone back from the dead?" asked Ana Maria.

"I have," said Hades. "But, unless that person was made immortal and taken outside of the hands of fate, it never sticks. Something always happens to them and they end up back in the Underworld. I think the longest anyone lasted was about a day."

"But, you're a god," said Johnny. "Can't you just snap your fingers and make anything happen?"

"We gods have great power," said Hades, "but there are limits to what we can do and there are forces that we cannot overcome."

"So, what's the point of you then?" asked Johnny rudely.

"Gods and goddesses help to order the world," said Macaria testily. "We provide direction for the primal forces of nature and protect humanity from unseen and destructive influence. Being a god is about responsibility, not self-gratification."

"Thank you Macaria," said Hades. "That will be enough of that."

"Didn't Athena say that all things would be within our collective powers?" asked Ashley haughtily.

"She also said there were a few exceptions," said Hades. "Death just happens to be one of them."

"Lame," said Johnny.

Macaria and Hecate both opened their mouths to say something, but Ana Maria cut them off.

"You said that the Underworld rejects life. But then, how are we able to be here?"

"You are protected by your divinity," said Hades. "And, even if you weren't, the effects are not immediate. When a mortal enters the Underworld, their life force is slowly drained away from them. If they were to stay too long without some kind of divine protection, then they would die. Fortunately, you do not have to worry about that."

"What would have happened if Sara's father had stayed in the living world?"

"I'm not sure. All I know is that some sort of tragedy would have befallen him, and he would have been sent back down to the Underworld. At least, with Thanatos coming to collect him, it prevented the possibility of him bring others with him from collateral damage." The new gods exchanged looks of concern at the heaviness of Hades' words. None of them knew exactly what to say or do next.

# Chapter Sixteen

"Perhaps it would be best if we changed the subject," suggested Persephone, eyeing Sara with concern. "Maybe to a more cheerful subject? I understand that you all are being trained in your powers by Hecate and in combat by Heracles. How is that going?"

"Except for Matthew, they are all underperforming," said Hecate immediately. "Gavin and Benjamin especially have made almost no progress since we first began training last month."

There was an immediate uproar at these words as several of the new gods sought to defend themselves against Hecate's comments."

"We have made plenty of progress!"

"We've only been training for a month, what the hell do you expect?"

"Maybe if you learned to teach instead of just standing around and criticizing us, we would be further along!"

"Everyone, calm yourselves," said Hades, holding up his hands for silence. "You too Hecate." He turned reproving eyes to the goddess of magic, who was glaring murderously at the new gods.

"Why don't you all tell me what you've learned so far?" suggested Persephone diplomatically. "Ben, why don't you start us off?"

"Ummm," said Ben, caught off-guard by being called on first. "Well, I think I've figured out how to summon a spirit. Or resurrection, I guess. Oh, sorry." He shot a look at Sara to make sure that his words had not upset her.

"It's fine," said Sara. "Really."

"Okay. Well apart from that, I haven't really figured anything else out. I mean, what else is there besides that?"

"Is that the only thing you think being the god of the dead entails?" asked Persephone.

"Yeah, kind of."

Persephone turned to look at her husband reproachfully.

"He's supposed to figure it out for himself," said Hades calmly, though he was actively avoiding his wife's eye.

"And you agree with this?" asked Persephone, rounding on her mother.

"We had to learn how our powers worked for ourselves," said Demeter. "I see no reason why it should be any different for them."

Persephone let out a long sigh of exasperation. "Hades isn't just the god of the dead," she said. "He's also the god of the riches of the earth. This means he has power over the stones, rocks, gems, crystals, minerals, dirt, soil, mud, sand, and ore. On top of that he, along with the other thirteen Olympians, has the ability to utilize the powers of those in his court. In Hades' case, this means anything from Hecate's magic to Hypnos' ability to induce slumber. Something for you all to think about."

"Why couldn't you tell us all this before?" asked Andrew, annoyed.

"It is not your place to question the decision of the gods!" spat Hecate.

"That's enough Hecate," snapped Hades. "They have the right to ask any question they want. And, like I said before, you were supposed to figure out your powers on your own. Zeus, in particular, was very insistent upon this point. I think he wanted you to prove yourselves worthy of the powers we are bestowing upon you."

"And you all went along with it?" asked Ashley.

"Many of us agreed with him," said Demeter. "Or, at the very least, found it reasonable. As for those who dissented, Zeus can be a very troublesome opponent. One must pick one's battles carefully."

"So why are you telling us?" asked Lance, look at Persephone.

"I don't care what Zeus thinks," said Persephone coldly. "Besides, I have an ulterior motive for helping Ben master his powers."

"What's that?" asked Ben.

"The sooner you take over as King of the Underworld, the sooner Hades and I can go on a ten-year vacation," said Persephone matter-of-factly.

Everyone chuckled at this.

"So, Sara, what have you learned?" asked Persephone.

"I can get plants to grow and move how I want them to," said Sara. "And when I was angry at Thanatos, I made the wooden table and chairs in the dining room move. But that's it."

"A good start," said Persephone with a warm smile. "And you Reneé."

"I can summon and change clozing. And I 'ave power over my 'air. I can style it, gwo it, or shorten it."

"Wonderful," said Persephone. "How about you Gavin? What can you do?"

"Crash into walls," muttered Hecate.

"That's enough of that," said Hades warningly.

"I can run fast," mumbled Gavin. "But I have problems controlling it. I could probably stop if it I had enough time to slow down naturally but—" He trailed off dispiritedly.

"Just because you are going to be the future god of speed doesn't mean you have to be in a rush," said Persephone. "There is no shame in taking your time. In fact, far too many people rush through life. Trust me, as the Queen of the Underworld, I would know." She smiled kindly at Gavin, who smiled back at her.

"How about you Ana Maria? From what I understand you were able to create a force field while fighting the Cetus."

"Yes," said Ana Maria. "I've also been working on moving objects around with my mind like Irene. So far, I've only managed to move things that are under two kilos."

"It's a start," said Persephone. "How about you Irene? How much can you move?"

"I don't know," said Irene. "I've never tested. Mostly I just move pots and pans around while I'm cooking. The heaviest thing I've moved was that table we used while on the yacht."

"Is that the only one of you powers that you've mastered?" asked Persephone.

"I can start a small fire," said Irene. "But nothing else apart from that."

"I think that's very good for only a month's work," said Persephone. "Can you do anything with fire, Lance?"

"I can produce it, yeah," said Lance. "I'm also a lot stronger than I used to be. I can lift about a hundred more kilos than I used to be able to. I'm also starting to be able to attract bits of metal towards me, but that's more hit or miss."

"Very good," said Persephone. "It sounds like you're getting a good handle on your powers. Johnny, am I correct in assuming you are stronger too?"

"Yeah," said Johnny proudly. "I used to bench like two hundred. Now I can get up to 'round six hundred."

"Impressive," said Persephone.

"And I can pull swords out of thin air," added Johnny.

"That is very good," said Persephone. "Sophia, your powers are physical too, correct?"

"Yes," said Sophia. "I don't bench press or nothin' but I have noticed that my punches are gettin' stronger. I'm also a lot faster and more flexible than I used to be. Unfortunately, I can't do anythin' showy yet."

"I wouldn't worry about that," said Persephone. "As the goddess of the hunt, your powers will be mostly physical. And I'm sure you'll be able to figure out your other powers in time. Now, can anyone else conjure like Johnny?"

"Me," said Vincent. "I can make any bottle of alcoholic beverage I've ever tasted, which is pretty much every kind of alcohol, pop into existence. And I can refill them, so I never run out. Very cost-efficient."

"Glad to see you are benefitting in multiple ways," said Persephone. "Now, who haven't we heard from yet? Sammy, how about you?"

"I can make and move water," said Sammy. "And I can breathe underwater too. And I've gotten faster at swimming. My swim coach is super excited about that. Umm, I think that's everything with me."

"Very good," said Persephone. "It's nice to see that your interests are playing a part in your training. How about you Andrew? I believe Ben told Hades you were trying to learn how to fly?"

"Yes," said Andrew, "but it's not going well. I've tried to just lift myself off the ground by sheer force of will, but it hasn't worked. I can get some height if I use the wind to propel me, but I can't control it very well."

"But you have managed to gain some mastery over the wind?" prompted Persephone encouragingly.

"Yes," said Andrew. "I can create blasts of wind and make miniature tornados. But, if I'm not careful, the tornados get too big and I lose control of them. Hecate's had to bail me out a few times."

"At least you are learning your limits," said Persephone. "That is a very important lesson to learn, especially for you. Losing control of the weather can have disastrous results."

"I know," said Andrew. "I try to be as careful with my powers as I can be."

"Very wise of you," said Persephone. She turned to face Ashley. "And how about you dear?"

Everyone turned to look at Ashley too. None of them could ever remember Ashley using her powers.

"I have no interest in discussing my training," said Ashley coolly, her head high.

"Oh come on," said Johnny. "We've all talked about what we've learned. Why don't you wanna? Do you suck that much?"

Ashley turned to glare daggers as Johnny.

"I will not speak about my training," said Ashley, her voice as cold as ice. "And I have no interest in discussing the reasons why with a baboon like you."

Johnny's face flushed. He opened his mouth to say something, but Persephone cut him off. "You don't have to talk about it if you don't want to," she said quickly.

"Thank you," said Ashley, flashing a final cold look at Johnny before returning to her food.

"That just leaves you, Matthew," said Persephone. "From what Hecate's said, you've made the most progress?"

"I guess," said Matthew. "I don't really think I've done that much."

"Don't be modest," said Persephone. "You should celebrate your success. What have you managed to master so far?"

"Well," said Matthew hesitantly, "I guess I've mastered the ability to manipulate light. I can project it, bend it, change its color, use it to create illusions, concentrate it into blasts and beams, create a defense aura with it, and even use it move objects. And I've recently started working on manipulating sound. I'm not quite as skilled with that yet but I can mimic any sound I've heard before without much issue. I can also heal. I wouldn't go so far as to say I can heal anything, but I think I can say with confidence that I can heal most major injuries. And I can hover too. Almost forgot about that."

He stopped, noticing that all the other new gods were looking at him with mixed expressions of envy and respect.

"Sorry," he muttered.

"Don't apologize," said Persephone. "You should be proud of everything you've achieved. You only started training last month and you've already mastered a considerable amount of your powers. That is very impressive isn't it?" She turned towards the others, her eyebrows raised.

Everyone, except Johnny, nodded in agreement.

"I don't care how good he is at usin' his powers," said Johnny. "I'm not goin' be impressed by a fucking perv."

"Can't you give that a rest?" snapped Sara coldly.

"I'm sorry?" asked Persephone in confusion. "What is this?"

"Johnny doesn't like the fact that Vincent, Matthew, and I are gay," said Sophia.

"Technically, I'm bi," said Vincent.

"You are?" asked Lance.

"Yes," said Vincent. "Is there something wrong with that?"

"No," said Lance. He opened his mouth to say something else but then changed his mind and closed it.

"It's not natural," said Johnny. He turned to the gods. "Y'all have been around for a while. Tell them that this is not how it's supposed to be."

"You are talking to the wrong people," said Hades. "We gods don't care about stuff like that. Almost every single god I know has had lovers of either gender, except for those who have taken vows of eternal celibacy."

"What?" demanded Johnny."

"Sorry to burst your bubble," said Hades.

"But... how... what... when..." Johnny was desperately struggling to wrap his head around what he'd just learned.

"Dionysus has often been viewed as the patron god of homosexuals, intersexuals, and transsexuals," said Persephone, an evil glint in her normally kind eyes.

"Eros, who's the god of desire, is the protector of homosexual men," said Demeter.

"Zeus' cupbearer Ganymede is a symbol for homosexual love between men," chimed in Macaria.

"Hermaphroditus is the god of effeminate men," added Melinoë quietly.

"What about lesbians?" asked Sophia.

"Aphrodite is usually the one that looks after them," said Hades. "And I suppose you could call Callisto the original lesbian martyr. Unfortunately, even among us deities, lesbians are underrepresented."

"Of course," grumbled Sophia.

"Blame Zeus," said Demeter. "He's very patriarchal."

"I encourage you to do something about it when you become a goddess," said Hades. "There are plenty of people to choose from if you wanted to create a goddess of lesbianism."

"Believe me, I will be doing something about it," said Sophia determinedly.

"What the hell is wrong with all of you?" demanded Johnny. "How can you all be okay with this?"

"I think," said Hades, "the better question is, why aren't *you* okay with this?"

"*Parce qu'il est u âne*," said Vincent.

Reneé, Ana Maria, and Matthew all choked with laughter.

"Hey," snapped Johnny, jumping at any chance to change the subject, "if you've got something to say, say it in a language we can all understand. Just because you four can speak French doesn't mean everyone else can."

"Actually, since I'm French-Canadian, I speak Québécois," said Lance. "It's not exactly like real French, but it's close enough."

"Okay, five French speakers," grumbled Johnny. "Big whoop. Just because you guys can speak two languages doesn't mean you have to show off all the time."

"Actually, I can speak eight different languages," said Ana Maria. "Well, you don't really speak Latin, but I know it."

"That's one more than me," said Vincent, raising his glass in a salute to Ana Maria. "Unless you count sign language. Then we are tied."

"And those five aren't the only ones who can speak two languages," said Andrew. "I'm Greek on my mom's side so she taught it to me when I was younger."

"Same with me and Italian," chimed in Sophia.

"My father does a lot of business with China," said Ashley. "I ended up picking up the language. It wasn't hard."

"My family's Jewish, so I actually know Yiddish and Hebrew," said Ben.

"You're Jewish?" asked Sammy. "But I've seen you eat bacon."

"I didn't say I was good at it," said Ben, defiantly cutting into a pork chop.

Sammy snorted with laughter.

"I learned Japanese so I could watch anime without subtitles," said Gavin.

"And my family works a lot with indigenous people from New Zealand, so I picked up some Māori," added Sara.

Johnny stared around the table in shock. "So, you mean that except for me, Cinderella, and Fish-boy, everyone knows another language?"

"Not quite," said Sammy. "I'm fluent in Spanish."

"And I know Afrikaans," added Irene.

Everyone turned to look at her.

"I'm part South African."

"So, I'm the only one who only speaks one language?" asked Johnny in annoyance.

"Shocking, isn't it?" asked Vincent rhetorically.

"Well whatever," said Johnny grumpily. "Either way, I think you should all speak English. Having private conversations in foreign languages is rude."

"And you'd know all about being rude, wouldn't you," muttered Vincent to the amusement of Matthew and Reneé

"What was that?" demanded Johnny, turning to glare at Vincent.

"Nothing to concern yourself about," said Vincent as he took a drink from his wine glass. He turned to look at Ana Maria. "So, what other languages do you know?"

"Spanish, Chinese, Greek, Japanese, and German. I am also thinking about learning Italian. It should be easy since I already know Spanish and Latin."

"Rather an interesting collection of languages," said Matthew

"You never know what information could be useful," said Ana Maria with a shrug. "Which reminds me, Hades is it possible for us to have a tour of the Underworld? I understand if you are busy, but I thought that, since we are already here, it would be a convenient time."

"Of course," said Hades genially. "Although you're right, I am busy at the moment. Well, maybe not at this moment but I will be after dinner concludes. But maybe someone else can show you around?" He looked around the table.

"I can show you my garden," offered Persephone, "but I'm afraid I cannot do much more than that. My absence during the spring and summer months always leaves my garden in desperate need of attention. Perhaps someone else can show you the rest of the Underworld afterward?"

"I'll be helping Hades catch up on his duties," said Hecate. "And even if I didn't have work, I still wouldn't do it."

"I still have souls to reincarnate," said Lethe, "and Hypnos has offered to help me."

"I have to supervise some training," said Macaria.

"I can take them," said Melinoë quietly, her eyes downcast as usual. "I have nothing else to do."

"Excellent," beamed Hades. "You couldn't ask for a better guide. Melinoë knows the Underworld almost as well as I do."

"Well now that that's settled," said Persephone as she stood up from the table, "is everyone finished? Wonderful, then if you would all follow me, my garden awaits its mistress' return."

# Chapter Seventeen

Persephone's garden was a stark contrast to the dark and forbidding edifice of Hades' palace. Plants of every kind stretched as far as the eye could see, though their color and vitality seemed somewhat muted. A myriad of weak fragrances assaulted the noses of the new gods, who looked around the garden with varying levels of interest.

"Not really that impressive, is it?" asked Ashley under her breath as she stared down at a half-wilted rose bush.

"Wait," said Melinoë, her eyes on her mother, "it still sleeps."

Persephone, having left the group behind, was walking further into the sea of plant life. As she moved passed them, the flowers, trees, bushes, and shrubs all seemed to stretch out towards her, sending out their tendrils, stems, roots, and branches, all in an attempt to be closer to the radiance that was their goddess. Persephone, noticing the attention that her greenery was bestowing on her, stopped. Soft, pale energy flowed out from her, twining around the outstretched flora with a gentle grace.

Immediately, the color of the plants touched by Persephone's power became fuller and stronger. Flowers blossomed into full bloom, their petals popping opening in unabashed excitement. The trunks of trees straightened to their full height as all manner of fruits began to ripen upon their large, spreading branches. Scrubs and bushes rustled about, their leaves growing darker in color and large in size. Within moments what had once been a somewhat subdued patch of vegetation had become a wild sea of unruly growth, vibrant colors, and powerful fragrances.

"This is wonderful," said Sara as she gently caressed the luminescent petal of a large, unknown, blue flower. "I've never even seen half these plants before."

"Some of them are extinct in the mortal world," explained Persephone as she walked back towards the group, "like that *Araucaria mirabilis* over there. That was last seen during the Jurassic period. Others, like that *Hyacinthum nocturnum* you're admiring, were created by various nature deities. These butterfly flowers, for example, were one of my creations."

Persephone pointed down towards the cluster of multicolor flowers with wing-like petals.

"Blow on them," suggested Persephone to Sara. Sara leaned down and let out a soft stream of air. The flowers instantly sprang to life, flapping their petals madly as they flew into the air and fluttered around Sara's head.

"Why aren't these in the living world?" asked Sara as she watched the flowers flitting about in awe.

"They are, but only in places where they won't be discovered. Remember, the gods wish to remain a secret from the mortals. Now, if you will excuse me, my garden requires more of my attention," said Persephone. "But please, stay as long as you would like."

Persephone gave them all a warm smile before vanishing in a swirl of white petals.

"When you are ready to leave you need only inform me as such," said Melinoë as she took a seat on a marble bench.

The others wandered around the garden, taking in the beauty around them. Nothing any of them had ever seen on

Earth could compare to Persephone's garden. Everything seemed more real, more appealing, more alive.

As they ambled about, they would catch the occasional glimpse of Persephone tending to her various plants. Ashley saw her moving streams of water through the air so as to hydrate a collection of parched ferns. Vincent saw her instructing several spades to dig new plots for an assortment of flowers. Ana Maria saw her commanding vines to grow along a trellis in intricate patterns. No matter how intense her concentration, however, each time someone spotted her she would look up from her task to wave and smile at them.

Eventually the novelty of Persephone's garden began to wear off. Soon enough it was only Sara and Ana Maria who were still inspecting and studying the various flora around them. The rest of the group were all huddled around Melinoë, waiting for the curious duo to join them.

"Are you two done yet?" snapped Ashley in annoyance, her impatience finally getting the better of her. "I mean, wasn't it *your* idea to take a tour of the Underworld, Ana?"

"Can you blame me for being interested?" asked Ana Maria as she scribbled away in a notebook. "There are plants here that haven't been alive for millions of years."

"Yes, but your interest is holding everyone else up," chided Ashley. "If you two don't get your asses over here in the next minute we are going to leave without you."

"All right already," said Sara in exasperation as she and Ana Maria moved to join the others. "We're coming."

"Are you all ready to go?" asked Melinoë as she rose to her feet.

"Yes," said Sara, "even if it's somewhat against our wills."

Melinoë clapped her hands together. A chariot tied to several black, winged horses revolved into existence in front of them. Melinoë waved her hand and the dimensions of the chariot expand to accommodate her and the fourteen new gods.

"I hope that none of you are frightened by heights," said Melinoë as she stepped onto the chariot. "I thought an aerial view would be best."

Once the new gods had all clambered into the chariot Melinoë gave the reins a quick flick. The winged horses galloped forward several yards, their wings beating furiously, before takeoff up into the clear, gray skies.

The whole of the Underworld stretched out below them, its many islands of earth floating about lazily over the void that was Tartarus. Soon a massive island came into view. Its surface was covered in healthy, verdant fields of grass and crystal-clear lakes of sparkling water. As they flew over, they could see several spirits taking their ease beside a riverbank or picnicking in a tranquil meadow, totally at peace in their own personal paradise.

"The Elysium," said Melinoë, "home to the souls of departed heroes."

"Seems idyllic," said Matthew.

"Of the many places for a soul's eternal rest, none is more idyllic than the Elysium."

"Is that Macaria?" asked Sophia, pointing ahead of them towards a large group of souls who looked to be practicing combat drills.

"Yes. As she is the goddess in charge of the Elysium, and general for the army of the dead, it is her responsibility to keep the heroes up to snuff."

"Is there really a need for an army of the dead?" asked Sara.

"There used to be. Not so much these days though. But it does not hurt to have one in case of unexpected incidents."

They flew onwards passed the Elysium and, in time, came upon a corkscrew-shaped island. One half of the island was bare, and the other half was covered in poppies. There were also a pair of caves on the island. Milky white water flowed out of the mouths of both caves and joined together to form a river, which traveled along the surface of the island and then down its twisting slopes. As the new gods flew past, they could just make out the miniature figures of Lethe and Hypnos as they dunked spirits into the river and then hung them, like washing, on a line to dry.

"What are they doing?" asked Ana Maria.

"Preparing spirits to be reincarnated. The waters of the River Lethe strip away all memories. Once the souls have dried, they are sent back to the world of the living to begin life again."

"So, it's okay to reincarnate a soul but not to resurrect it?" demanded Sara hotly.

"Resurrection returns to life what should be dead," explained Melinoë. "Reincarnation starts life anew. The souls that are sent back to the world of the living are not the same as they were when they first lived. Their memories, their experience, their essence has been washed away. Where resurrection interrupts the natural cycle of life and death, reincarnation simple restarts it."

They traveled on without any further discussion on the topic. Eventually they came upon a collection of fourteen tiered floating islands. With a firm grip on the reins, Melinoë flew them through the gaps between the stony masses. The lowest island, which hovered mere inches above the emptiness of Tartarus, was a barren, dismal stretch of colorless earth. Innumerable spirits could be seen upon its desolate surface, all as still as the grave.

"These are the Asphodel Meadows," explained Melinoë. "The spirits of all those whose lives lacked a hero's glory or a sinner's shame reside here." The chariot soared upwards. Each new tier they came upon was slightly more pleasant and colorful than the one before it. The final tier looked almost as tranquil as the Elysium.

"What is the difference between this tier and the Elysium?" asked Ana Maria.

"The luxuries are not quite as exquisite," replied Melinoë. "The final tier is for those who are nearly heroes."

"Who determines that?" asked Andrew.

"The judges of the Underworld. Although I'm not sure exactly what the rubric is."

"What's that?" asked Ana Maria, pointing towards a solitary, rock float several yards away from the Meadows.

"The Mourning Fields," replied Melinoë. "The domain of Achlys. She reigns over the souls of those who wasted their lives chasing unrequited love. Their misery is a sweet nectar to her."

"That's horrible," said Sophia in indignation.

"Death is often horrible," said Melinoë. "Unfortunate spirits they may be but, they choose their lives and thus must suffer for those choices."

"But why make them suffer for eternity? Just because they were obsessed with someone in life doesn't mean that they have to suffer now that they're dead. You should just let them move on with their lives, or afterlives in this case."

"If they could move on, they would not have been sent to the Mourning Fields in the first place."

"Melinoë, I was wondering if we could set down somewhere and take a closer look at things?" asked Ana Maria, cutting off Sophia before she had a chance to continue her argument with Melinoë.

"If you so wish," said Melinoë.

She guided the chariot down towards a large rock. Most of its surface was taken up with a large lake. Melinoë set down the reins and exited the chariot. Everyone else followed her, except Ashley. She looked down at the dusty, barren ground below her and clicked her tongue in disapproval.

"Problem?" asked Matthew.

"I'm not messing up a perfectly good dress by walking around this dusty hellhole," said Ashley haughtily. "And I'm wearing the wrong shoes for a walking tour."

"We will not be walking," reassured Melinoë. "I merely wished to start our journey here. We will be voyaging the rest of the way."

"Voyaging?" demanded Ashley. "As in, on a boat? Honey if you think I'm making a fuss out of getting dirt on this dress, just wait and see what happens if it gets wet."

"I zink I can handle zis pwoblem," said Reneé. Raising her hands, she waved them delicately through the air. The new gods' clothes were momentarily covered in pink sparkles. When they'd faded, however, nothing seemed to have changed.

"Was something supposed to happen?" asked Ashley derisively. "Or did you just feeling like playing with glitter?"

"Give me a second," said Reneé. "I've never done zis before."

Reneé closed her eyes and took a deep breath. Opening her eyes, she waved her arms again. The new gods' clothes began to sparkle again but, this time, when sparkles faded their formal clothing had been replaced with more casual attire.

"*Brava*," said Matthew.

"*Merci*," said Reneé with a smile.

"I suppose this works," said Ashley pompously as she finally stepped off the chariot.

Melinoë clapped her hands and the chariot and horse twisted away into nothingness.

"Where did they go?" asked Ana Maria.

"I have returned them to the stables," said Melinoë, as she waved her hands over herself.

The beautiful gown of white faded into a simple dress of gray ash and her hair regained its tumbleweed like appearance.

"You should have stayed the other way," said Ashley. "You may have looked like a corpse, but at least you were a pretty one."

"I prefer this form," said Melinoë. "It is more comfortable."

"So where are we exactly?" asked Ana Maria, cutting across Ashley like she had Sophia.

"The lake of Styx," explained Melinoë, "my favorite haunt within the Underworld. This basin holds the accumulated waters of the River Styx."

"I thought Hades said the River Styx flowed outside the Underworld?" questioned Ben.

"There are many holes in reality," said Melinoë. "Though the main body of the river does exist in the mortal world, a small tributary flows into this lake. The same holds true for all the rivers of the Underworld, except for the River Cocytus, which flows out of the Underworld instead of in."

"Melinoë, can I ask you a personal question?" inquired Ana Maria.

"Of course."

"What do you do in the Underworld?"

"I have no defined role in the Underworld," said Melinoë. "I merely help out where I—" Melinoë suddenly stopped talking, her eyes narrowing.

They all turned to see what had drawn her attention. A hooded figure had appeared before them.

"No one should be here," said Melinoë in confusion.

"Who are you?" demanded Andrew.

The cloaked figure looked over at Andrew before reaching up and lowering her hood.

"Medea," whispered Melinoë.

# Chapter Eighteen

Hades dropped heavily into a chair, his formal attire melting away into more comfortable clothing. The dinner was over, the servants were cleaning up the dining room, all his guests were off enjoying themselves, and he, Hades, was stuck in a meeting with Hecate. Hades looked up at the goddess of magic, still dressed in her snake-skin dress, and contemplated the woman before him. Hecate was many things: unpleasant, cold, cruel, ostentatious, judgmental, but she was also extremely dedicated to the Underworld. No one else in his court was more focused and determined in their work, except maybe Achlys.

"You can change out of that dress you know," said Hades as Hecate conjured a scroll into existence. "It can't be terribly comfortable. It looks so tight."

As Hecate unfurled the scroll, she tapped the head of her boa constrictor boa. The snake slithered down her body, taking her green dress with it and leaving more traditional witch's garb in its place. As the snake glided out of the room, Hecate pulled a pointed hat out of thin air and placed it on her head.

"Is this better, my lord?" asked Hecate, looking up at him for the first time.

Hades let out a sigh of resignation. He knew this outfit well. It was the one she pulled out whenever she felt her sartorial tastes were being insulted.

"There's no need to be catty," said Hades. "I just wanted you to be comfortable. Something tells me we'll be here for a while."

"Whatever makes you say that, my lord?" asked Hecate as the bottom of the scroll fell from her hand, hit the floor, and then rolled across the length of the room.

"As you can see, my lord, we only have a few things to deal with."

"Lucky me," said Hades moodily.

Hecate began to read from her list, conjuring papers for Hades to sign as she went. Hades was only half listening as he absentmindedly signed everything Hecate passed him with lazy flicks of his finger. Ever since Zeus had suggested the idea of giving up their powers and positions Hades had found it difficult to concentrate on his work.

For millennia he had served dutifully as the god of the Underworld, working on every problem that arose without complaint or qualm. It was his duty and responsibility, a burden that he had to perform. But now, there was a way out. Once Ben was ready to take over the Underworld, Hades would be free. Free from the never-ending irritations of the dead. Free to travel the world above. Free to spend as much time as he would like with dear Persephone. Free to live a life of his own making for the first time since he was born. The feeling filled him with such a sense of expectation that he could no longer find joy in the monotony of ruling the Underworld.

And yet, though Hades yearned for his freedom, a small part of him wondered if what he was doing was truly fair to Ben. Yes, Ben had chosen to replace Hades of his own free will but Hades wasn't sure that Ben fully understood what he was getting himself into. Before Persephone's intervention, the Underworld had been simple. Spirits arrived, were sent to their respective afterlives, and that was that. The

Asphodel Meadows had been nothing more than an open field where the spirits of the dead wandered about for all eternity. And then Persephone asked him to change it. How could he refuse the woman he loved? Unfortunately, that was when all the headaches began. Now that the dead were active, they were full of complaints, requests, and suggestions regarding *his* Underworld.

And the dead weren't even the worst of his problems. Besides them, Hades had to deal with the over-inflated egos of seventeen other gods, his daughters and Persephone not included. The amount of infighting between the members of his court was staggering. If it weren't for the fact that they were all immortal, Hades was sure that they would have killed each other by now. Yes, running the Underworld was a thankless, insipid job that garnered no reward or respect. In fact, despite his rather genial personality for a god, Hades still recalled the fear and hatred he'd received from mortals, just because he was the god of the dead. Hades had been one of the only gods who was pleased with the advent of Christianity. Being forgotten was far better than being hated.

He didn't really blame the mortals for their opinion of him. At least not anymore. There had been a time when he resented them for their treatment of him. Though not as prone to cursing mortals as his kin, during these moments of bitterness, Hades had sent his share of plagues, famines, and misfortunes up to the mortals. He'd come to regret his actions, as much as a god could regret anything, and now he yearned to make amends for his poor judgment in some way.

This was the reason he had voted for the gods to be replaced by mortals. True, he knew that his own children were uninterested in taking over the Underworld but, if truth be told, it was a guilty conscience that guided his decision. He still remembered the meeting of the gods.

The fact that he was invited at all was a surprise. He and Hestia were not normally included in the workings of Olympus. But Zeus had said that he had something to discuss that would affect them all. When Zeus had finally revealed his plan, the response had been explosive. Several gods found the idea laughable. Other's considered it an insult and were nigh upon ready to strike at Zeus for even suggesting such a thing. Eventually, however, cooler heads prevailed and those in opposition soon found that their objections were driven by foolish pride. In the end, it seemed that none of the gods were truly happy with the current state of affairs and the thought of leaving their responsibilities to another was not only pleasant, but acceptable.

The real problems began when the question was posed as to who should replace them. The obvious path would have been handing over their powers to their divine offsprings. This created a flurry of contention. Several of the gods did not have any children at all and some that did didn't trust that any of their offspring would be a right fit. At the suggestion from Zeus that those without children could simply parent one without much fuss, Artemis had shot an arrow at him in disgust. Though she'd intentionally missed her shot, her actions led to a rather uproarious fight. Had it not been for the intervention of Hestia, Hades doubted they would have ever made a decision.

Of all the gods on Olympus Hestia was the most well-liked. Even Zeus liked her, though he treated her like a servant. In her own way, Hestia was the most powerful of all the deities. She alone was able to end any conflict within their ranks, an ability that, unfortunately, she had to use quite often. It was Hestia who came up with the idea to give their powers over to mortals.

"Who better to rule over the mortal world than those who were once mortals themselves," she had said. The discussion that had followed Hestia's suggestion was one of the longest Hades had ever experienced. Only two came to mind as being longer. The first was how to punish the Titans that had sided with Cronus, and the second was how to deal with mankind after Prometheus had given them fire. After days of deliberation, a vote was finally called for. On one side, the gods would hand their powers over to an appropriate god or demigod. On the other, the gods would give their powers over to mortals.

In the end, it was eight to six in favor of granting their powers to mortals, with Zeus, Hera, Poseidon, Ares, Hephaestus, and Artemis all voting against the idea. And so, the plan to find fourteen young mortals to give their powers to was created.

The gods ran into a snag almost immediately. When they looked upon the mortal world, they found that they could not find a single mortal that they trusted with their divinity. And so, mere moments after the first plan was created, a new plan was formed. They would consult with the Fates and create their own heirs by intervening in the lives of the mortals. And now, one hundred years later, their plans had come to fruition. The new gods were being trained in their powers and responsibilities. Soon enough they would take over, and Hades would be free from the confines of his eternal servitude. And yet, though this thought filled Hades with elation, he still felt a nagging sense of guilt.

"You seem troubled, my lord," commented Hecate.

So lost was Hades in his own thoughts that he did not hear her. It wasn't until a jolt of electricity shot through him that he turned his attention back to Hecate.

"Ow," complained Hades, though the jolt hadn't really hurt at all. "What did you do that for?"

"To regain your attention," said Hecate. "Your mind seems to have wandered away from the job at hand."

"Your concern is touching Hecate, but perhaps next time, you could come up with a less invasive method of getting my attention."

They returned to their work, Hades paying more attention to what Hecate was having him sign this time around. She had just placed a request from Michelangelo to construct yet another statue when the door to his office burst open, and Ascalaphus came flying in.

"My Lord Hades," croaked Ascalaphus, "please forgive the interruption but something has happened that requires your immediate attention."

"What is it Ascalaphus," asked Hades as he rose up from his chair.

"Something has happened to Tartarus, my lord. The pit has been opened."

Hades' eyes widened with shock. In an instant he was standing outside his palace, looking down over the island's edge. Below him was the vast pit of Tartarus, its bowels exposed. The darkness that had suffused every inch of it had vanished completely. Hades could see each of the black stone cells that housed the various souls that had been sentenced to eternal torment.

As Hades stared down into the pit in disbelief a small speck of movement caught his eye. Something was rising up from the depths of the abyss, growing larger and larger every moment. Soon a massive creature, all claws and teeth, came soaring up out the pit. Hades raised his hand and shot a stream of black fire at the monster, but it simply swerved out of the way. Hades shot out more streams of fire, but the creature avoided each and every one of them.

As Hades readied another fiery blast, a strange gurgling sound caught his ears. It was as if someone had pulled the plug out of a large tub full of water. Hades' eyes flitted about, trying to find the source. And then he saw it. A dark vortex was forming, a swirling maelstrom of warped space, in the center of which shone a radiant white light. The monstrous creature let out a screech as it flew directly at the whirling vortex. Hades shot another jet of fire after the beast, but it was too late, the monster had been sucked into the gaping eddy of blackness. A look of horror spread across Hades' face as he realized just what that vortex must be.

It was a hole. A hole in space and time. A hole in reality. A hole in the Underworld which led, he could only assume, into the mortal world. A cold chill ran down Hades' spine. Something had escaped the Underworld. With a roar of fury, Hades released another stream of black fire, this time aimed at the portal. The flames slammed into the whirling vortex, consuming it in flames, and sealing it shut. Hades breathed a short-lived sigh of relief.

A second later, he heard the strange gurgling sound again, only this time it was considerably louder. Portals were beginning to open all across the Underworld. Hades watched in horror as the very fabric of reality was ripped apart before his very eyes.

New sounds began to float up from the pit below him. Looking down Hades saw that the horrors trapped within Tartarus were spilling out of their cells, their voices raised in roars of triumph and shrieks of glee. Some began to jump from cell to cell, while those who could fly simply soared through the open air. But, whether by foot or by air, they all had the same goal, get to a portal.

Hades held his hand out in front of him, palms down. Energy rippled out from his outstretched hands, covering the pit with a film of darkness. Hades watched as the monsters pushed against his divine seal, unable to break through. And yet, he knew this was not a permanent solution. There were forces far stronger than him held prisoner deep within the pit and, without Tartarus to keep them at bay, there was nothing stopping them from breaking free.

So intent was Hades in his attempt to keep the creatures of the pit inside that he failed to notice a lone spirit appear behind him. The spirit crept forward, silently and cautiously, towards Hades, a spectral dagger in his hand. Just as the spirit was poised to stab Hades, he was struck by a jet of pale green light. The spirit was sent flying sideways. He landed with a loud thump on the earthern ground. The spirit looked up to see who had attacked him.

"Don't you dare try and harm my husband."

Persephone had arrived, and she was livid. She glared down at the spirit, her green eyes flashing dangerously.

"Who sent you?" demanded Persephone.

Before the spirit could answer, a portal opened up under him. Flowery vines erupted from the tips of Persephone's fingers, but it was too late. The spirit slipped away through the gap in reality, just as Persephone's vines were about to wrap themselves around him.

"Drat," snapped Persephone as her vines retracted. She moved to stand next to her husband. "What is happening? Where is Tartarus?"

"I don't know," replied Hades, most of his attention still focused on maintaining his seal over the pit. "But we can't let anything else out of this pit."

Suddenly they both heard a trio of sounds: a booming bark, a menacing snarl, and a chilling howl.

"Cerberus," they said in unison.

"Persephone, show me what's happening at the gates," ordered Hades.

Persephone waved her hand. A large, shimmering window appeared in front of them. Through it, they could see that the gates of the Underworld were under siege. Thousands upon thousands of spirits were charging towards the gates, with only Cerberus blocking their path. Standing as tall as the gate, he was batting away spirits with his massive front paw while two of his three heads unleashed a seemingly endless torrent of fire upon the rampaging horde. And yet, despite his best efforts, it was clear that the sheer number of would-be escapees would eventually overwhelm him.

"Hypnos!" roared Hades. "Lethe! To me now!"

# Heir to the Underworld

Hypnos and Lethe appeared immediately, their expressions turning from mild confusion to utter shock at the scene before them.

"A myriad of spirits are trying to leave the Underworld," said Hades hurriedly. "Cerberus is keeping them at bay for now but eventually he will be overrun. I want you both to go to the gates and assist him. Make sure that not one spirit leaves the Underworld."

"Of course, my lord," said Hypnos and Lethe in unison, before they both teleported away. Through their window, Persephone and Hades watched as the god of sleep and the goddess of forgetfulness arrived at the gates and went to work subduing the stampeding mob of spirits.

"With Hypnos and Lethe covering the gates we shouldn't have any other problems. Unless—"

Before Hades could finish his thought the seal over the pit was shattered. Both Hades and Persephone watched as creatures started flooding out of the pit.

"Macaria! Hecate! Thanatos!"

They each appeared at Hades' call.

"We need to stop this, and we need to stop this now. Macaria, gather the army of the dead as fast as you can. Hecate and Thanatos, keep these horrors from leaving by any means necessary. I'll work to close these portals."

"And what should we do, brother of mine?" asked Demeter as she appeared next to Persephone.

"Keep that at bay," said Hades.

*That* was a massive, fifty-foot tall fiery monstrosity and it was headed straight towards the palace on a chariot pulled by at least ten harpies. As Hecate and Thanatos teleported away to deal with the denizens of the pit and Macaria leapt away to gather her army, Demeter and Persephone stepped forward, their arms outstretched. Long, thick vines erupted out of the ground under their feet, stretching out through the empty air towards the giant and his flock of harpies.

The vines wrapped themselves around the harpies, binding their wings and pulling them from the chariot. The flaming giant let out a cacophonous roar and jumped forwards, sailing through the air, and landing upon a large, floating rock. Stabilizing his footing, the giant began to hurl balls of fire at Demeter and Persephone, who conjured up barriers of energy to defend themselves.

"Are you alright, Daughter?" asked Demeter.

"You needn't worry about me, Mother," said Persephone. "I can hold my own against the likes of this creature."

"True as this may be, I think you should leave the fighting to me. My brother may need your strength."

"Are you sure Mother?" asked Persephone. "You were never one for combat."

"You needn't worry about me either, daughter. Autumn has come and I'm at my strongest. Go to your husband and leave this to mother."

Without another word Demeter shrunk into the ground and disappeared. A moment later she erupted up out of the ground behind the giant. Taking a deep breath, Demeter exhaled a mighty gust of wind so strong it sent the giant in front of her flying forward over the edge of the rock and back down into the pit.

As the bellowing giant plummeted through the air, Demeter raised hands that were alight with flickering, green flames. Thick trunks began to grow up from the ground and form themselves into arboreal warriors. Once fully grown, the wooden soldiers wrenched themselves free from the earth that had borne them and leapt down into the pit. Large, leafy wings exploded open from their backs as they fell. The timber troops glided down to engage the monsters of the pit in combat, slashing at them with swords of sharpened wood.

At Demeter's command, a large leaf grew out of the edge of the rock that she stood upon. Once she'd stepped onto the leaf, it detached itself from the earth and sailed down into the pit. From her lofty perch above the fray, Demeter began calling vines and brambles up out of the stone cells. They snaked about through the air, entangling anything they came in contact with.

Yet, despite Demeter's presence, more and more monsters were flocking out of the pit and, though Hecate and Thanatos were fighting them back as best they could, several had already managed to escape. The battle at the gates was going no better. Lethe and Hypnos could easily corral the spirits of the dead, but the prisoners from the pit of Tartarus were proving to be a challenge. Unlike the spirits of the dead, several of these monsters found themselves immune to Lethe and Hypnos's particular charms. Fortunately, they had reinforcements. The gods of death had joined the fray.

Geras and Nosoi had joined Hypnos and Lethe in their effects to halt the escaping dead. Phobos had engaged another massive giant in combat, growing in size to match his gargantuan opponent. Algea was dancing about the battlefield, her claws leaving her victims in crippling pain. High in the air Limos, Aporia, Penthos, and Oizys were raining down blasts of divine energy upon the would-be escapees. Yet, despite their best efforts, there were simply too many portals from which the spirits of the dead and horrors of the pit could escape through. Every time Hades closed a hole in reality, three more took its place. None of the gods, not even Hecate who could split herself into three, could cover them all.

"I can't close these portals fast enough," growled Hades in frustration.

"Perhaps if you closed all the portals at once?" suggest Persephone.

"It won't help. Whoever is creating these portals will just make more."

"Then stop them from making them altogether."

"And how do you expect me to do that when I don't even know where they are?"

"Whoever is making these portals is obviously exploiting holes within reality. That means that the barrier between the Underworld and the mortal world has been damaged or weakened somehow. If you can fix the damage, you can stop them from creating portals."

"Yes," said Hades, a glimmer of hope in his eyes. "But mending the barrier between the worlds will take a considerable amount of energy. I don't know if I can do it alone. Perhaps in my true form, I might have the power."

"You needn't resort to such things," said Persephone as she took her husband's hand. "Your queen is ready to stand by your side."

"There is no greater blessing in this world than having you for a wife," said Hades as he kissed Persephone's hand.

"We can talk sentiments later, my love," said Persephone, her cheeks reddening. "For now, we have work to do."

Hades nodded. They both closed their eyes and raised their free hands up over their heads. Power radiated out from the divine couple as flames of pale green and inky black bellowed around them. The sky of the Underworld began to glimmer as they went to work mending the damaged veil between worlds. Slowly the portals began to fade away, causing the monsters from the pit to howl in panic and fear. Those confined to the ground charged forward wildly, desperate to reach a portal and escape. Those who could fly, however, rushed towards Persephone and Hades. Just as the first of the monsters was about the reach the sovereign duo, however, a clear clarion horn was sounded.

A new portal, far larger than any yet seen and made of radiant white light, opened up above Persephone and Hades. Macaria, dressed in gleaming armor and wielding a sword of shimmering light, charged out of the portal, cutting down any monster in her path. Behind her followed an army of heroic spirits, each clad in glittering armor and wielding shining weapons. They poured out of the portal like a flood, crashing into the horde of horrors mercilessly. As the army of the dead pushed back against the rebellious swarm of creatures from the pit, the last of the portals out of the Underworld closed.

Hades and Persephone opened their eyes. They both staggered a little but managed to keep their footing. They looked out upon the conflicts below them. Macaria was cutting a swath through the enemy lines. Hecate, split into three, was chanting her way across the battlefield. Thanatos had taken it upon himself to strike down some of the largest horrors, draw away their life force until they were so weak they fell back into the depths of the pit. Demeter had created a vast network of forests that stretched from cell to cell, inside of which could be seen numerous ensnared monstrosities. The battle at the gates continued to rage, but it was clear that the gods had the upper hand, especially now that Achlys had joined the fray. She waded through the enemy line, leaving only misery in her wake.

"It will soon be night," said Hades. "Once Nyx joins the battle this fight will be over."

"Good," said Persephone. "The faster this is taken care of the better. This is not the impression I wanted to make on our guests."

Both Persephone and Hades froze as the full import of her words hit them. They both turned to look at each other, horror in their eyes.

"The children!"

# Chapter Nineteen

"Hello Melinoë, it's been too long." Medea's voice was mocking and imperious. An evil smile played across her otherwise lovely face.

"How came you to this place?" demanded Melinoë. "For your crimes, you were condemned to Tartarus for all of eternity."

Medea's smile widened. "That does not matter," she said with an airy wave of her hand. "What matters is what I plan to do now that I'm free. So, little Melinoë, why don't you stand aside and let me claim my prize."

"What prize is this?" asked Melinoë, her eyes narrowing.

"The little Hera, of course. Just give her to me and I'll be on my way."

"What do you want with me?" snapped Ashley, her head held high and her eyes flashing.

"Your patron bound me to wed an unfaithful wretch of a man. And then, she and the rest of the gods abandoned me when I sought my revenge upon him. So now I plan to repay the favor."

There was a flurry of movement as Andrew, Lance, Sophia, and Ana Maria closed in around Ashley. The sight of this made Medea laugh, a wild, cruel, twisted cackle devoid of all sense of decency.

# Heir to the Underworld

"You have no idea who I am, little gods. I will have the little Hera no matter what you try." Medea raised her right hand. "*Ελάτε σε μένα, μικρή Ήρα.*"

Ashley let out a scream as she was yanked forward by an unseen force. Lance and Andrew grabbed her, trying to pull her back, only to be dragged forward along with her. There was a flash of ash gray light, and Ashley stopped moving. Melinoë had sent a bolt of energy at Medea, blasting her off her feet.

"Let her be Medea," said Melinoë.

"You do not scare me, little Melinoë. Perhaps if you were anything like your dear sister Macaria you would stand a chance, but no. You are pitiful, weak, broken, a fragile weed waiting to be plucked from the ground."

"Enough," said Melinoë, her voice as cold as winter.

Drawing herself up to her full height Melinoë locked eyes with Medea. For a moment the world around them grew cold and still. Medea withered under Melinoë frigid gaze, all color and vitality draining from her face. And then the moment passed. Warmth and motion returned to the world and Medea was laughing her high, cold laugh.

"*Από τα πόδια σου.*"

Melinoë was blasted off her feet as a jet of purple energy shot forth from Medea's outstretched hand.

"I'm afraid that won't work on me, little Melinoë," crowed Medea. "You see, I'm already mad."

Melinoë got to her feet, eyes blazing with fury.

"I do not wish a fight with you Medea. Return to the pit of Tartarus where you belong."

"You have no authority over me anymore, little Melinoë. If you want me to return to Tartarus, you're going to have to make me. Although, by now, there's not much of a Tartarus left to return to."

"And what do you mean by that?" asked Melinoë.

"Oh, nothing much," said Medea as she absentmindedly played with the black-jeweled pendant she wore around her neck. "Only that the great pit of Tartarus, prison for the darkest of souls, is due for an exodus."

"What have you done?" gasped Melinoë.

Medea cackled with maniacal laughter, the twisted smile returning to her face.

"Oh little Melinoë, you shouldn't concern yourself with such things. Especially since you won't be around to see what becomes of your father's precious Underworld. *Κάψτε τη φλόγα του ήλιου.*"

A stream of golden fire erupted from Medea's eyes and streaked towards Melinoë, who raised a barrier of gray ash in defense.

As the flames subsided and the barrier of ash fell, thorny tendrils began to grow out of Melinoë's arms. At the tip of each tendril, a large bub emerged. The buds started growing and growing until they were large enough for a grown man to fit into them. Slowly, the petals opened to reveal rows upon rows of thin, spiny teeth. The earth hissed and smoked as acid dripped down upon it from the gapping, floral maws.

"If roots my madness cannot take, then nourishment you shall be for my garden," said Melinoë.

The carnivorous flowers surged forwards, the jaw-like buds snapping hungrily.

"*Από τον Δία, επιτρέψτε μου να πετάξω,*" cried Medea. Medea soared up into the air, avoiding a flower's snapping jaw by inches. "*Κάψτε τη φλόγα του ήλιου.*"

Golden fire erupted from Medea's eyes again, burning away any flower in their line of sight. The fire didn't seem to bother Melinoë's creophagous creations. The burnt bits of flora simple fell away as new growth took their place. The new gods watched as Medea sailed through the air, dodging the raptorial onslaught of Melinoë flowers.

"I grow tired of these games, little Melinoë," said Medea as she barely managed to avoid being pincered.

Medea grasped the pendant around her neck with one hand and raised the other towards the oncoming swarm of tendrils. Her whole body was quickly engulfed in a dark aura.

"*Ξηρά και πεθαίνουν!*"

A wave of energy erupted from Medea's outstretched hand and struck Melinoë's flowers, which withered away into dust. Melinoë staggered backward, a pained expression on her face. Once she had settled herself, she glared up at Medea as more tendrils started to sprout from her arms again.

"Don't look at me like that Melinoë. In fact, don't look at me at all. *Στο όνομα της Εκάτης, μετατρέψτε αυτή τη θεά σε πέτρα.*"

There was a flash of vile green light from Medea's eyes. Melinoë let out a small gasp as her body stiffened and the hem of her dress turned stony. Slowly the petrifaction began to creep up the rest of her body. Melinoë stared in shock at Medea, who was laughing maniacally. Melinoë was now completely stone from her knees down. She turned to look at the new gods behind her. At the sight of their frightened faces, a look of determination came over Melinoë. She turned back to Medea; her head held high. As the petrification began to creep up her chest, Melinoë let out a long, shrill whistle. The whistle hung in the air, even after Melinoë had been completely turned to stone.

"*Θρυμματίζω,*" said Medea lazily.

The statue of Melinoë exploded, sending pieces of stone flying in all directions.

"Well now that Melinoë isn't here to interrupt us anymore, I'll be taking the little Hera with me."

"Stay away from her," said Andrew, stepping forward to put himself between Ashley and Medea.

"Aren't you protective? But it matters not. I have little interest in dealing with false gods."

Medea clasped her hands together in front of her chest and closed her eyes.

"*Φέρτε μου τα δόντια ενός δράκου.*" She flung her hands forwards, sending several large, jagged, white teeth flying out in front of her.

"*Αφήστε τώρα να γεννηθεί ένας στρατός.*"

The teeth burrowed into the ground. Nothing happened for a few seconds and then suddenly the earth near Medea's feet broke as a skeletal hand burst forth. More hands broke through the surface of the earth, clawing at the barren ground as they struggled to escape their earthen confines. Within seconds, a small army of skeletal warriors was standing in the open space between Medea and the new gods.

"Bring me the little Hera," commanded Medea. "And kill anyone who gets your way."

The skeletons began to move forward, their weapons poised and ready to strike.

"Back off," ordered Andrew as he thrust his arm forward.

A tight funnel of wind exploded out from his outstretched hand, sending a line of skeletons flying in its wake.

"Impressive, little Zeus, but, ultimately, useless."

The skeletal warriors' bones, which had been scattered after Andrew's attack, rose up into the air and began to reform. The newly reconstructed warriors quickly fell back into line.

"Oh crap," said Andrew as he took a faltering step backward.

"Here, let me have a go," said Ben, stepping swiftly around Andrew. He held out his hand, palm forward.

"Stop!"

The skeleton froze in their tracks. There was a moment of stunned silence.

"Kill him!" ordered Medea.

The skeletons began to move forward again.

"Stop!" ordered Ben.

Again, the skeletons froze.

"Kill him! Kill him! Kill him now!"

The skeletons rushed forward.

"Stop and don't listen to Medea anymore!"

The skeletons stopped, their swords inches away from Ben.

"Listen to me and kill him now!" shrieked Medea.

The skeletons remained stationary.

"Guess future god of the dead beats psychotic witch," said Ben with a smile. "Skeletons, I order you to subdue Medea."

The skeletal horde turned and marched towards Medea.

"Don't think yourself so clever, little Hades," said Medea, a sneer curling her lips. "I brought them to life, and I can end it just as easily. *Επιστρέψτε στη γη.*"

The skeletons collapsed into heaps of bone and armor.

"It seems I'll have to deal with you my—" began Medea, but she was interrupted by something slamming into the side of her head.

There was massive shockwave as Medea was sent flying several feet away. In the space behind where Medea had stood was Charon, his paddle in hand.

"Well that's an interesting development," said Ben.

"Not that I'm complaining," said Ashley, "but um, who's the person in the tacky robe and holding the big stick?"

"That's Charon," said Ben. "He ferries souls to the Underworld."

Black lights shone as Medea rose up to hover several inches in the air, her face livid and her hand clutching the pendant around her neck.

"*Δώσε μου το κουπί.*"

The paddle wrenched itself out of Charon's skeletal hand and flew into Medea's. A satisfied smile stretched across Medea's face. Suddenly Medea had teleported herself behind Charon. Before he could even react, she'd struck him with his own paddle. Charon was blasted away, sailed through the air, and landed in the lake with a large splash. Medea yanked the pendant from her neck and turned her eyes towards the paddle, the head of which warped and twisted itself into a small nest. Medea placed the pendant inside the twisted head of the paddle. The new gods staggered backward slightly as a wave of dark energy rippled out of the newly formed staff.

"It seems that fortune favors me today," said Medea, an evil smile on her face. "Now, I'll take my prize."

She tapped the butt of her staff against the ground. The piles of bone began to glow with a purple light, which slowly began to bleed into the ground. For a moment all was still and silent, save for the sound of the water lapping against the shore. Then the ground began to rumble. Mounds of earth began to rise up and take the shapes of deformed giant men. In a matter of seconds, an army of golems stood before the new gods.

"Crush them all."

The golems surged forward. Ana Maria stepped forward and spread her arms wide. A dome of gray energy erupted around the group. The golems slammed their giant fists against the barrier, trying with all their strength to break through.

"Anyone who's willing to fight, come with me," ordered Andrew. "Everyone else, stay here and stay safe."

Raising his hand again Andrew blasted a path through the golems and charged forward, Lance, Sammy, Sophia, and Johnny on his heels.

Charging towards the nearest golem Johnny raised his hands above his head. There was a flash of red light and a sword appeared in his hands. The golem raised a fist to strike at Johnny, but he dodged to one side and quickly sliced through the golem's arm. With another quick stroke, he cut through the rest of the golem and then moved on to the next one.

Sophia darted from golem to golem, striking them with her bare hands. Though she wasn't strong enough to shatter them with a single hit, her punches left massive cracks in them. By darting between multiple golems, dodging their attacks, and striking repeatedly at their cracked exteriors, she was able to bring down several golems at once.

While Johnny and Sophia were busy exerting their physical dominance over the golems, Lance, Sammy, and Andrew were hurling streams of fire, water, and wind at the oncoming horde. No matter what any of them did, however, any destroyed golem would simply rise up again.

"Anyone got any idea how to stop these things?" yelled Johnny as he hacked down another golem.

"If I did, we wouldn't be here right now," yelled Andrew over the sound of whirling winds.

As Johnny moved to the next golem, he, unintentionally, left himself open for attack by the golem he had just defeated, which was quickly reconstituting. The golem in front of him was proving to be somewhat difficult, evading his sword with ease. With Johnny's full attention focused on trying to hit his opponent, he wasn't able to notice that the golem behind him was raising its arms to strike him down.

Gavin had noticed though. It was far too loud for him to yell out a warning and, even if he could be heard over the raging battle, there wouldn't be enough time for Johnny to react. And yet, despite knowing that Johnny would hate him if he knew the truth about him, Gavin knew he had to save him if he could. Gavin dropped down into a runner's crouch.

"Gavin what are you doing?" asked Sara.

Gavin ignored her. He locked his eyes on Johnny, lined up a clear path, and took a deep breath. Just as

Johnny was finally able to land a clean, powerful strike onto the golem in front of him, Gavin shot forward. For the briefest of moments, the world slowed down around him. Compared to him, everyone and everything seemed to be moving in slow motion. For the briefest of moments, Gavin felt as though he'd finally gotten a handle of his powers. And then he collided with Johnny. The force of Gavin slamming full speed into Johnny was enough to send both of them flying a good ten feet. As they soared through the air, the massive stone fists of the golem came crashing down, slamming into the ground where Johnny had been standing not a second before.

They both hit the ground hard. Gavin rolled off of Johnny, his head reeling madly. He just laid there, his heart thumping wildly in his chest, waiting for the world to stop spinning. Johnny, on the other hand, was already up on his feet. He reached down, pulled Gavin upright, and held him by his shoulders to keep his steady.

"Thanks, zippy," said Johnny with sincerity.

He turned to face the golem that Gavin had saved him from, which was now barreling towards them. Johnny stepped in front of Gavin sword poised and ready. As the golem swung down at them, there was a sudden burst of golden light. The golem exploded, sending chunks of rock and dirt showering down upon them. Matthew had stepped out of the barrier, his entire body aglow with shimmering golden light.

"Close your eyes, everyone," warned Matthew as his radiance began to intensify.

A dazzling wave of light pulsed out of Matthew, blasting the golem army to rubble. Matthew raised his hands in front of him. A beam of concentrated light shot forth towards Medea, who conjured a barrier of darkness to block it.

"You think you can stop me with a display of pretty lights, little Apollo," said Medea. "Do not think yourself strong. You know not what powers you face."

The head of Medea's staff flashed. A wave of energy billowed out, blasting away Matthew's light and sending him flying backward several feet before he managed to steady himself, in mid-air. Matthew, now hovering several feet above the ground, looked towards Medea and smiled.

"Perhaps I am not strong enough to bring you down on my own but together, I think we have a chance."

Andrew, Lance, and Sammy had moved to stand next to Matthew. Together, the four of them let loose their elemental energies upon Medea, who was forced to conjure another, stronger, barrier to defend against their combined assaults.

The golems had begun to reform by now. Johnny and Sophia tried to keep them at bay, but there were simply too many for the two of them to handle. A few managed to break through the duo's defenses. As the first golem was about to strike at Lance, it found itself unable to move its arm. Long strands of golden hair and thick vines of ivy had wrapped themselves around the golem's body.

Reneé and Sara, whilst still inside Ana Maria's barrier, had joined the fray and were working together to keep the golem army at bay. Reneé's hair was rapidly growing in length as it snaked through the air in search of golems to tie up. At the same time, thick vines of ivy were growing up out of the earth at Sara's feet. The vines slithered about the ground like snakes seeking golems to ensnare, just like Reneé's hair. Between the two of them, they soon had the entire golem army restrained. With the golems taken care of, Johnny, Gavin, and Sophia started hurling rocks at Medea.

"ENOUGH OF THIS!" snared Medea.

The head of her staff grew darker and darker until it finally releasing a colossal wave of black energy. The blast sent Medea's seven assailants crashing to the ground and shattered the barrier around the rest of the new gods.

"I have had enough of your little games."

Medea pointed the head of her staff at Matthew. Just as she was about to fire a blast of energy from her staff, there was a soft popping sound. Medea yelped in pain as something small and light-colored struck her dead in the right eye. The blast of energy from her staff went wild.

"Sorry," said Vincent.

In his hand he held a bottle of wine, vapor still rising from its recently opened top.

"You shot a cork at her?" asked Ashley incredulously.

"Accident," said Vincent. "You never know where those things are going to go."

"You die first!" roared Medea, slashing her staff through the air.

A blade of dark energy sailed towards Vincent, only to be blocked, at the last second, by a wall of pale green light.

"Persephone," hissed Medea.

"Hello Medea," said Persephone, appearing out of thin air in a swirl of flower petals. "It has been a long time since last we met. Still as deranged as ever I see."

"You do not scare me, little queen. Your daughter was no match for me, and neither are you."

Persephone's eyes darted over the shattered remains of Melinoë, her normally kind face a mask-like grimace.

"You've attacked my family and my guests all in one fell swoop Medea. I admire your gumption. But if you think you are leaving the Underworld, you are sorely mistaken. You *will* answer for your crimes."

"And who will make me? You, the little goddess of spring growth? Don't make me laugh. Queen of the Underworld you may be, but you are no threat to me."

"As much as I would love to be the one to take you down, I'm afraid that, at least today, I am not your opponent. He, however, is."

A deafening roar split the air as Medea was engulfed in an explosion black flame. Hades had arrived, and he was livid.

# Chapter Twenty

The genial host of an hour ago had been replaced by an irate king, his jaw set and his eyes burning with fury. With a dismissive wave of his hand, Hades turned Medea's golem army to dust. He then turned his gaze upon the raging inferno that had consumed Medea. The flames bulged and then exploded outwards, scattering through the air like leaves on the wind. In the wake of the fire was Medea, her skin charred black as coals, her eyes filled with hate, and the head of her staff aglow. Medea's charred flesh began to mend, turning from charcoal black to creamy white. Within seconds Medea stood, fully healed, in front of Hades.

"If you had an issue with my hospitality, Medea, you should have filed a complaint," said Hades evenly, his civility belying his rage.

"You have no power over me Hades," taunted Medea, her eyes flashing dangerously. "I'm no longer one of your precious dead souls."

"This is still my Underworld Medea. This is still my domain. And you will return to Tartarus where you belong."

"What Tartarus? By now the pit has been emptied. Your coming to protect the little children has allowed the darkest of the dark to crawl out into the mortal world. So much for the great Lord of the Underworld."

"This was your problem in life Medea. You never truly understood how to trust in others. It was always about you. I, on the other hand, realize that even a king must have help from time to time. As we speak, my court, in collaboration with my sister Demeter, is working to keep those horrors in check, leaving me free to deal with you."

With a flick of his wrist, he sent a ball of black fire soaring at Medea. It struck her squarely in the chest and sent her flying into the sky. As she sailed through the air a giant hand of earth erupted from the ground and swatted her out of the air. She crashed into the ground with enough force to make a small crater.

"Your arrogance was always your greatest downfall Medea," said Hades. "You think you can strike at me and come away unscathed? I am a god! And you, you are but a foolish witch who's let her own power go to her head."

Medea struggled to her feet, her bones popping themselves back into place. With a furious roar, she sent a beam of concentrated darkness towards Hades, which he blocked with a wall of black flames.

"Is this truly the best you can do Medea?" taunted Hades. "How disappointing."

Hades reached out and tapped the fire wall with the tip of his finger. The flames shot forward, cutting through Medea's dark beam as it went. Pulling up her staff, Medea conjured a shield at the last second. There was a massive explosion of black fire. When the flame cleared it was only to find that, though Medea's barrier had been broken, she was unharmed.

"Enough of this Medea. If you surrender now and provide me with information as to who perpetrated this grand scheme I shall show you leniency. Otherwise, I can assure you that whatever hells you experienced in Tartarus before now will pale in comparison to the fresh horrors in store for you."

"Your ignorance is almost as great at your arrogance," spat Medea.

"Very well. Upon your own head be it."

Tongues of black flame billowed out from Hades' hands and snaked towards Medea, who raised another shield of energy. The flames burned through it within seconds and wrapped themselves around her wrists and ankles. For a moment it seemed as though Medea was trapped, bound by the black flames of Hades. And then she began to laugh.

"Ignorant god of the dead!" cried Medea, her face twisted with savage glee. "You have no idea what you have done."

As she spoke the flames that bound her began to bleed into her. Veins of darkness started to creep up her arms and across her face. Hades clenched his fists, dousing the flames, but the damage had already been done. The dark veins faded, only to be replaced by dozens of black runes, which appeared all across Medea's face and arms.

"Persephone, protect the children," ordered Hades, a note of concern in his voice.

Immediately, pale green energy flowed out from Persephone, encircling the new gods in a lily-shaped barrier. There was a sudden flash of black light, and Hades was blasted backward. Having managed to catch Hades unawares, Medea was now raining down bolts of dark energy at him, giving him no chance to do anything other than defend himself from her onslaught. Black flames danced around Hades, blocking each oncoming bolt of energy.

"Come now Hades, is that truly the best you can do?"

The attacks from Medea were growing in intensity, each blast exploding on impact. Hades had now encased himself in a barrier of black fire.

"You've grown soft Hades. Where is the fabled god of the dead, the warrior who fought against the Titans, the god who helped bring down his own father? All I see before me is a washed-up shell of a god."

"You want to see a god Medea?" Hades' voice, cold and menacing, came, not from the swirling barrier of black flames, but from the earth and sky around them.

Medea halted her bombardment and lowered her staff, a look of genuine fear on her face.

"Very well Medea. I'll show you a god."

The barrier of fire whirled upwards, forming a pillar of searing black flames. The temperature began to rise until the air was shimmering and the ground was cracking. Medea grasped her staff in both hands, conjuring forth an ice blue barrier around herself. Though Persephone's barrier protected the new gods from the heat of Hades' fire, it did not prevent the feeling of foreboding that emanated from the flaming pillar from taking hold. Every one of the new gods felt an inexplicable urge to turn tail and run. And then, the pillar collapsed. Where Hades had stood, only the devil remained.

Standing ten feet tall he had large, leathery wings, pointed, black horns, and a long, thin tail. Each of his nails was six inches long and black as night. The only article of clothing he wore was a sarong, leaving his upper body and unshod feet exposed. His skin was golden and around his head floated a crown of jagged black stones. When the devil turned to face the new gods, they saw that it was indeed Hades, though there was nothing friendly or familiar in his cold, hard face or his pitiless, black eyes.

"What, the hell, is that?" asked Johnny, a note of fear in his voice.

"It's Hades' true divine form," said Persephone. "We gods take a human form only as a matter of convenience, but it limits our powers. In this form, Hades has access to his full array of powers."

"Is this what you wanted Medea?" asked Hades, his voice still cold, still menacing, still omnipresent. "Well, as your host, I feel obliged to honor your request."

## Heir to the Underworld

With a lazy flick of the wrist, Hades sent a fireball towards Medea who teleported away to avoid it.

"Oh, I don't think so Medea," said Hades as he reached out with one hand. "You wanted this fight. No running away for you."

Hades pulled his hand back. Medea immediately reappeared, her eyes wide with shock and horror.

"*Στο όνομα του Ερμή, σε συνδέω σε αυτό το σημείο,*" chanted Hades.

Medea glowed briefly bronze. She tried to teleport away again only to find that she was unable to do so. Her body flickered with purple light, but it was to no avail. She was stuck.

"Have some problems Medea?" asked Hades contemptuously. "Here, let me give you a hand."

In the blink of an eye, Hades was standing directly in front of Medea. Before she could even react, Hades had reached out and flicked her with one of his long, sharp, black nails.

There was a small shockwave as Medea was sent flying through the air at a speed faster than sound. As Medea soared through the air, a slab of earth erupted up out the ground, slamming into Medea and redirecting her flight upwards. Hades flexed his wings. An instant later he was floating in the sky directly above Medea's flight path. Once she'd grown close enough, Hades' lashed his tail, sending Medea plummeting to the ground. The crater from this collision was twice the size of the one before.

Hades wasn't done with Medea yet. As the dust cleared and Medea started to try and get to her feet, Hades appeared next to her. He reached down, picked her up, and hurried across the island and into a wall of rock that had risen up to meet her. As Medea slid down the earthen wall cracks began to form across its face. A second later the entire thing collapsed on top of her, burying her under a ton of rubble.

"I should thank you Medea," said Hades as he slowly advanced upon the pile of stone. "It's been a considerable amount of time since I've gotten to spread my wings, so to speak."

The stones under which Medea was buried began to rise up into the air leaving Medea, battered and bruised, in their wake. She was standing, though barely, her staff clutched in her hand and her eyes livid. With a primal scream of fury, Medea sent the floating rocks hurling at Hades, who turned them all to dust with a wave of his hand.

"Are you ready to surrender Medea or shall I take this game to the next level?"

"I will never surrender to you Hades," spat Medea.

"As you wish," said Hades, a small ball of black fire alighting on the tip of one of his long nails.

Pointing the flaming finger at Medea, Hades gave a lazy twist of the wrist. The ground under Medea exploded as a pillar of black flames erupted upwards, devouring Medea in its remorseless inferno. The crackling roar of the flames was barely loud enough to drown out the shrieks of pain coming from within them as Medea was roasted alive in Hades' hellish blaze.

For a moment it seemed the battle was over, but Medea still had some fight left in her. She flew out of the blazing pillar, her body slowly healing itself from the searing heat as she sailed through the skies. More pillars of fire erupted from the ground as she flew, following her path relentlessly. As Medea swerved through the air to avoid the roaring columns of hellfire, giant slabs of earth wrenched themselves up from the ground and hurled themselves at her. Medea's flight path grew even more erratic as she desperately tried to dodge flying rocks and scorching flames simultaneously.

"Στο όνομα του Εκάτης, καλώ την καυτή βροχή," chanted Hades, raising a hand to the sky.

Dark clouds formed over the area, blotting out the endless sky above. Droplets of fire began to fall like rain, scorching the ground in a burning shower. Medea let out a scream of pain as the flaming droplets hit her skin. At the same moment, tongues of black fire rose up from Hades' hands, shaping themselves into blazing claws and burning maws. They streaked through the air after Medea, snapping and snatching at her as she flew about. Though her aerial maneuvers were exceptional, it was only a matter of time before Medea would succumb to Hades' overwhelming onslaught.

"You can't escape me Medea. This is my Underworld. This is *my* domain."

"We shall see," cried Medea as she soared over the lake of Styx. As she sailed over the dark water of the divine lake, she swung her staff above her head. Water from the lake rose up to form a bubble around her. Encasing herself in a protective bubble of Stygian water, Medea ceased trying to evade Hades attacks, all of which fizzled and died upon meeting the barrier.

"A clever ploy Medea," said Hades. "What does that make, four augmentations just to deal with me?"

"I will use every trick I know, ever spell I can conceive, if it means that I may leave the Underworld," spat Medea. "You gods think you have the right to govern mortal's lives. Where's your power now? You cannot defeat me, Hades. And as you sit here and struggle against me Tartarus is being emptied. Your court cannot contain the horrors within the pit forever."

"As it is now, perhaps you are right Medea," said Hades evenly. "But there is something you fail to realize."

As Hades spoke the dark clouds that covered the sky melted away.

"And what would be Hades?"

A smile spread across Hades' face.

"Night has fallen."

At Hades' words a wave of pure power rolled through the Underworld. The gray light that seemed to suffuse the entire Underworld was snuffed out, leaving only crushing darkness in its wake. And then, from out of the suffocating darkness, a single point of light bloomed into existence. Within seconds, that single point of light was joined by several more, filling the darkness that surrounded the Underworld with a galaxy of twinkling stars. With each new star that appeared, the force exerted by the darkness grew stronger and stronger. Several of the new gods fell to their knees, their breathing ragged as they fought against the power of the night. Persephone reached up and placed a hand upon her barrier, which began to glow brighter. The crushing pressure was immediately alleviated.

"Nyx," whispered Medea.

Though they couldn't see her face, the new gods could hear a note of defeat in her voice.

"Yes," said Hades calmly as he conjured several glowing lanterns into existence.

They floated through the air, illuminating the scene so that the new gods could still see what was happening between Hades and Medea. With sight returned to them the new gods could see a look of abject fear upon Medea's face. It seemed that the very thought of Nyx was enough to scare even someone as insane as Medea.

"So much for your plans," said Hades, lazily examining his long nails. "Tartarus may not be around, but I think that the primordial goddess of the night is more than capable of handling anything that might try and escape the pit."

"Enough of your arrogance Hades," commanded Medea, trying and failing to regain her lost composure. "I'm not beaten yet."

"You've already lost Medea," said Hades. "You lost the moment you opposed me. You lost the moment you entered the Underworld. You lost the moment you killed your own children in retaliation for Jason leaving you. Not even your blessed grandfather Helios could save you from your fate after that. Give up Medea. You will never win."

"ENOUGH!" screamed Medea as she slashed her staff wildly through the air, sending blades of darkness at Hades, who blocked them all with deft flicks of his wrist.

Medea, shrieking in frustration, now sent arrows of dark energy arcing towards Hades, who folded his wings in front of himself in defense. The arrows slammed ineffectually against Hades' winged barrier.

As the rain of arrows subsided, black lightning began to blossom out from the head of Medea's staff, crackling madly as it crawled up her arm and over her body. Gathering the lightning into a ball she hurled it at Hades. Hades responded by lowering his winged barrier and stopping the ball of lightning with a single outstretched hand, before crushing it into nothingness.

"This is an exercise in futility Medea," said Hades. "You cannot win against a god."

"We shall see which one of us is the victor today, Hades."

The head of Medea's staff began to darken, as did the runes upon her skin. Dark energy began to swirl around her, creating an eddy of murky blackness. Grasping her staff with both hands Medea pointed it at Hades and released a beam of concentrated darkness, into which she poured all of her power and hatred. Black flames sprung forth from Hades' right hand and twisted up into an ornate bident of black stone. A ball of black fire hovered in-between the bident's prongs. Hades directed the head of his bident towards Medea and a blazing stream of fire soared forth to meet Medea's beam of darkness.

The two attacks slammed into each other, each one vying for control over the other. The combination of divine fire and dark magic was clearly an unstable mixture. Pulses of energy were emanating from the point where the two attacks met. As the waves of energy slammed into Persephone's barrier, cracks began to appear upon its surface.

"That's not good," said Gavin as the cracks in the barrier grew larger. Persephone raised her hands and closed her eyes. The lily-shaped shield glowed brightly, and the cracks faded away. For a moment all was fine, and then the next wave of energy hit, and the cracks reappeared, larger than ever.

"Persephone, do you need help?" asked Ana Maria. "I can make barriers too. Maybe we can mix our powers or something. Just tell me what to do."

"There is no need for that," said Persephone through clenched teeth. "I can do this."

"Obviously not," said Ashley, backing away from a particularly large crack that seemed ready to split open.

"I am Persephone, goddess of the spring growth and Queen of the Underworld. I am the daughter of Demeter, goddess of the harvest, and wife of Hades, god of the dead. As your hostess, it is my duty to protect you, and it is a duty I shall fulfill."

Persephone opened her eyes, which were now aglow with pale green light. All color drained from her. Her face, though still beautiful, grew gaunt and cold. It was as if she was a long-forgotten beauty in a black and white photograph, a lovely image trapped in time for all eternity. She was as gloriously beautiful as she was heartbreakingly sad. Spring flowers, as colorless as she was, sprang to life around her feet, all as equally beautiful as they were depressing. The barrier around the group shone with greater intensity and the cracks melted away. A sense of tranquility washed over them all.

"What was I so upset about a moment ago?" asked Ashley dreamily. "I can't even remember."

"No idea," said Andrew, his mind adrift.

"Look at the pretty lights," said Matthew, pointing up at the standoff between Medea and Hades.

"Do not let the peace of death take hold of you," cautioned Persephone, her voice distant and forlorn. "If you allow it to take root the world of living may be lost to you forever."

Slowly the new gods broke out of their tranquil stupor. As calm ebbed away, fear and anxiety returned. The group clustered together; their eyes fixed upon the warring duo. Matthew took this opportunity to slip behind Vincent.

"Thank you," whispered Matthew as he wrapped Vincent in his arms.

"For what?" asked Vincent, also in a whisper.

"For shooting Medea in the eye with a cork."

"Like I said, it was an accident. You never know where those things will fly."

The battle between Hades and Medea continued to rage, with each new pulse of energy growing stronger than the one before it.

"Shouldn't Hades have won by now?" complained Ashley. "I mean he is a god after all."

"From what it's looking like Medea has found a way to increase her own power," said Ana Maria. "And whatever spell she did on the water is helping to protect her."

"It's not a spell," said Persephone. "It's just the properties of the water. Stygian waters have miraculous powers."

"Really?" asked Ana Maria, her interest piqued in spite of the dire situation. "What's so special about them?"

"The power of the goddess Styx flow into her river and her lake. In fact, she rests within the lake as we speak."

"Wait, what?" asked Ben. "Styx is there now?"

"Yes. It seems even a raging battle is not enough to wake the sleeping river goddess."

Ben, an idea forming in his mind, turned to face the lake.

"Styx," he called out, yelling with his might. "I command you to aid Hades."

Nothing happened. Closing his eyes Ben summoned as much inner strength as he could.

"Styx! I am Benjamin Darke, future god of the Underworld! I order you to rise up now and aid Hades!"

"The hold of her slumber is too strong," said Persephone.

Ben let out a growl of exasperation. He turned to look back at the fight between Hades and Medea as a wave of energy pulsed out again. A new plan came to him, and he started counting in his head. Another pulse was released. *About ten seconds between pulses*, he thought. Would that be enough? He would have to try one way or the other. No matter what she said to the contrary, Ben was sure that Persephone could not hold her barrier indefinitely.

For most of his life, Ben had been ignored by those around him. It wasn't really anyone's fault; it was just a fact of life for him. For a while he had resented it but, eventually, he grew to accept it, and even use it to his advantage. After all, you can't get in trouble for something if people don't even notice you're there. And now, with everyone's attention focused on either the battle between Hades and Medea or the battle between Persephone and the energy waves, Ben had the best opportunity to use his inconspicuousness to his advantage.

Slowly, silently, Ben slid back from the group, retreating towards the very edge of Persephone's barrier. As another wave of energy pulsed Ben steeled himself, waiting for just the right moment. Another pulse of energy burst forward. As it struck the barrier Ben shot forward, running with all his might towards the lake.

He knew he wasn't going to make it. He knew another pulse was coming already. He could almost feel it in his bones. He was twenty feet away from the water's edge when the wave of energy was let loose. It slammed into Ben hard, sending him flying forward several feet. He landed heavily on the earthen ground. Ben groaned in pain. His back felt like one solid bruise. He wouldn't have been surprised if his spine had snapped. Fortunately, not only did everything seem to still be working but, the wave of energy had knocked Ben within two feet of the water's edge. Feeling another wave coming Ben got hurriedly to his feet. Backing up a few steps, Ben took a deep breath and made a running dive into the water, breaking through the surface just as another pulse of energy was unleashed.

The water was like nothing he had ever felt before. It clawed at him with biting cold one moment, then scalded him with boiling heat the next. Ben pushed past the pain and swam forward, straining his eyes to see through the inky waters. He had to find her. She was their only hope. He had to find her. Ben focused his mind on that one thought, driving all doubt from his mind. To Ben's surprise, the dark waters parted in front of him, granting him a greater range of vision. It was as though his determination had swayed the water into accommodating him. Ben kept swimming, his eyes now scanning the clear water until, finally, he spotted her.

Styx was lying at the very bottom of the lake, her eyes closed and her face tranquil. Her long, black hair billowed around her in the gentle motions of the water. Swimming down to her Ben was able to get a full, unobstructed look at her. Styx was tiny and delicate. It looked like even the lightest of touches would shatter her completely. And yet, a sense of power radiated from her, a hidden strength behind her innocence and fragile facade.

"*Styx!*" screamed Ben in his mind, hoping that he wouldn't have to open his mouth. "*Wake up!*"

Nothing happened. Styx remained as motionless as the dead. Plucking up his courage Ben opened his mouth and yelled, "STYX!"

All that came out was a mass of bubbles. Still, the sleeping goddess did not stir. Now out of air, Ben began to panic. His body hurt from the water, and he could feel the gnawing pains of hypoxia course through him. Desperately Ben reached out and grabbed Styx by the arm. A searing pain shot up Ben's arm as Styx, finally, opened her eyes.

Above the surface of the water, Medea and Hades continue their duel. The waves of energy that still emanated from their attack continued to slam against Persephone's barrier. Though no new cracks had yet to appear upon the barrier's surface, it was clear the strain of the fight was taking its toll on Persephone. Her normally tranquil and lovely face was contorted with pain and determination, and her soft, flowing hair had turned dry and brittle.

"It seems your wife cannot take much more of this Hades," hissed Medea. "She weakens with every passing wave of energy. How sad it must be to have such a pathetic queen by your side."

"Persephone is neither weak nor pathetic," said Hades, his eyes flashing. "She is my queen, and she can hold out against any onslaught for as long as she needs to."

"Your faith is misplaced."

"Any faith I have in my love is never misplaced, Medea. If you had any understanding of love, you would know that. But you never did understand that did you? It's a wonder Jason was able to put up with you for so long. But then again, Hera was the one who brought you two together. How else would you have gotten a man?"

Medea snarled menacing, her beam of darkness growing darker still.

"Have I touched a nerve, Medea," said Hades coolly. "I'm so sorry. I'd forgotten. You did manage to find another husband. What was his name again? Aegeus wasn't it? I don't think I need to remind you how well that turned out."

"I will take great pleasure in your suffering Hades," spat Medea, her eyes flashing. "Almost as much as the pleasure I will take in Hera's."

"Oh, I'm not overly concerned Medea. Besides, this battle's already decided."

"So confident in your own abilities Hades, how foolish."

"It's it has nothing to do with me Medea and everything to do with *her*."

For the briefest of moments, Medea's face was clouded by confusion. Her unspoken question was soon answered as a giant wave of water roared up from the lake and surged towards her. Medea's eyes widened in shock as the tidal wave of Stygian water consume her barrier and crashed into her, driving her out of the skies and into the lake below.

Medea's head broke the surface of the water for a moment, just long enough for her to take a breath before the waters dragged her back down again. The waters began to glow with a strange shimmering light. Again, Medea managed to force her way to surface, and again, the water pulled her back under. Now the waters were churning as though in the grips of a great storm. After a minute of battering Medea around in its heaving waters, the lake spat her out onto the shore.

Hades began to move towards Medea as she lay upon the barren earth, sputtering and dripping. However, when she caught sight of Hades, Medea turned to strike at him with a spell, only to find that she had lost her staff in the raging waters of Styx. What's more, the water had also washed away the runes that had once decorated her skin. A look of utter panic overtook her face. Medea tried to rise, but her legs would not support her. Desperately she turned to crawl away, but it was far too late for that.

Chains of fire flowed from the tips of Hades' long nails and wrapped themselves around Medea's wrist and ankles. As Hades grabbed the chains with both hands, they changed from black fire to black metal. Medea rose up into the air, thrashing and screaming against her bonds but to no avail. The chains began to wrap around her, spinning her into a cocoon of dark metal. Once she had been fully ensnared Hades released his ends of the chains, which snaked forward and disappeared into the many coils of the chain cocoon.

"Ben!" Hades whipped his head around.

Persephone had let down her barrier and several of the new gods were running towards the lake's edge where Ben had been deposited. He wasn't moving. In an instant

Hades was at Ben's side, the others catching up seconds later.

Ben was a mess. His body was badly burnt in some places and frostbitten in others. Though he had been slight to begin with, any definition Ben had before going into the water seemed to have been washed away, leaving him emaciated and frail. His once dark hair had turned chalk white, his face was haggard and wan, and his right arm looked rotten and dead. Worst of all, he wasn't breathing.

"Someone do CPR," order Matthew as he placed glowing hands on Ben, trying, in vain, to heal him.

"That won't work," said Hades. "Not for these injuries. Nor will CPR clear these waters from his lungs."

"Then what do we do?" asked Sara.

Hades held a hand over Ben and closed his eyes. Water began to rise up out of Ben and pool around Hades' outstretched hand. As the water rose up out of him Ben's injuries began to fade away. His skin was once again whole, his hair darkened, his face became full once more. He still looked skeletally thin and fragile, but color had at least returned to him. Only his right arm remained unchanged. As the last of the water left his body, Ben gasped, his body arching upwards and his eyes flying open.

"Dude, are you ok?" asked Sammy.

For a moment Ben lay on the ground, his chest heaving as his lungs worked to get air back to his oxygen-deprived body. Finally, he spoke.

"Did we win?" he asked before falling unconscious again.

"Will he be okay?" asked Matthew, his eyes fixed on Ben's grisly arm.

"I believe so," said Hades, though concern lined his face. "I'll make sure that he gets the best of care. But first, I need to attend to certain matters." Hades raised a hand above his head. A second later the staff Medea had been using shot out of the waters of the lake and into Hades waiting hand. Hades pulled the pendant out from the head of the staff, which immediately returned to its original paddle shape.

Hades let out a long, shrill whistle. A moment later several objects flew out of the water. They soared through the air towards Hades before coming together to form the skeletal shape of Charon. As the last of the bones fell into place, black robes erupted into existence around Charon, covering his bony frame from view.

"I believe this belongs to you," said Hades as he handed over the paddle to Charon. "I thank you for your attempt to defend the children."

Charon nodded before heading back towards his barge, which was docked on the shores of the lake. As Charon moved away, Hades clenched his fists around the pendant. The crumbled remains of Melinoë rose up into the air and reformed. There was a flash of green light, and Melinoë stony continence crumbled away. Melinoë fell forward with a gasp.

"It's alright dear," said Persephone, suddenly appearing at her daughter's side, "Mother's here."

"Is everyone okay," gasped Melinoë weakly, her body shaking uncontrollably.

"Everyone is fine," said Persephone sweetly. "You did a wonderful job trying to protect them, my dear."

"Had Medea not had this, you would have been more than a match for her," said Hades, holding up the pendant for Melinoë to see.

"What is that?" asked Ana Maria.

"Tartarus," said Hades as he crushed the pendant in his hand. A wave of pure darkness exploded out of Hades' hand and covered the whole of the Underworld. The darkness was so all-consuming that it even blotted out the light from the stars that had arrived with Nyx. As the darkness began to fade away, a furious roar echoed through the Underworld. Tartarus was free once more.

# Chapter Twenty-One

"The impudence! The insolence! That someone would dare to bind a primordial inside a crystal is beyond egregious! When I find out who was responsible, I will make them suffer for all of eternity!"

The new gods watched as Tartarus stalked back and forth down the length of the meeting hall. He was in a towering temper and had been for the past hour. His voice echoed off the walls as he bellowed at the assembled gods. The Olympian deities, with the exception of Hestia, had all descended from on high to attend a meeting in the Underworld. Though they were all dressed in their traditional ancient Grecian garb, they had elected to keep their size at a more human level.

Tartarus was another matter. Standing twenty feet tall, he towered over the gods, old and new. His skin was pallid gray, his hair was chalk white, and his eyes were nothing but black voids. A pair of large, curved horns grew out of the top of his head and, instead of hands and feet, he sported claws of pure darkness. The only pieces of clothing he wore were a pair of black beeches and a long, tattered, black coat that left his cadaverous torso exposed.

"He sure can go on," muttered Ashley as Tartarus continued to stomp around the room, his horns narrowly avoiding collision with a crystal chandelier. "He's sworn vengeance at least a hundred times by now."

"Do not mock me, mortal," roared Tartarus, rounding on Ashley. "I have existed for far longer than you can even comprehend. I have already received a grave insult today; I will not tolerate another!"

"ENOUGH!" roared Hades as he rose to his feet.

Though he did not grow in height, his presence seemed to fill the room.

"We have heard your complaints Tartarus, and will we see to it that those that have wronged you will be punished. That being said, remember that this is *my* palace and *my* part of the Underworld and you will not threaten or mistreat *my* guest. Do I make myself clear?"

Tartarus turned to glare down at Hades, who glared back unflinchingly. The new gods held their collective breaths as the god of the dead and the god of the pit engaged in a silent battle of wills. Finally, after what seemed like an eternity, Tartarus shrank down to a more manageable size. He then took a seat among the other gods of the Underworld.

"Now then," said Hades as he sat back down, "we have much to discuss."

"I believe the first thing we should consider is the implications of Tartarus' imprisonment," began Athena. "Of all the problems before us, I believe this is the one that poses the greatest concern."

"Why is that?" asked Dionysus.

"Because binding a primordial requires a significant amount of power," explained Athena. "You would either need several gods, or Titans, working together, or another primordial."

"Are you implying that one of my brethren was responsible for imprisoning me?" asked Tartarus, his voice cold and menacing."

"Unfortunately, I am," said Athena heavily. "A primordial could easily slip in and out of the Underworld undetected. Had a gang of gods or Titans tried to enter the Underworld, they would have been detected immediately. This leaves a primordial as the only culprit. Though which one it was, I could not tell you."

A tense silence fell upon the assembled gods. Many of them looked uneasy at the idea of having a primordial as an enemy. Eventually, Apollo broke the silence.

"Will your boy recover, Hades?"

"Ben? Yes, I believe he will. Styx and Hecate are with him now. The damage to his arm was severe but Styx believes she can reverse most it. As of now, only time will tell if he will make a full recovery, but I'm optimistic."

"He was very brave," commented Artemis. "To dive into Stygian water, especially so close to the source of its power, is no mean feat."

"I agree," said Hades. "I only hope he knows how lucky he is to be alive. If he wakes up before a week has passed, I'll be shocked."

"Enough chattering," commanded Zeus. "Let us move on to more important matters."

For the next hour, the gods debated. It became apparent to the watching mortals that the gods weren't going to get anything done anytime soon. Arguments sprung up over even the tiniest perceived insult, real or imagined, halting all discussion about the topic at hand as the gods bickered. The new gods were, literally and metaphorically, in Hell.

It was Persephone who came to their rescue. After an hour of pointless discussion had passed, Persephone looked over towards the news gods. Seeing the expression of totally boredom on their faces she excused herself from the table and walked over to the new gods and ushered them out of the room.

"I'm so sorry," she said once they had all exited the room. "I got so caught up in the meeting that I forgot you were all there. You must all be bored stiff."

"That's one way of putting it," said Vincent, who had managed to go through six bottles worth of wine while he sat listening to the gods argue with one another.

"We gods sometimes forget about the concept of time," explained Persephone apologetically. "To us, four hours can seem no longer than forty minutes. But that's not important. You don't need to be here for this. I'm sure the gods will inform you of any developments."

"What about Ben?" asked Sammy anxiously. "What's gonna happen with him?"

"We will look after him," said Persephone. "And he'll stay here until he's ready to return to the mortal world."

"How long will that take?" asked Ana Maria. "He still has classes he has to attend."

"He almost died jumping into a lake to save us all, and you are worried about his class schedule?" asked Ashley incredulously.

"This is important," snapped Ana Maria. "If he makes a full recovery than he'll have to go back to classes and his teacher will be asking where he's been and why he's missed so much class time."

"Don't worry about that," said Persephone. "We'll take care of everything. I'm going to send you all back to the mortal world now. Try and get some rest."

Persephone waved her arms through the air, and the new gods vanished in a swirl of flower petals.

It did, in fact, take Ben a week to regain consciousness. For seven days he slept, half-dead, trapped in an endless abyss of nothingness. And then, one day, awareness began to return to him. At first, there was nothing, no sense of where or when, just empty blackness. And then, slowly, he began feeling something soft all around him.

*That's strange*, he thought. Last he remembered he had been lying on the barren ground. The smell of flowers wafted into his nose. But how? He was in the Underworld. What were flowers doing in the

Underworld? The only thing that made sense to his confused brain was the silence. But wait, even that wasn't right. Hadn't he been near a lake? There should have been the sound of sloshing water. Slowly Ben opened his eyes.

He was in a grandiose bedroom that looked straight out of Versailles. But what was he doing in France? Slowly his brain began to catch up. He wasn't in France. This had to be a room in Hades' palace. As he turned his head to look around the room, he realized that his body ached from head to toe, especially his right arm. He let out a soft groan of discomfort.

"Awake I see," said a voice he recognized.

Hoping against hope that he was wrong he turned his head towards the voice and found himself staring at Hecate. She sat, dressed in an old-fashioned nurse's uniform, on a gilded chair next to his bed. Ben wasn't sure whether this image filled him with dread or relief. Upon reconsideration, he found himself firmly entrenched in dread.

"How long was I out for?" asked Ben weakly.

"A week," said Hecate. "I wouldn't have been surprised if you had never woken up. By all accounts, you should be dead. It seems you have a strong will to live."

She reached out and touched his forehead with one of her long, talon-like hands. A strange sensation flowed through Ben's body, like electricity surging through cold water. After a moment Hecate removed her finger, and the sensation faded away.

"How is he," said a new voice, one Ben didn't recognize. It was surprisingly brisk and authoritative, while also sweet and sincere.

"He still needs time to recover," said Hecate. "But, as a whole, he's fine."

Ben turned his head to face the new voice. Sitting upon another gilded chair was a small woman. It took Ben a while to recognize who it was, Styx. She sat with her back perfectly straight and her hands folded in her lap, the image of a respectable young lady. And yet, despite her refined decorum, she was completely drenched. Water dripped from her face, clung to her clothes, and plastered her long, black hair flat against her body. A small puddle had already formed under the chair on which she sat.

"You were very brave," said Styx, her blue-green eyes staring at Ben in admiration. "Few would dare to dive into my waters so freely."

"Well, I didn't expect it to hurt so much," said Ben as he tried, painfully, to sit up.

"It seems Hades left out a few details when you first visited the Underworld. Where Lethe is the river of forgetfulness, Cocytus the river of wailing, Phlegethon the river of fire, and Acheron the river of pain, my river is the river of hatred."

"Shouldn't it have just made me angry," asked Ben, "instead of whatever the hell happened?"

"Hatred damages the soul. It burns you up from the inside out and freezes your heart. Had you jumped into the waters of the River Acheron I can assure you that you would know the difference between pain and hatred."

"Is there anything in the Underworld that isn't depressing, painful, or soul-crushing?" asked Ben, giving up his fight to sit up and laying back against his pillows.

"Persephone's garden is rather nice," said Hecate. "But apart from that, I'd have to say no, not really."

"Great."

"I shall take my leave," said Styx, getting to her feet. "I merely wanted to see that you were well. Take it easy Benjamin. It will take time for the after-effects of my power to leave your system. Do not try and rush your recovery. The consequence of doing so may be severe."

With those parting words, Styx collapsed into a puddle of water.

"As much as it pains me to say this," said Hecate, "I do have to echo Styx. You were very brave. Reckless, but brave. You have the thanks for the entire Underworld for aiding Hades, mine included."

"You're welcome, I think," said Ben.

He hadn't expected this. Hecate had never complimented him before. It was a rather unnerving experience. Hecate reached up, pulled a book out of thin air, and handed it to Ben.

"This is for you."

"What is it?" asked Ben.

He tried to pick up the book with his right hand but found it too painful to move, so he grabbed it with his left instead.

"It's a book of beginner spells," said Hecate as she rose from her seat. "As future King of the Underworld, any power your court possesses is at your disposal. This includes my ability to use magic. Study the spells in that book. Learn from it. Maybe next time you can come up with a better idea than diving headfirst into water full of divine energy. Now, if you will excuse me, I'm going to go inform Hades that you've woken up."

Ben opened the book Hecate had given him to a random page.

"Hey," said Ben as Hecate opened the door to leave. "This book is written in Greek. I can't understand a word of it."

Hecate turned to look at Ben, an evil glint in her eye.

"I know," said Hecate as she closed the door behind her.

Grumbling Ben flipped one-handedly through the book, trying in vain to make sense of it. As he finally gave up and closed the book the door opened, and Hades entered.

"You are an idiot," said Hades as he closed the door behind him. "A complete and utter idiot. What were you thinking, jumping into the water like that?"

"I was trying to help," snapped Ben, an unexpected sense of indignation surging through him. "You aren't very grateful for someone whose butt I saved."

"I am a god!" snapped Hades. "Whatever augments Medea may have been using pale in comparison to my power. I would have triumphed in the end."

"Persephone wasn't going to be able to take much more of those shockwaves."

"Persephone would have been fine. Why does everyone always think she's some delicate flower? She's a lot stronger than she looks, you know. And heroic intentions aside, you still shouldn't have jumped into that water."

"Well, how was I supposed to know it might kill me?"

"This is the Underworld! Everything can kill you. That's kind of the point of the whole place. I told you before that living things don't do well here."

"Well, you didn't say shit about the waters of the River Styx being dangerous."

"Did-didn't-didn't say! I told you there were many dangers in the Underworld. I told you about the River Lethe. Hell, you've even seen the River Phlegethon in action. What? Did you think the River Styx was unique? It's the one river that wouldn't have some adverse effect on you if you jumped in?"

"Okay, so I wasn't thinking. I admit it. I was trying to be heroic and save the day. Are you happy now? Go on, chew me out some more if you want."

Hades let out a sigh of frustration.

"I didn't come here to chew you out," said Hades as he sank into a chair. "And I'm sorry for yelling. In truth I was worried. I was worried that you wouldn't make."

"And if I didn't make it that would be mean you couldn't retire."

A pained look flitted around across Hades.

"I won't lie to you. That was part of the reason I was so worried. But it wasn't the main one. In truth, I felt guilty about dragging you into this mess."

"You expect me to believe that a god feels guilty about messing with a mortal's life?" asked Ben sarcastically. "I might believe you if I'd never met another god but after meeting Zeus, Hecate, and Thanatos you'll have to excuse me if I'm a little skeptical."

Hades locked eyes with Ben. For a moment they stared at each other, one full of anger and the other full of woe. Finally, Hades spoke.

"I'm sorry."

The sheer amount of sincerity that Hades was able to put into those two words was astounding. Slowly, Ben's temper began to wane.

"I'm sorry too," said Ben, once sanity had returned. "I don't know why I said that."

"I'm afraid that you are still suffering from the effects of the River Styx," explained Hades. "Hatred is a powerful thing, and it may take some time for the stain of it to fade away. And don't apologize. There is some truth to what you said. We gods are selfish and petty creatures. We care only about ourselves. True, there are exceptions but, as a whole, our only concern is our own self-interest. And yet, when I saw you lying there on the ground, half-dead and breathless, my heart plummeted. I was scared of losing you, and not just because it would mean I'd have to start my retirement plan over. I've grown rather fond of you Ben, and I've come to see you as a son."

"But we haven't known each other that long."

"Half-true. You haven't known me that long, but I've known you. I was there when you were born. I watched you learn to walk, to talk, to eat solid food, and even to ride a bike. I watched as you accepted that you were to be ignored throughout your whole life. I watched as you grew up into the man I see before me."

"That's a little creepy."

"Perhaps. But as much as I want to retire, and trust me I really want to retire, I wasn't going to give my kingdom over to just anyone. I had to make sure that you were the one for the job. So I watched you. I watched you to make sure that you were the one who could take my place. And low and behold here you are, lying in front of me. You've proved that I chose the right person. Foolish and reckless as you were, you were willing to sacrifice yourself for others. You could have left the waters after the first sting, given up the idea although together. But you didn't. You kept going. You persevered. And I couldn't be prouder."

"Then why did you come in here and call me an idiot?"

"Because I was scared. I love my daughters dearly and one of the greatest blessings I've had as a parent is that I've never had to worry about their safety. They are immortal goddesses, deathless and enduring. But you, you are still mortal. You are still susceptible to death. I have never in my life felt the kind of fear and anxiety that I felt when I saw you on the shores of the Styx."

"I'm sorry I worried you," said Ben, his eyes downcast. "I just wanted to help."

"Don't be sorry," said Hades. "You did a noble and heroic thing. You should be proud. I know I am."

Ben looked up to see Hades smiling affectionately at him.

"Can you explain something to me?" asked Ben. "Why does my right arm hurt like hell?"

"The aftereffects of grabbing Styx I'm afraid. You touched raw divine power when you grabbed her arm. It's a miracle she was able to heal it at all. It will take some time for it to recover completely. Apart from your arm though, how are you feeling? I probably should have asked that a while ago."

"I hurt but not as bad as when I first woke up."

"Well, that's something at least. You'll stay here while you recover. Hecate has offered to be your nurse. Oh, don't give me that look. It won't be that bad. You've managed to earn her respect so, at the very least, she won't be as cross."

"Lucky me," muttered Ben.

Hades snorted with laughter.

"What about going to the bathroom?"

"We handled that. Hecate placed an enchantment on you to deal with such things. I think it's in chapter twelve of that book she gave you, actually."

"Fat lotta help that'll do me," said Ben as he picked up the book. "I can't read a word."

"Maybe Andrew can translate it for you," said Hades.

"How's Melinoë," asked Ben as he put down the book, "and Charon."

"They are both fine. Melinoë is admittedly a little upset that she was not able to protect you all better than she did."

"Why was Medea so powerful anyway? What was that pendant?"

"Oh right, you weren't awake for that reveal. It seems that someone had trapped Tartarus within that pendant. Medea was using his strength to augment her own."

"Well then it's not Melinoë fault that she wasn't able to protect us," said Ben. "Medea was cheating."

"I've told her that, but she's still downcast about it."

"Well bring her in here, and I'll tell her," snapped Ben. "There's no reason she should be beating herself up over this."

Hades smiled at Ben.

"What?"

"Nothing," said Hades. "Nothing at all."

Silence fell between them. It wasn't exactly a comfortable silence, nor an awkward one. There was just nothing to say. So they sat there, together, neither speaking a word until, eventually, Ben fell back asleep.

It took another week for Ben's arm to recover enough for him to leave the Underworld. Between visits from Persephone, Hades, Hecate, Macaria, and Melinoë, he was well looked after. Even Thanatos dropped by once to wish him a speedy recovery, in his own macabre way. Despite all the attention, Ben was happy to leave. Comfortable as his bed was, lying in it for days on end had grown tiresome.

The only one around when Ben walked through the closet portal was Matthew. He was seated on one the more rigid armchairs, aimlessly strumming a guitar. Ben watched him for a few moments before speaking up.

"You know any songs yet?"

Matthew looked up from his instrument, a smile stretching across his face.

"Well, look who's back from the dead."

"You heard me," observed Ben, somewhat shocked. "Normally it'd take me a few tries to get anyone's attention."

"I think you'll find us a touch more receptive to your presence from now on," said Matthew as he placed his guitar on the floor and stood up. "You gave us all a scare."

"All?"

"Well maybe not Johnny or Ashley," admitted Matthew. "But everyone else was worried. How are you feeling anyway?"

"I could be better. Could be worse. Have been worse actually. But all in all, not much to complain about."

"Well it's good to have you back," said Matthew. "Um, you good for a hug or no?"

"I like hugs," said Ben. "Don't get a lot admittedly but—"

Matthew cut off Ben by pulling him in a warm, gentle embrace. Standing there, in Matthew's arms, Ben felt an unexplainable sense of relaxation wash over him, as well as the scent of expensive perfume. It was several moments before Matthew released his hold on Ben, who was somewhat disappointed that the experience had to end.

"So, what have we got to eat around here?" asked Ben.

"Not sure," said Matthew. "We can check the kit— speak of the kitchen devil."

Irene had just walked into the room. Though she never looked exactly well-groomed or stylish, Irene looked even more out of sorts than normal. Her clothes were streaked with dirt and grease, her hair was matted, and her face wore a deeply cross expression. Upon seeing Ben, however, her expression changed to immediate delight.

"You're back!" she said happily. "I'd give you a hug but I'm kind of a mess."

"What happened?" asked Matthew. "You fall into a trash can or something?"

"I was the only one who stuck around to clean after class," said Irene in exasperation. "And some of my classmates make quite a mess when they cook."

"That sucks," said Ben sympathetically.

"It is what it is," said Irene with a shrug. "At least my clothes weren't expensive, so I don't feel so bad about ruining them."

"You know, Reneé and I have both offer to take you shopping for new clothes," said Matthew. "Our treat. Your apparel could really use an update."

"And I've told you both, I don't want you to waste your money. The culinary arts and *couture* don't exactly mesh well, especially around my classmates. But enough about me, what about you, Ben? Are you hungry? Let me get a quick shower and a change and I'll whip something up for you."

"Thanks," said Ben. "That would be great."

Irene smiled at Ben again before scurrying off to her room.

"So, you're learning the guitar?" asked Ben, turned to face Matthew, who was gazing after Irene with narrowed eyes. "Something wrong?"

"No," said Matthew as he turned to face Ben. "I was just under the impression that her cooking classes were on Monday/Wednesday/Friday, not Tuesday/Thursday. Must have gotten my days wrong."

"Oh," said Ben. "So, the guitar?"

"Right. I thought it would be fun to learn some instruments since I'm going to be the god of music. I started last week. At the rate I'm going, I think I'll master it before the month is out."

# Heir to the Underworld

Ben and Matthew chatted for a while, mostly about what Ben had missed while he was recovering in the Underworld. The biggest surprise, at least for Ben, was that Gavin and Johnny seemed to have formed an unlikely friendship. It seemed that Gavin had earned Johnny's respect in some way. Though Johnny continued to be as unpleasant as he had always been to everyone else, he was considerably kinder and friendlier to Gavin.

"It's so weird to see," said Matthew with a light chuckle. "I guess even bullies like Johnny have heart, even if it's buried under a ton of stupidity."

"What do you think got him to open up?" asked Ben.

"Well, Gavin thinks it's because he saved Johnny from getting clobbered by a golem, which makes sense. I tried to ask Johnny, but you know how he is."

"Insulted your sexuality and ignored the question?"

"Bingo."

"Food's ready," called Irene.

Ben and Matthew entered the dining room to find the table groaning under the weight of what seemed to be every one of Ben's favorite dishes, though Ben did not remember ever mentioning them to Irene.

"I can't possibly eat all that!" cried Ben, his eyes widening in shock as he sat down at the table.

"Well eat what you can and everyone else will have some. They should all be heading home anyway. Besides, have you seen yourself? You're all skin and bones since you took a dip in the Styx River."

"*Tu devrais parler*," muttered Matthew under his breath as he took a seat next to Ben.

"Whoa, what's with the smorgasbord?" Sammy had just walked into the room, his hair still damp from swim practice.

"It's for Ben," said Irene.

"Yo, Benny! Welcome back man."

"Thanks," said Ben as he filled up his plate full of food. "You can have something if you want. There's no way I can finish all this."

"Don't mind if I do, man," said Sammy as he took a seat. "Swim practice works up one heck of an appetite."

"Maybe I should make more," mused Irene, already turning back towards the kitchen.

"NO!" cried the others in unison.

"The sentiment is appreciated," added Matthew, "but I'd rather not experience death by dinner if it's all the same to you."

"But if everyone's going to be having some—,"

"Calm down dude," reassured Sammy. "There will be enough for everyone. Trust me. Just take a seat and start pigging out."

Irene ruefully joined the three boys, though she didn't eat much. Her concern was, of course, completely unwarranted. As the rest of the household slowly trickled in and took their seats at the table, it became apparent that not only was there enough food for everyone, but they would also have several days of leftovers once everyone had finished.

"My stomach hurts," complained Johnny once everyone had finished eating.

"Well that's what you get for eating three whole pizzas by yourself," chided Ashley. "Honestly, do you have any sense of decorum or decency?"

For answer, Johnny let out a loud, satisfied belch.

"I guess not," said Ashley in disgust.

"So, what do you think guys?" asked Andrew. "Is it time?"

The others nodded in agreement.

"Time for what?" asked Ben.

"You'll see in a second," said Matthew as he and the others filed out of the room.

"Sit," commanded Ashley when Ben tried to get up.

"But—"

"Sit and wait."

Ben plopped back down into his seat. A few seconds later the others returned, all of them holding presents.

"Happy belated birthday!" they all chorused.

"You guys didn't have to get me presents," said Ben, a huge smile spreading across his face.

"Of course we did," said Vincent. "Now shut up and open them."

Happily, Ben started unwrapping his presents. He got a water-resistant watch from Vincent, a leather-bound copy of Grimm's Fairy Tales from Matthew, a hand-woven bracelet from Sara, a collection of CDs from Sammy, one hundred euro in cash from Ashley, noise-canceling headphones from Gavin, a pocket knife from Johnny, three jackets (in leather, suede, and cotton) from Reneé, a variety of gift cards from Andrew, a tool kit from Lance, a cowboy hat and boots from Sophia, a book on mineralogy from Ana Maria, and a hand-knitted scarf from Irene.

"This was so nice of you all," said Ben.

"You jumped into a lake of death to try and save us all," said Andrew. "Giving you a few birthday gifts is the least we can do."

"Literally," muttered Vincent.

"That's enough out of you," said Matthew grabbing a carrot from the table and shoving it into Vincent's mouth.

As Ben stared down admiringly at his gifts, and Vincent started to begrudgingly eat the carrot, there came a loud knocking sound. An instant later Hades erupted out of the ground.

"What did I forget my toothbrush or something?" asked Ben sardonically

"I didn't come here for you," said Hades dryly. "At least not specifically. I just figured that since you were all gathered together, it would be a good time to update you all on certain matters."

"Isn't that Hermes' job?" asked Ashley. "What's the point of having a messenger for the gods if he doesn't do his job?"

"As this has to do with the Underworld, I'm able to give more particulars than Hermes," said Hades. "Now, as you all know, Medea broke out of Tartarus because someone was able to trap him inside a pendant. As a result, several of the prisoners within the pit tried to escape. We managed to keep most of them from escaping, but I'm afraid to say that some wayward souls were able to find a way out of the Underworld."

"Wait," interjected Ana Maria. "Are you telling us that there are more people as twisted and crazy as Medea running around up here?"

"No, I'm telling you there are things much worse than Medea running around up here. Fortunately, the most dangerous of Tartarus' residences remain imprisoned. Had they managed to escape, who knows what horrors would have been in-store for the world."

"Who are these dangerous prisoners?" asked Ana Maria.

"Cronus and Typhon. Had either of those two been allowed to escape the world would have been in grave peril."

"So, who did break out?" asked Sara.

"We are still checking but you probably wouldn't know most of them anyway."

"So, what are we going to do about it?" asked Andrew.

"*You* will do nothing," said Hades sternly. "This is a matter for the gods."

"But—" began Andrew but Hades cut him off.

"No. You are still mortals. Death is still a very real possibility for each and every one of you, as Ben almost found out. And just because I am the god of the dead does not mean I will be resurrecting you if you die. Life is not a game that you can restart on a whim. Death is supposed to be final. And it is my job to make sure it stays that way. As such, you will leave this to the gods. Do we understand each other?"

"Yes," said the group as a whole, though many looked unhappy about it.

"This brings us to another topic, winter break. I don't know if you all have plans, but we would prefer it if you would all stay here for the winter vacation. Or at least for most of it."

"But Christmas," said Sophia. "I haven't missed Christmas with my family since I was born."

The group all began to speak at once, creating a noisy din of complaints and objections. Finally, Hades held up a hand for silence, which fell immediately.

"I understand that you want to spend time with your families. And I think we can make arrangements so that you can at least have Christmas day with them. Assuming you celebrate Christmas of course. But please understand that this is for your own protection."

"Do you think these people will come after us?" asked Lance.

"It's a possibility. Loathe as I am to admit it, we gods were a bit arrogant to believe that this transfer of power would go off without a hitch. We have many enemies and if there was ever a time to strike against us, now would be it. Every day the powers of the gods weaken. And while it is true that every day you all get stronger, it's nowhere near fast enough. There are true dangers in this world, even ignoring the escapees from Tartarus. Monsters, Titans, giants, and all other manner of unpleasantness lurk in the shadows, just waiting to pounce."

"Well we have to do something," said Andrew. "I can't just sit here and do nothing."

"You are doing something. You are training. You are learning how to use the new powers that have been bestowed upon you. Had Medea not been using Tartarus and Charon's paddle to augment her powers, I have every confidence that you would have been able to defeat her on your own. But again, there are worse things in the world than a crazy witch with a god complex."

"I'll stay here," said Ben quietly.

Whereas before his words would have been lost in the sea of voices that were his fellow new gods, now all attention was on him.

"I'll stay here over break. If I can get away for some of *Chanukah* that would be great but yeah, I'll stay here."

Under the table, Ben's right hand was shaking furiously. Though Styx had managed to heal the damage that had been done when he grabbed her, his arm had yet to fully recover from the shock. As he clutched at it with his left hand, trying to lessen the shaking, he wondered if it ever would.

"Well if you think I'm going to let you stay here without any company you're just insane," said Matthew, reaching over to put a hand on Ben's right arm.

A warm, gentle sensation flowed down Ben's arm. The tremors in his right hand, though still present, lessened considerably. Ben looked up at Matthew, who smiled down at him knowingly.

"We'll all stay," declared Andrew as he too put a hand on Ben's shoulder.

The rest of the group agreed to say as well. They all huddled reassuringly around Ben. A smile crept across his face. For the first time since Medea's attack, Ben truly felt at peace.

Made in the USA
Coppell, TX
12 December 2021

68199177R00162